Everything
Turns
Invisible

Gerry Hadden

For my moms

PART ONE

Wimple, Maine, September 1985

One morning you're just stewing in juvi cracking wise to the universe until, as a matter of course, some amoeba-brained bunkmates come round and hammer you to the floor for the seven hundred and thirty fourth time. The next you're on a bus rolling towards some college near the North Pole with the guy next to you playing spelling bee. Against himself. You never could have made sense of it, much less recognized it for the second chance that it supposedly was. Yet there you were. Rolling with the punches instead of taking them.

"M-A-DOUBLE-S-A-C-H-U-S-E-DOUBLE-T-S," the guy says. "Sean Patrick Sullivan. Barnstable, Massachusetts."

"Why'd you spell it?"

"Can you spell it?"

"You could just abbreviate. Like the postal system."

"So. A smart-guy."

I had an aisle seat. There was not one thing to look at but woods. "Slide your window open," I said. "It's hot as hell."

"Enjoy it while you can," Massachusetts said. The guy was about my age, I guessed. But that's where the similarities ended. He was huge and red-haired and taking up half the bench. His pale-green button down dress shirt stretched skin-tight against his upper arms. Like he was four fifths of the way to the Hulk. "Soon it's gonna start snowin'," he said, "and it's not gonna stop snowin till next summer."

"Summer," I said. "S-U-DOUBLE-M-E-R. Summer."

"Next stop, Wimple College!" came Powders' voice over the bus intercom. Dr. Horace Powders, the guy running this pilot project: Achieving in Maine, or just AIM. None of us knew yet what it was really about, only that it had just snatched each of us off our own, custom-made runaway chariots of trouble. That is, it had gotten us out of lock-up. Exactly one day earlier. I was twitching like some lucky lab rabbit with its cage door left open.

"I didn't see your parents at the drop-off," Massachusetts said.

"Yeah? You didn't?"

"So, what, you're like an orphan?"

"Sullivan! Prieto! Bowles!" Powders said. "Grab your parachutes, we are over the target."

Said target we'd learned about just that morning, at AIM's first and only orientation, a meet-and-greet for the thirteen trouble-makers who organizers had drudged up and dragged to this press event in a motel off I-95 outside Augusta, Maine. Smile for the cameras, kids. Apparently, our respective penal institutions had nominated us for this experimental scholarship because at some point in our lives we'd shown a glimmer, however faint, of academic promise. And I can only guess that academic promise implied general promise. As in, we might figure out how to live right generally. Like getting a job. Paying money for stuff. Learning to prepare food, to clean up after ourselves. Maybe washing your own actual car on a Sunday morning instead of wrecking someone else's the night before. All the mundane, mysterious stuff you could see other people doing so naturally, month after month, year after year, until the day they died and someone would notice.

We were supposed to be watching Powders. Mostly we were staring at each other. Like we were all sharing one of those escape-from-jail dreams that ends so cruelly. Standing next to Powders was a Maine State Police Captain, one Leon Bigelot. Our liaison. If Massachusetts was big, Bigelot was monolithic. His crew-cutted Easter Island head. He looked strong enough to lift me by the strap of my underwear with one hand and set me atop a Christmas tree.

"This is a first, gentlemen," Powders was saying. "If Achieving in Maine Works - and I'm sure it will - this fine state, and Mr. Cal Joiner, will have shown America that second chances matter." The same way we weren't really looking at Powders he wasn't looking at us. His eyes kept drifting to the two reporters and the photographer at the back of the conference room.

"Excuse me," a pony-tailed kid interrupted. He was in the front row, half standing, waving his hand.

"It's gonna be tough going," Powders said. "Because you're all the kind of stupid who think you're smart." That got the press chuckling. "That is, you're already smart. You've just been playing stupid. Which is stupid. You're smarter than that."

Ponytail still had his hand up. His other hand was on a guitar case. "Excuse me. *Pardon. Oui.*" You had to be kidding. I mean you could see he was off, and definitely dressed for a beating in those ironed jeans and the billowing white silk shirt. But what, French? You'd think he'd have kept his head down.

"If you need to take a leak," Powders said, gesturing for the door. Frenchy did not move. Bigelot was staring at him now.

Massachusetts leaned over. "Some encouragement this guy is".

"Yeah, like one of those Calvinist pre-destination nut-jobs."

"A nut what?"

"Excuse me," Frenchy said again.

"What is it, son?"

"Do these schools recognize us as regular students?"

"Under the program, you are being released from detention early and placed in the custody of the State of Maine. Your school credits will count toward a degree, thanks to Mr. Joiner's generosity. And his close cooperation with state lawmakers and college regents. But it's still up to you to make it through."

"Then we can go on semesters abroad. Like everyone else."

Abroad? That caught my attention good. Abroad had a wide-open ring to it. A one-way resonance. Abroad could be a place so far away there'd be no trace of your trail. No way they could drag you back.

"Focus on surviving in Maine," Powders said, "before you consider bushwacking through Borneo." He walked to a table and picked up a book. I could just make out the title as he waved it around: Gone Fishin' - For Trouble.

"Now, who among you knows who Cal Joiner is?" No one even blinked. "Joiner Sports? Anyone? Well I'll tell you. He's your savior. That's all you need to know. But read his book. Guy starts out building kayaks in the old Pembscott Home for Young Men, ends up owning 47 outdoor sports stores in 11 states."

"Where is he?" said a kid in a Michael Jackson-style bomber with a purple birth-stain covering a full third of his face.

"He wanted to come," Powders said, "but he's running a multi-million-dollar business. However he firmly believes you can benefit from the same second chance he got."

"What was he in for?" I asked.

"Fishing on Lake Chebago," Powders said. "With dynamite. Three times. It's in the book."

"Multiple homicide!" someone yelled. The photographer's flash was strobing up the room.

"That's enough," Powders said, thumping the book. "Now, you've all got your school assignments. Three of you are going to Wimple, seven to Horwitz and the other three all the way up to Zane." He raised his voice. "Second chances mean different things to different people," he said. "Some of you might achieve something academically. Others might simply learn not to attack people with forks. Please do not forget what *not* achieving is. That would be anything that causes Captain Bigelot's telephone to ring."

Powders swept one arm forward like he was presenting us with a Yeti. "Let the public rest assured that we will be keeping a very close eye on you boys."

So crossing paths with Bigelot again would mean we'd blown it. A return trip to juvenile detention, no credit for time served in the free world. Even though I had no idea what this free new world held in store. But I was going to hold the line, keep my hands clean. Until my moment presented itself. And then I would trip the high-tension spring coiled inside me and catapult my tail to freedom. To some place with no eyes on us at all. So fast and so quiet they'd wonder if I'd ever been there at all. As for after that? It did not matter even slightly.

As we filed out into the motel parking lot Powders wouldn't let us talk to the reporters. They trailed us anyway, their pens wagging.

"Hey fellahs, what were you in for?"

"How does it feel to be free?"

"Do you feel prepared for college?"

"Question is, is college prepared for us?" some kid yelled.

We got back on the bus and started up the interstate in silence. Bigelot followed behind us, his lights flashing. Forty-five minutes later we pulled off the interstate and wound along a two-lane road climbing past farms. We passed a wooden sign that read in carved letters "Wimple College. Founded 1789."

"1789!" yelled the French kid.

Then, like entering someone else's promised land, we were rolling by terraced lawns dotted with three-story red-brick dorms. The bus pulled into a cul-de-sac and stopped.

"Be good, gents," Powders said as me, Frenchy and Massachusetts stood up. "You've got the literature to read over. And Joiner's book. I'll be checking in on you later in the week." He slapped me on the back as we climbed off the bus, then put a hand on my shoulder. "I'm counting on you, Prieto," he whispered. "You make AIM work."

"How do I do that?"

"Listen." He leaned toward me. His breath smelled like donuts. "Sullivan. You be careful around him. That's my advice. I got a sense for these things. When his ship goes down you'd best be clear of the whirlpool."

"What'd he do?"

"Confidential," he said. Then he was shooing me down the bus steps.

Sullivan seemed nice enough. My gut told me Powders had the guy wrong. I had a soft spot for guys gotten wrong. But Massachusetts and Frenchy were already heading across campus, in opposite directions, each led by a student with a clipboard.

"Don't worry, we'll get you oriented too."

"What the - ?"

I spun around. There in front of me, my very own Student-with-Clipboard. Except.

"You get to get oriented too."

"Who are you?"

"Halsey."

"Whussup. I'm -."

"Milano Prieto. I know."

My alarm bells sounded. "Okay."

"Full name's Halsey Zehra Taylor. People just call me Hal. It's my nickname. You might get one. But maybe not. Depends on how long you last. You ready?"

Halsey Something Taylor regarded me with disdain. Or was it derision or boredom. Or all three? Her look was so deadpan it was hard to tell. She reminded me of Lurch from The Adams Family except for not so tall and her synapse-frying good looks. I didn't know where to look myself. But she saved me by starting off down a flagstone path, moving across campus in some kind of swishing skirt which if I'd ever seen such a thing it was probably in National Geographic. She was barefoot. Her skin the exact color of a Marathon Bar. Her hair, black. I swung my duffle over my shoulder and followed.

"Long way from The Bronx, isn't it."

"About eight hours on the bus."

"Ah, right. Travel-wise."

'Qué tu sabe', hermana?'

She stopped, turned. "That was Spanish. Where did you learn it?"

"At home."

"What method?"

"Total immersion."

We reached a dorm and Halsey opened the door. Up some stairs, to the left, down a hall, Halsey walking ahead. Room 204. She opened the door. "Welcome to your new home."

I set my bag down by the single bed and walked to the window. Outside kids and their parents were busy unloading station wagons. Lugging skis and stereo speakers into the dorms.

Halsey was standing in the doorway. Looking at me in Lurch mode again. Her mouth slightly downturned.

"So, Spanish."

"This looks like a double room."

"It's a triple."

"But there's only one bed."

"Lucky you," she said, pressing her pen against her lip. "Total immersion. That's really the key isn't it."

I sat down. "So, now what do I do?"

Halsey looked down the hall, then stepped into the room and closed the door. "My question is, what did you do?"

"When?"

"I know I'm not supposed to ask. But to end up here."

"Some dumb shit."

"I'd like very much to hear the story."

But there was no time to tell it because suddenly Halsey lurched for real. Right onto my lap. She kissed my cheek. "I am so sick of this place. And it's only day one. This forest of frat boys. All talk and talk and…" Her hands moved to my belt. For my part I was frozen. Among many other firsts, this was the first time I'd smelled a white girl up close. Which, I know, is a strange thing for a white kid to say. But what wasn't strange about my life?

"What did you do?"

Her shirt went up.

"Tax fraud," I said, feeling short on oxygen.

Her skirt came down.

"Seriously." She pushed me back on the bed.

"I punched a police horse."

That stopped her, her breasts in my face. But only for a second. Then she did something. I tried to look, to be sure, before just giving in to the wonder of it. The unimaginable overload. This new kind of losing control, like a rollercoaster drop but not in your stomach. And all the while the eye contact making it seem actually connected to me. Like she was connecting with me. This couldn't possibly be a mistake, or some fevered dream. Could it? If it was I wasn't going to let on. Worse mistakes had been made. And fewer dreams had ever been better. To be honest, none I'd ever had even came close.

"Well?" she whispered. There was some urgency in her voice. "Mr. Total. Immersion. What. Did. You. Do…"

"Murdered," I gasped. "I, cold-bloodedly, murdered."

The dream lasted about four minutes. Or maybe fourteen. What did I know? I was knocked sideways. Before I knew it Halsey was fixing her hair and writing her dorm room number on a slip of paper.

Like nothing had happened. If I hadn't been so stunned I might have said thank you. For popping my cherry.

"Why are you sick of it here?" I said. Just to say something. To put off what appeared to be her preparations for leaving.

"Give it time." She stood and pulled up her her skirt. "I knew you were different," she said. My nerves jangled again. What did she know? She kissed my nose but the empty look had returned. Like, this won't be happening twice. Or was it a look of pity? I remained on that bed, starting to brood, my pants half-masted, silent. What else was I going to say? Here I am. Here I am. I wasn't calling the shots. I hadn't even seen the shots coming. Halsey was way out of my league. Classy beyond anyone I'd ever talked to. Like out of a magazine. You could tell just by how she held her head. By the clear, direct way she spoke. Also, she was at least a sophomore.

"So now what?" I said. "Do we go to the library?"

"That's for after classes start," she said, bowing out the door. "I'm glad you're here. I'll be back. For now, just tidy up. And make yourself at home."

"And that would mean – " But she had already ducked out.

"See you later, assassin!" she called from bottom of the stairwell. "Hahaha! Manslaughter, or first degree?"

I kicked the door shut and lay back down on my bed, listening to the revelry outside, the footsteps in the hall. Different, she'd called me. As in, a criminal to be had? Was I a first for her, as she'd been for me? Something for her to check off on her clipboard? Her soapy smell was all over. I remembered the note card she'd just written her number on. She hadn't given it to me. What the hell? Was that on purpose? Would she really come back? Had I just made love for the first time or, surprise surprise, been test-driven for my freakishness? This was how easily I could start to spiral. This was my problem. Correction: This was the inside symptom of my problems. Which tended to lead to outside problems. Did I like this about me? No. It was the worst side of my lost-ass self, this self-pitying. These psychological seizures of abandonment. But I couldn't control them. My gut churned darkly.

Stop it, I told myself. Stop. This is your chance. As more students arrived I tried repeating what Halsey had said, just for kicks: Make yourself at home. Make yourself at home. It was no use. The urge only rose. The urge to get up and walk outside and punch the first nice enough kid I saw in the throat. For no reason whatsoever that he might understand. The less reason, the more hurt. Surprise had always been my only advantage. But with all my strength I lay there, resisting. Because I knew where that path led. I'd supposedly just stepped off it.

The murder path was another story. The murder path you never got off. Laugh all you want, Halsey Taylor. I went out to find Massachusetts and Frenchy.

There was Massachusetts playing Frisbee on one of the big lawns. His partner, one of the campus security guards. A guy who appeared not to know what a Frisbee was. He grinned at me and made a V sign with two fingers.

"You realize you may have to arrest that guy one day," I said.

"Come on, now," the guard said. "No need for that kinda...uh..." This kid was way too young to offer anyone security. His uniform hung like a big suit on a small hanger. "We have a little unwitten wule in security," he said. "Oh, man. Un*written rule*. And that is, you don't mess with us, we don't mess with you."

I pinched my fingers together and raised my eyebrows.

"Yeah? Right on."

We went and sat down next to a row of birch trees and Massachusetts joined us. Security produced a sad looking joint, twisted it taught. I lit up. The marijuana was skunked and made me cough.

"Sorry. Tough little bud. We have a short growing season in Maine."

"What's your name, Security?"

"Don."

"You from around here?"

"I ain't moved a goddamn inch in my life."

"You got a bitchin' gig."

"The only gig in town," Don said. "You don't work for Wimple, you're either a crook, a cripple or dumber than a box a dirt."

Don hugged his knees, his smile going funny for a split-second. Maybe he was thinking about his crappy dope. Or maybe about the goddamn inch that was his universe. But probably he was just doing the math on us. For one, if you analyzed it even for a second, we did not fit the figure of any of the Wimple students we'd seen so far: a guy like me and another dressed like a Salvation Army Client-of-the-Month sitting under a bone-white birch smoking a roach.

"It's crooks then," Don said finally, "with that new crooks program."

"How'd you guess?" I said.

"Well you ain't from Choate."

I thought to ask what that was but I started giggling. The weed was kicking in. Pretty soon my ribs hurt. What was funny? Nothing and everything. That day, my life. Things were getting weird at such a pace. Compared to the bone-aching boredom of life on the inside, where the only change might be where they hit you or what time it was when they hit you, events here were moving at the speed of light. *Madre mía,* five minutes in and I'm being laid by some out-of-my-leaguer with the softest delta of fuzz just below her bellybutton. So what if she didn't follow through with the small talk I would have imagined? A blown kiss from the sidewalk below or something. A second knock at the door. Hey, I brought us lunch.

For the moment it was all worth a laugh, the real and the imagined. I was going to sit there and giggle until stopping was like Rip Van Winkle opening his eyes on a one-hundred percent reset world.

"Say, what'd you do anyway," Massachusetts said, "fall into in a thresher?"

"Yeah," I said. "On my farm in the north Bronx. *Comemierdas.*"

That stopped him like Halsey. "What are you then? Some kind of Mexican albino orphan?"

"I ain't albino."

We were on our way to the dining hall. Still stoned. We passed an old sun-filled chapel, its doors open. In front of a dorm students in aviator sunglasses sat in beach chairs drinking beer from a silver keg.

"I never even heard of Wimple College," Massachusetts said.

"I was gonna ask you," I said. "You know, not to tell me how you got locked up. Since it's confidential."

"Right. Ok. It was not for assaulting anyone."

"Why am I not surprised?"

"I did not punch a guy with designs on my girl straight into the hospital. You?"

"I did not steal a countless number of cars."

"Not knowing is much better," Massachusetts said. Then, "You? Really?"

He held the big glass door for me. Inside the dining hall there were students coming and going and it smelled like fish sticks.

"You talk yet with the other guy?" I said.

"Nah."

"What could a Frog have done to end up here, anyway?"

"Whuddever he did," Massachusetts said, grabbing a food tray, "it pisses me off to no end that he would do it in America."

"Why?"

"Cuz this is America, mothuhfuckuh. What we need to do is go to France. Commit some felony or something. Restore the balance."

"I'm in. There's an architect over there I need to punch anyway."

"Yeah? You got a strong enough right to make up for the left?"

"Not even close," I said. "But I go down swinging."

Nathan Hale Rehabilitation Center for Boys, The Bronx.
Six months earlier

"Hey Orphan. Go get me a coke."

"Heya dipshit. What am I not?"

"What'd you call me?"

"You are a piece of lab meat with two eye-holes."

"I'm Swope to you, you honky cripple-ass motherfucker. Swope the Great Black Hope."

"Ow! Ow, ouuuuch!"

"Now get me my coke before I slap your other goddamn ear clear off."

"Throw in a Mountain Dew for me and you got a deal, fuck-face."

"You makin this too easy, Orphan Boy."

The other boys crowded around. I should have been scared

instead of all excited. Some things did scare me. Like quiet families from the suburbs, or those big oil rigs that bob up and down like dinosaurs in the desert. Why do they do that? Getting a beat-down always hurt but I never did get all shaky over it. Because for some reason I always held out the hope of winning. I could actually imagine it. Clearly enough to reach for it. To swing for it. But win or lose the deeper truth was that this was attention. From fists and feet but also from the boys surrounding us, then the guards and finally the juvi doctor and his Phillipina nurse, Patricia. With each punch, prod or suture, whether they liked it or not, they were acknowledging me. And that alone, given where I stood, was my prescription-free drug of choice.

"Go fuck yourself Swopey," I said. "Fuck you and your crack smoking street dealing black ass." I missed his jaw with my Hail-Mary last-chance roundhouse, then just curled up for it.

I unbuckled my duffle and stacked my clothes according to type on my bed, then went drawer by drawer putting things in their place. Like pieces of a puzzle.

"Take your sweet time."

"It's comforting."

Massachusetts was circling the place, his arms outstretched like he was measuring it. I pulled a pewter flask from my duffle. Then the cigar in the old yellow handkerchief and the resin statuette of Ogún, dressed in black and green and wielding his sword. My life-long companion. Or jailer. Spiritual, that is, not brick and steel. Which was actually even tougher to escape from. I still didn't know why I hadn't just tossed all this stuff in the trash when I'd got sprung. Maybe it was to have something familiar in this strange new place, even if that familiarity was the sucky kind.

I centered Ogún on top of the chest. To his right I set the cock on the pedestal with his tiny anvil. Then I unwrapped the cigar and lay it before the Orisha. I squeezed the flask between my knees and unscrewed the cap.

"You got anything iron on you?" I said.

"Anything iron? Like a clothes iron?"

"Smaller. A railroad spike, an old horseshoe, even a nail."

"I do not have an old horseshoe on me. Sorry."

I knelt and poured a thin stream of the rum on to the floor. It splattered and pooled on the linoleum. I handed Massachusetts the flask.

"Which super hero is that?"

"Ogún. The wounded warrior."

"You're a god damned witch doctor."

"Whatever you say."

"Voodoo."

"Voodoo is from Haiti," I said. "Santería's from Cuba."

"So you're a Cuban albino?"

"I ain't – "

"I know. You ain't albino."

"And I ain't Cuban and I ain't no orphan."

Saying what I wasn't came so easily.

Massachusetts stepped out to use the communal bathroom down the hall. I reached back into my duffle and fished out the main thing. What everything else was wrapped around. The doubled plastic lunch bags sealed with the green twisty. I held it up to the light. The mystery. I came from a world of shared symbols and talismans but these were mine alone: Eight nickel-alloy washers and five matching lugnuts, 3/8 inch. The first washer had arrived when I was five, in an envelope addressed to me and left in our lobby mail slot. No return address or postal mark.

My dad, Hipólito, had brought it into the kitchen and opened it. "You got ghost mail," he'd said, peeking quickly into the envelope. "Empty." He handed it over. Of course not another ounce of curiosity about it. About it, or about me. I peered inside and shrugged and put it in the garbage and waited. My face all red. Hipólito went back to the living room, to the variety show on the TV with the old frog-faced Argentine and the models in bikinis. I took the envelope out of the trash, walked to my room, shut the door and dumped out the tiny metal ring onto my pillow. My heart racing. Hipólito had obviously missed it. I hadn't had much contact with anyone over the last several months, except with my friend Ronny and his sadist dad and Hipólito himself, which was more like contact's opposite. Now someone had sent me, well, something. No note, but still. I pinched the dark ring between two fingers, picked it up. I let it roll into the palm of my hand where it lay like a tiny flattened donut, unmarked, perfect, the size of a nickel across but lighter. Ghost mail, my dad had said. It might just be, I thought. Goosebumps rose on my skin and I started to cry, then sob. Mucous inglorious. The wounds were still so red-raw. I closed my eyes so that in my head I was falling into the dark hole again. Towards that last chance. It was true that I'd squandered it, but now there was this. I squeezed my hand tight around the ring. A ghost from beyond the grave, I thought. A gift or a message. From Miriam herself. My mom.

New York City, December 25th, 1971

I was riding Hipólito's shoulders, hanging on for life. Hundreds
of people milled around us, pushing and chanting. Some even
wearing Santa hats but most in normal clothes – normal clothes for
recently-arrived Cubans experiencing winter for real: big second-hand
army coats or hooded parkas with rings of fur hiding their faces,
scarves wrapped willy-nilly around heads, mismatched gloves over
gloves, moon boots with plastic bags tied over them. Any shit they
could scrounge against the cold. Cubans tasting their first New York
winter took some time to learn how to stay warm. They seemed to
nearly panic over it. What took them longest to learn, Miriam said
once, was that the cold air wasn't some slime from a horror movie.
Being wrapped up in it for an hour wasn't going to kill you. It was a
dry cold here in New York, she used to tell them, unlike the deadly
damp cold you found, say, inside Cuban prisons.

This was not a Christmas celebration. But it was no accident that the protest had been called for December 25th. Back home Fidel Castro had long banned Christmas, along with all the shopping for presents that went along with it. Shopping for presents was a capitalist undertaking, my dad told me.

"What's capitalist?"

"Capitalism? It's when you work and get paid for it."

Holding this protest on Christmas Day was simply a bonus jab, another way to stick it to the man who'd caused all these people to have to leave home in the first place. We were walking back and forth crammed within a perimeter of blue, wooden police barriers. Across the street stood the glass and steel headquarters of the United Nations with all of its colorful flapping flags. We were protesting that day against Fidel Castro's attempts to export socialism to some country in South America, I'm not sure where. Every week it seemed to change. Sitting there on my dad's narrow, muscled shoulders I was more or less at eye level with the hundreds of raised fists clenched and pumping the air like the bobbing heads of ostriches. I was four.

"Viva Cuba!" chanted the crowd, over and over. *"Cuba sí, Castro no! Fidel Castro has to go!"*

I was sucking on a cherry Blowpop Hipólito had bought me, taking in the excitement, when it slipped from my mouth. It happened so fast I could only watch it drop to the sidewalk. Except it never reached the sidewalk. Instead it struck a big furry boot and stuck to it like Velcro. Wearing that boot was a girl with frizzy brown hair parted dramatically to one side. She looked up. I wanted to point but was afraid I would fall if I let go of my dad's p-coat.

"Grita, Milano!" shouted Hipólito over his shoulder. *"Grita!"*

"I am yelling, *papi!"* I yelled. *"Ya estoy gritando!"*

I had never been to Cuba, had only the most marginal idea of what it was like there, but I understood that the people in the high complex across the street somehow had the power to help my parents with what they wanted. And that was to go home. To go home and to take me with them. This was my parents' dream so from a very early age I'd made it my own. I believed that getting to Cuba could be a way of filling the hole inside of me. It could be a homecoming for everyone, me included. Binding me to a real family history.

"Mejor Ford que un dictador!" my father was yelling. I was getting

pretty cold as the morning wore on, and tired from all this screaming, despite the atmosphere and all the police looking on like we were the center of the universe. Also, I hadn't gotten any Christmas presents yet. My father had taken me early to this rally, consoling me with the promise that Santa would come while we were out. As would my Uncle Three Bags, who was at the apartment for just about every holiday you could imagine and lots of days in between.

"Why didn't Three Bags or Santa come last night?" I'd asked at sunrise.

"Cuz if they had you wouldn't have come with me now."

I'd been so excited all morning that now I was beginning to crash. Which is why when I felt my left sneaker slipping from my heel I reacted slowly. By the time I did jerk my foot up the shoe was off. I looked down. The girl with the frizzy hair. She was holding it. My white sock steamed embarrassingly.

"*Oye!*" I said.

The girl smiled sweetly and dropped my sneaker to the street and scampered away. She did not look back and was lost in the crowd. The fast-moving crowd. I kept my mouth shut, afraid we'd be trampled if my dad were to try to wade back through the multitudes to fetch one downed blue Ked. Also, I didn't want him to know a girl had bested me. It was only when we were already on the subway heading back to VertiVille that he noticed.

"Milano, *dónde está tu zapato?*"

"I don't know," I said, trying to look surprised. Like my foot wasn't still aching from the cold.

"How is it possible that you do not know?"

"A boy stole it off my foot," I said. "I don't know where it is."

"When?"

"Just now during the march."

"Why didn't you say anything?"

"I did but you were yelling. And he ran off with it really fast."

"This is a strange country," Hipólito said, flexing his wrists forward and back — a hand drummer's habit. "Why would one boy steal another boy's shoe?"

"Maybe he has a little brother."

"With one foot? The chances of that."

"Maybe he was a Commist."

"A communist?" Hipólito said. "That's one for our next

21

rehearsal, Milano. We'll make a song out of that." He rubbed my head. The way people did when I said something they liked.

When we got home we were going to tell my mother and Three Bags the story of the Commist agitator and how close I'd come to falling into enemy hands. We were sometimes allies like that, early on. But there were presents on the floor in our living room. I nearly forgot about the morning's politics and intrigue. Beneath our puny plastic tree, which Hipólito had nailed to an upside-down fruit crate, sat a set of bongos and clave and an old rusty *campana* that rang so round and so true when I struck it that I would have sworn Santa had stolen that bell straight off one of his own reindeer.

"Wow," Three Bags said, inspecting the drums. "These are the real deal. Do you think you can handle that?"

"Botnitz?" I said.

"Botnitz," Hipólito said.

I wore an idiot's smile as I spun in a slow circle and bowed to everyone. I did not need a single other thing in the world after that, because one day I was going to be the *bongocero* in my parents' group, *Los Balseros de la Bahía.* The Bay Rafters.

The rafts were a nod to the rafts Cubans built to flee for Florida. The Bay referred to Pelham Bay, close to where we lived. We were subletting just across a small, smelly river called the Hutchinson, where at sundown rats came out from the reeds to fuss along the sludge-black banks. It was an experimental housing complex called VertiVille. The experiment consisted in taking a lot of poor and middle-class people and stacking them, one family on top of another, in very high, cylinder-shaped apartment towers. They looked like rocket ships from a 1950's science fiction movie. We were cut off from the rest of the city by the confluence of two highways on one side and the Long Island Sound on the other. 1,584 subsidized housing units in eight high-rises that were already beginning to fall apart even as politicians were cutting the inaugural ribbon and lucky renters went rushing toward the elevators carrying TVs. We got there two years after the complex opened, moving into a two-bedroom apartment on the 3rd floor of Elder Tower. A friend of my parents, Dago Martinez, a successful jazz pianist from the Dominican Republic, had turned them on to the place. Dago, like most of the Dominicans in VertiVille, also lived in Elder Tower. Elder was basically a giant grey-green silo packed with nothing but Latinos. Not because elder trees grew in Latin America or anything poetic. People just ended up there by word of mouth. Like us, after nearly a year of couch-surfing the boroughs. In the same way, Maple, Elm and Willow had quickly become mostly Black buildings. Spruce, the closest tower to the river and the last finished, in 1969, was all sorts of Asian although the Koreans controlled the stairwell and the building administration, from the chain mail welcome mat outside to the TV antennas on the roof. You could see lots of Korean flags fluttering from clotheslines. The northernmost three towers, Oak, Redwood and Birch, were occupied by working class whites, mainly Irish and Italian Americans. The whites were well-organized, especially when it came to complaining to city housing authorities about this water leak or that broken handrail. We would complain about the same shit but only to ourselves. And so the whites' towers always got fixed first, and for this they were worthy of our collective resentment.

I'm not saying there wasn't some racial mixing in the complex, but it was rare. Put it this way: I never heard of anyone ever envying a Hmong family toughing it out in Spruce or a Nigerian couple making the best of it in Oak. Or my white friend, Ronny Linky, for that matter, whose family had ended up in Elder where basically no one spoke, or felt like speaking, English. These people were simply not going to find the sense of community city planners had hoped to achieve. And so, almost immediately, people had begun swapping apartments to be closer to their kind, a sort of internal migration within that uncharted principate. It wasn't uncommon in those early years to see a white couple and latino couple pass each other on the commons, each carrying their own belongings to the other's officially designated flat. As they passed each other they might nod discreetly.

The key to making this work was not to alert the housing authorities; because once the city had assigned you a subsidized unit it was impossible to move. The chances were higher that you'd lose your spot in Vertiville altogether. The waiting list to get in was long. Apartment exchanges happened on the sly, even if that meant a smaller bathroom or a floor lower than you might have wanted. The bottom line was that people felt better among their own. More welcome, safer, at home, what have you.

Funny how that same desire for belonging led to a state of eternally simmering tensions among the towers. Fights would start, for example, following the most mundane exchanges between kids from different buildings. One clever pretext for rumbling went something like this: *Whuhchoo lookin at honky? chink? gumbah? _____?* *(Add your own term of affection).* Then it'd be all dust and fists and occasionally, but hardly ever, sirens.

What kept things from getting out of hand was TSS, or Tower Self-Sufficiency. This was VertiVille's innovative genius, authorities said, although they admitted that they'd pinched the idea directly from some hot-shit French architect named Le Corbusier who'd done something similar in his country. Except in his version he gave people balconies. But we had nearly everything else you needed. On the fourth floor of each tower we had a grade school. A tiny but real public school. On the ground floor were shops and cheap-o restaurants facing outdoor underpasses; in Elder you could eat Mexican tacos *al pastor* or *papusas* from El Salvador or rice and beans with *ropa vieja.* In Elm there was a ribs stand with five levels of spicy and who knows what else. Two of the towers, Willow and Birch, had small Gristedes supermarkets. You had halls of worship on the thirty-third floors – closest to God - that you could sign out in advance; a gym and health clinics on floor two along with beauty and nail salons and a small pharmacy. On the groundfloor of each was a liquor store open till midnight and a Help Desk that closed at 5pm if it opened at all. The idea, city officials said, was to create a sense of community and "ownership" within your own tower. And to create jobs for residents. But I think planners stacked all that stuff up like that mainly to compensate for VertiVille's isolation. Imagine those eight tall round towers set in a wide, perfect circle, standing out on a vast former landfill that could not produce grass no matter what they sprayed on it. From the sky the complex looked like the open cylinder on a revolver. Each tower a chamber waiting for some hammer to fall.

We were out there in the proverbial pot but we were not melting. At least this was how my friend Ronny Linky, who was two years older than me, and his drunk-ass parents described it. They'd been in the building since day one. My arrival, Ronny told me, had been a godsend. "You're a godsend," he said, when he saw me for the first time, by the elevator bays. Mistaking me for something I wasn't. "Hellified! Another white boy!" he yelled. His mother shushed him, but there he was dragging me and my parents up to his apartment on the 32nd floor before I'd even had a chance to answer him.

"What's a godzen?" I said finally. We were sitting on his bed trying to toss Leggo pieces into each other's mouths.

"We gotta stick together," he said. His Benji t-shirt had Kool-Aid stains all over it.

"Benji! Guau, guau!!"

"Dogs say bark-bark. Listen, I'm telling you we gotta stick together. Alone, they'll get you."

"Grrrrrr. Who? Bark-bark."

"Somebody who's not one of you," he said. I didn't understand this boy at all. But afterwards he let me play Hot Wheels with him while his folks and mine chatted stiffly – my parents' English was survival level - and drank beer in their bright orange galley kitchen. At some point Ronny's Dad came in and said, "So you're bi-lingual, Milo? You know in America what bi-lingual means, right? One language too many."

In the beginning VertiVille was a pretty nice place to live. My mom said we'd been blessed to find our way into something so spacious for so cheap. Plus, Elder Tower turned out to be packed with musicians, which is how she and Hipólito got Los Balseros together so quickly. On any given floor you were bound to hear the muffled bleat of a trumpet or the tinkling of a *montuno* on some electric keyboard. The low plunk of a stand-up bass. The hollow woodpecker *tock* of the clave. Soon after moving in they started using the 2nd floor gym as a rehearsal space during the afternoons. Miriam said that all that luck had coincided with them adopting me. She said that it couldn't have been a coincidence. She made me feel like a talisman.

VertiVille wasn't supposed to have been so cut off. The original plans called for bringing the subway out to us. But it never happened. If you wanted to leave you had to walk to the nearest subway stop on the other side of the I-95 freeway, more than a mile away. You got there by crossing a green steel pedestrian bridge whose stairs could be as crowded as those in Grand Central Station in the mornings, or via a long, urine drenched tunnel if you had a car. There, on the other side, in the real world without limits, The Bronx extended forever, block after block until it became something else and something else and then Canada. On the far side of 95 you were free. You could go

wild, me and Ronny would learn. You could buy produce from a
Polish grocer named Janski or get a hat made by a gypsy man from
Armenia who also sold expensive cognac under the table or bus it up
towards Westchester to the Korvettes department store, and leave
with some stupid little thing you liked tucked tax-free under your
shirt.

Or you could simply head out to wreck someone's day.

One of the first storefronts you passed crossing the bridge was a
beauty salon for people with kinky hair. At Afro Solutions the ladies
did three things well: straightening afros so that they didn't look like
afros, controlling afros so that they didn't become too unwieldy, and
teasing out afros until they were huge and puffy like chocolate ice
cream cones balanced on heads. In the 14 years I lived in VertiVille I
never saw a single white person enter Afro Solutions. Except me. My
parents both got their hair cut there. Hipólito for a trim, Miriam for
the ice cream cone. I was more than welcome, since my parents were
as well. They were Hispanics but Afro-Cuban – read, black – and
they were mostly treated politely in the African American
community.

There was another reason I was welcome: I was a flat-out
novelty. Being a novelty was great because it helped cover up the
opposite feeling, which was that you were an addendum, not part of
anyone's plan. Kaylie the hairdresser, originally from Cameroon, and
the owner, Mrs. Potter, an elderly, slender American from Georgia,
used to joke over who'd get to cut my hair.

"It's like duck feathers," Kaylie told me once as she gave me a
trim. She was running her chubby, ringed fingers along my scalp as I
reclined in one of her puffy chairs, my eyes closed. "It reminds me of
being back home," she said. I came to imagine Cameroon as a place
where people massaged ducks. I wanted to go there. Kaylie was really
black – nearly purple - and had a long neck and kept her head shaved.
She paid attention to me the way most people didn't.

"You look different today Milo," she might say, if I'd lost a tooth.
Or, "Morning Milo. Nice new book bag." Or whatever.

Hanging out at Afro Solutions after school made me feel safe,
surrounded by witnesses to my legitimacy. By people who took more
than a passing interest in my towhead hair or, later, my left
shirtsleeve. I could also get that feeling at home, or hanging out with
Ronny Linky. When I didn't feel that way was when I was moving

anonymously around VertiVille. This part of what Ronny had told me when we met was true. I was a white kid with hair so white-blond you could practically read by it in the dark. At first the Asians and Blacks and Hispanics would look at me with puzzlement, like I was some kid who'd wandered away from his Icelandic parents at JFK. It made me a target for teasing and, later, a hell load of roughing up. So Afro Solutions was a haven. One result of hanging out there so much as a kid was that my hair was always very short. Dominican ladies and busty black women watched and joked about the fine white snips floating to the floor like seed, and they told me how I was going to go out into the world of white people one day and change how they thought. Because white people were unkind and indecent and white society as a whole needed some rewiring from the inside.

Sometimes when I played my cheap bongo drums the grownups on the music scene would ask me how I did it. Back then they used to say that I was on the road to promise. And that rumor spread even beyond Elder Tower. If it was true it was only because I was surrounded by the absolute best. In that accidental cauldron of musicality, it was normal to be practicing the way I practiced – just about constantly - even at four years old. There was encouragement and there were role models on just about every floor you stopped on. Kike Guerra, the Panamanian *timbalero* who famously refused to play with Ruben Blades because he wasn't roots enough, lived with his mother on 17. On 21, Paquito Flores, the legendary studio percussionist who recorded for forty years before deciding just like that to quit drums and learn trumpet, which he never got any good at. On 4, literally right above us, Jorge "El Topo" Santos. On 16, Ray Bourgesi and his little brother Vinnie. And of course in my own apartment, Hipólito Prieto, my dad, the skinny monster conga player and batá leader, the stern master drummer who had played with Fidel Castro's personal *babalawo* before the falling out.

"What's Communism?"

"It's when you work but don't get paid for it. Or when you get paid for not working."

My father was a multi-dimensional musician who could fiddle on the bongos better than most pros playing their hearts out. Not to mention the piano and *contrabajo*. He and my mom had studied music their whole lives in Cuba. Her instrument was the *tres*. And of course her voice.

There were eleven members in Los Balseros de la Bahía, but not everyone showed up for every gig or party. Like Hipólito, most players had day jobs or night jobs or both and it was the early days, before salsa and the latin jazz scene really took off. Before Roger Dawson's Sunday Salsa Show on WRVR or Pedro Navaja or the weekly gigs at the Village Gate where members of Los Balseros would sometimes sit in with the salsa stars. The Balseros were a mix of Cubans and other Latinos, and my parents quickly got them up to speed on the repertoire of their original son group, from Matanzas: Los Soneros de Matanzas.

It was Los Soneros that had impressed a Carnegie Hall audience one Fall night in 1966. A couple of years later, long after my parents had skipped out on their government chaperones while on tour in Europe, and after we'd moved to VertiVille, the group added the famous Norwegian jazz trombonist Gunnar Gunderson – my Uncle Three Bags - to its horn section, and soon they were making a living – no small feat back in those early days. Everyone called Gunderson Three Bags because that's what he was always carrying. His trombone case and two other bags. A tiny one with a tiny Buddha inside it, hanging from his neck. And a backpack with a change of clothes. Whether he was going to lunch or flying to Bergen.

He wasn't really my uncle but he was that close to us. To me, during that time, he was like a god. So tall, so sure of himself, so funny. He had not yet broken my heart. The first time he came to our apartment, at least that I knew about, I must have been three. He'd just joined the band. He knelt down in front of me before taking his coat off.

"You I have been waiting to meet - "

"Is that real?" I said.

29

" - since before you were born," he said in an accent I'd never heard before. "The emissary from another world! Is what real?"

I pulled on his mustache.

He pulled my hair.

"Gunnar," my mom said.

"I will show you real."

He set me like a parrot on his shoulder and waddled on his knees to the window. Outside, I could see all the way from the dirt fields below to the far blue line of the Sound.

"That!"

"A window?"

"No! What the window reveals." He spun me to the floor and put my hand to his mustache. It was like a hot paintbrush. "Yes, it's real," he said. Then my hand to his forehead. "Inside and out, it's all real! Or, none of it is! What's the difference, if you think about it?"

"Milano, meet a crazy person," Hipólito said. "Crazy person, Milano."

"But the most real goes like this. And it never stops, no matter where you are or what you're doing."

With a thumb under each of my arms Three Bags tapped out the palitos pattern for timbales. I knew that one already. I squirmed, looked up at his comic face. The Einstein shagginess. The pleasure and affection. What can I say? It was uncle at first sight.

Three Bags was the first person I looked at when I saw the old, dinged up pair of Valjes that Christmas. There they were, laid out in a soft black, second-hand case like uneven twins in a baby bed. When I unwrapped them I found the clave and cowbell tucked into the outer zip-pocket which made it – and me – feel mobile and complete. Like Robin Hood with a full quiver. Like I could just wander away, even though I could barely lift the bag's strap over my shoulder to carry it. But mostly it made me feel like my uncle himself, who on his frequent visits to our apartment would tell me that he carried his world with him because he never knew when the world was going to ask him to play. That seemed to me the best way to live.

Kitted out with my bongo set, I got to work improving my riffs off the *martillo* and the basic bell patterns. The son clave, the foundational rhythm, had already settled in my gut, ticking there like a syncopated wristwatch. It was all familiar ground. My parents had been bringing me to parties and *descargas* and religious *toques* since I was a baby. It was the same with the Orishas, the Cuban dieties who we turned to for guidance. To my ear the furious, crackling conversations of the three double-headed batá drums, meant to stir the dead, were like lullabies. Many nights I fell asleep in some steamy basement dance hall, draped over my mother's shoulder as she danced to Yemayá, the goddess of the ocean and protector of children. Miriam protected, me protected. Swaying back and forth, sweating from her forehead to her feet, soaking me like she'd carried me inside her own womb.

Later in the afternoon that Christmas, when Miriam suggested we all take the train into Manhattan to see the tree at Rockefeller Plaza, Hipólito and I remembered about my stolen sneaker.

"The boy leaves the house with two properly laced shoes," my mom said, trying to seem cross.

"*Oye linda*," Hipólito said, tipping his beer toward her. "It was a dangerous mission. You knew that."

"Only a boy with a foot in two worlds could lose a shoe like that," Three Bags said, winking from the corduroy love seat. "Your bravery knows no limits!"

"Hmmm," Miriam said. Then she turned to me. "Milano?"

"Someone stole it right off my foot," I said. I glanced at Hipólito. The thing about my mother - that tall skinny woman who never ate enough and who sang to me and played her *tres* for me and who sent photos of me back to the family in Matanzas, the city she'd been forced to leave behind - the thing about her was that I could never lie to her. Not even by omission. I ratted myself out every time.

"My lollipop fell and stuck to this girl's shoe," I said. "So she stole mine."

"You said it was a boy," my father said.

"There was a boy too," I lied.

Hipólito watched me without expression. He wouldn't have cared less about it being a boy or a girl. But for some reason I'd lied. It wasn't the first time. At that age I loved him as much as I loved Miriam, and I probably tried even harder to impress him. Just as I tried with Three Bags and, later, with Massachusetts. All seemingly strong men who might have some strength to spare, who might scooch over and make room for me. So sometimes I'd bend the truth, to try to score more points. But I wasn't used to getting caught.

Hipólito's bored stare told me that I hadn't impressed him at all. I told myself I'd never tell him a white lie again. And I don't think I did. Not while Miriam was alive.

"Either way," Three Bags said, leaning forward and smiling, his big mustache spreading to expose his upper lip, "this boy deserves a combat medal."

Miriam handed Hipólito another beer. "Feliz Navidad."

"Feliz Navidad."

"Feliz Navidad," I said. I jumped up on Hipólito's lap. His sinewy, shipyard-rope arm around my waist. Miriam pushing second-hand winter boots onto my feet. Three Bags slipping on his parka. Our weird, walrus-mustached Ent of joy, our ever-present witness. Most of the other Latino kids I knew celebrated the visit of the Three Kings later in January. I lived with mine.

A few weeks later Hipólito brought over Los Balseros' *bongocero*, a Puerto Rican ex-cop named Rosario Justo. Rosario lived next to the chapel on the top floor of Elder, the 33rd, and had views all the way to Washington Heights and west to Bayview, on the island. They found me in the basement laundry room, as usual, playing along to the radio. Hipólito came through the swinging doors in his blue uniform from the airport, where he'd gotten a job loading luggage. Rosario was dressed, as usual, like he'd just come from the chapel itself: a pumpkin-colored three-piece suit, alligator shoes, and a white, wide-collared shirt, open at the neckline.

The laundry room was perfect for practicing. It was the only place noisier than the noise I made with my drums and bell. The only place that didn't either attract eager listeners – I was shy about playing in public – or piss off some Mexican trying to nap. That morning when I saw Rosario behind Hipólito I stopped flat out. I turned my Sony boom box cassette player down.

"Qué bolá?"

"Go on," Hipólito said, rubbing my head, turning the music back up. "Do what you do."

"Papá" I protested. Rosario came over and picked up the clave and began to tap out the two-three pattern, humming to the montuno. He smiled and moved his feet.

"Anda, chico," he said. *"Qué te pasa?"*

I waited for the train to pass a couple of times — that's how I imagined the music then - then jumped on with the *martillo*, the hammer, those three sharp strokes on the smaller drum head, the fourth a pat down low. My left hand marking the backbeat, a beat felt more than heard. Until it leapt out to sock you in the jaw. Rosario stepped in front of me, crouching a little, and shimmied his shoulders. My father stood behind him, humming along. *"Vamo', mi'jito."* Go on, son.

And then it wasn't really a train anymore, the music. It went airborne, like it sometimes could, something lifting you, a tremendous hawk or an angel that had caught you from behind, and I was soloing in the old school *son cubano* style, punching, backing off, a butterfly, a bee, like the wise guy Ali from the TV fights. My father said once that Mohammed Ali would have been a good bongocero. Light on his feet, deadly when you didn't expect it. You could translate that into music, he said. Everything always, inevitably, came back to the music in our world. In *the* world. Reduced at that moment to two dancing men and a bony boy making them laugh with respect.

When the song was over, Rosario lifted his sunglasses up, lifted his eyebrows, and looked at Hipólito. *"Sus manos prometen,"* he said. *His hands hold promise.* Then he and my father went up to our place to have an early lunch with Miriam and Three Bags. I stayed for another twenty minutes, trying to get airborne again. But my father and Rosario had taken that fickle, untamable energy with them. That was an early lesson. Music can't happen in a vacuum. Not ours, at least. It needs people. A critical mass. But not the people who were coming down now with baskets of dirty clothes. I packed my drums away and headed back for the apartment, a bounce in my step, knowing that I was in for more compliments and encouragement. Probably some advice too, and some teasing. Days like that were the happiest of my life. Days without any doubts about anything. With my life laid out so clearly before me.

I put down my sandwich and reached for my left shoulder. For the lost piece of the puzzle. My automatic response to anything that knocked me for a loop.

"Just look at them," Julien said, looking where I was looking. "Can the world take so much beauty?"

"Can the world take comments like that?"

We were at lunch in the dining hall. Ragged from the previous night's golf party. At Wimple a golf party had nothing to do with the clubs that would never have us. It was a drinking game. I could remember the bartenders marking our chit sheets after each boozy hole, eighteen in all. And Julien telling me how he'd gotten locked up for smuggling a bunch of drugs from Europe or Africa to somewhere in Connecticut.

"Look at my fork," Julien said, scraping it with his thumbnail, "There's dried egg on it. How can one live like this?"

"Another reason to blow his joint," I said for the zillionth time.

But actually, for the first time since I'd arrived, I wasn't really meaning it; how could I? There was Halsey. Her green eyes, the caramel skin. It was the first time I'd seen her since her orientation ambush two weeks earlier. She and her friends were selecting silverware from the utensil racks.

"Would you look at her. She appears to be *Hispanica*."

"Based on?"

"On things you would not understand."

"Are you about to lay some La Raza bullshit on me?"

Halsey and her friends disappeared into the kitchen, reemerged with their hot lunches steaming wildly in the chilly air of the hall. It was only the end of September but a cold spell remarkably similar to what I'd always understood to be winter had already set its icy backside on the state.

Julien stood up. *"Tu veux quelque chose?"*

"That means nothing to me."

He picked up his tray, leaving me alone at the long table. My wool hat down over my ears. I watched him make his way to the kitchen, legs slightly bowed above his black cowboy boots. The Frog Yank. The Yankee Frog. No matter how you arranged it, the mix — American dad, French mom - had apparently not served him well. Just my kind of guy, I was thinking. Then the cafeteria doors burst open. A guy in a football jacket carrying another guy on his shoulders stumbled in and smashed forehead-first into the central salad bar. They knocked bowls and carrots and iceberg lettuce and two other students to the floor. Including Halsey. Laughter spread through the dining hall. For a moment it felt like I was back in juvi.

And then she stood up, that gorgeous, class-act girl, a year older than me and a world apart, whose only mistake was being in the wrong place at the wrong time. I don't just mean at the salad bar, but by having been assigned to me that first day. She wiped julienned carrots from her face. She was perfect. I knew this based on my deep experience with the imperfect. The look on her face. She picked up her plastic tray and wacked it over the head of the bigger of the two doofuses. The guy was still on all fours. Smack, smack, smack she went, like someone putting out a fire. Corn nibblets flew from her hair. People started getting really riled. I was up and out of my seat. The guy raised an arm to block the blows. His face, when he saw it was a girl, got stuck somewhere between mortified and incredulous.

She kicked him once in the ribs with her funny rubber boots just as I reached him with my canvas high-top Chucky-T's. Lord those eyes. Let's do it again, they said. At least that's what I saw. I saw the two of us stomping on a thousand jock assholes as the sun set over a football stadium in flames. But she just dropped her tray and walked out, leaving me standing alone over our large and already stirring adversary. The students erupted in crazy applause. It was not cheering for the underdog. But for the violence that had arrived out of nowhere. So people everywhere got off on this. Even at the top of the heap.

I waved once then skedaddled myself, right behind Halsey. But just outside the main doors she'd vanished. Where had she gone? As much as I wanted to, there was no time to look for her. Surprise had been my ally once again, but now my physical integrity hinged on hightailing it into the deep woods.

Ten minutes out I found a Douglas fir and hid myself on the far side. To pass the time I got to thinking about all kinds of stuff, my mind wandering here and there. To the weird and out-of-my-reach Halsey. To what I might possibly say to her. To life and death. And the fact that, barring an angry frat-boy catching you, or deliberately jumping from a bridge into truck traffic or something, you really have no idea when or how you are going to die. It's unnerving if you think too much about it, and it was unnerving then. But if the end was cloaked in fear at least most people could take solace in their beginnings. It was their enviable birthright. A known thing they carried around with them all the time without even noticing. Like their own bodies. And surely that would make the ending easier to swallow.

What am I even talking about? It doesn't matter. Unless you never had a beginning. Then it's a conundrum you can't ignore. Because you're unanchored, with fear lurking beyond the last bend and stone-cold mystery concealing the start. No matter where you look you have zero footholds. You are a hologram, truth be told. Anyone who reaches out for you will realize this truth sooner or later. When their hands and hearts discover the nothingness inside you. The honest lack of substance. And when that happens they will walk.

How I longed for solidity. To be someone made of something. But I could only make my beginning up, or at least eliminate the most unlikely scenarios. Early on I ruled out that my conception had been the happy continuance of a story that begins with childhood sweethearts or college sweethearts or two people who fall in love at work or the beach or any other damn place, get married and, to dispel any doubts, make a baby. I could eliminate categories like that because fairy tales and meant-to-be relationships didn't generally end the way my life began: traded away for a green card.

Hipólito and Miriam never hid the fact of my adoption from me. Not that they could have anyway, given that I was the lone pistachio in a bowl of cashews. But they weren't exactly talking about stuff either. Until one day. The great I-wish-it'd-never-happened-but-can't-erase-it-now day. I was in the laundry room, five years old, playing my bongos in my usual winter spot: my back up against the boiler, keeping warm. In front of me, the deep slosh from the long bank of washing machines.

Miriam was emptying a load of dry laundry into a plastic hamper. And she was singing, making up lyrics to the rhythm.

"*A Milo le gustan las alcachofas…*" *Milo likes artichokes…*

"No!"

"But he doesn't like ice cream…"

"Mama," I said, looking up at her and her afro. It was positively colossal and made me think of my own weird, where-you-from-anyway hair. "Was my dad blond like me?" I asked.

"I don't know about your father," she said. She leaned against one of the washing machines, her arms folded across her chest. She hesitated. The air in the room changed. "But your mother was blond."

"She was? And who was she?"

"She was a woman with a hard life."

"What was she called?"

"I don't know."

"Sometimes they tease me."

"Who?"

"In the park," I said.

"What do they say?"

"Patico blanco!"

"Don't pay them any attention. My little duckie."

Miriam kneeled in front of me and put one hand on the bongo, the other on my shoulder. With gestures like that it was like she was completing a circuit. "Sometimes people get into trouble," she said. "That's what happened to your biological mother. She was very poor."

"Why?"

"I don't know. But she helped me and Hipólito. She probably saved us from having to live in a jail. Did you know that? Your mama was a hero."

I tried not to smile. A hero!

"And…was she also Cuban?"

"She was from here."

A hero from here!

"How did she help you to not live in the jail?"

"She invited us to Italy, then Spain, then to play here at Carnegie Hall. Imagine that."

"What's that? Where's Italy?"

"Carnegie Hall is close by. Italy, I'll show you on a map."

"Will you show me today?"

"I will."

"And, and…" My mind was racing. Now that I'd asked the first question, the first ever about this – and gotten an answer of sorts - I had a hundred more all piling into each other. I didn't want this talk to end. It was a dreadful and exhilarating new feeling. "And then what, mama?" I said. "What did my – she do next?"

"She helped us escape from the people who were trying to control us."

"And my mama was a hero, mama?"

"She got us to Spain. Then you were born and we adopted you. The last thing your mama did was invite us to New York. It was our chance."

"And, do you have other kids?"

I was running out of new things to say.

Miriam touched my face. "You've seen the pictures."

"Can they come live with us?"

She picked up the basket of clothes. "You're a hero, too."

"No, you're a hero! Why, mama? Why am I?"

She kissed my head. "You helped us to be a family again."

In the apartment Miriam pulled out an oversized book filled with nothing but maps and showed me Italy, then Milan, the city she'd fallen in love with, the first they'd reached after leaving Cuba on what was supposed to a short, state-sponsored tour, and after which they'd named me. Milan, *Milano*, meant a new beginning for them, a fresh start, an escape. And I was its enduring symbol.

But sitting next to Miriam, looking at that map, something else inside me stirred. Where everything about my past had been an abstraction, now there was this. The trailhead of a route for my imagination to follow. Even if the route had long grown cold. I could suddenly and for the first time imagine myself traveling the converging, accidental lines of destiny that had led to this very moment, and backwards too, to my conception: New York, Matanzas, Madrid, Milan, … each leg a step closer to the entry portal that no one remembers but which gives everyone such surety. A step closer to the woman who'd given birth to me. Actually seeing her in my head. What an image. What a terrible thing. There was a duplicate of myself, physically the same and happy - happier maybe? - kicking cans around a different housing complex, in a different life, with my real parents and their hard, heroic lives. Forgive me, Miriam. My mom who counted. But how it hurt. It hurt like homesickness. But how could I pine for a place that had never existed? For a person I'd never known? I tried to push the longing away but I couldn't. I suddenly didn't want to talk about such possibilities. Here was my mother. I leaned against Miriam's thin arm, then wrapped it around me to shield myself from the feeling. When that didn't work, I tried a new trick that's pretty much kept me on the fucked side of screwed ever since. I flipped my sense of betrayal and the shame over it into anger. A silent, unjustified anger that flamed against my ribs. Burning for any target to make up for my sorry-ass weakness. I aimed it first at the shadow figure of this unknown woman who'd suddenly sprung to life, into my inner life, making me feel for the first time that what I had somehow wasn't enough. And then at the woman hugging me now. For this lapse in our family defenses. Why did you answer my questions, mama? In doing so you exposed my turncoat heart. I tried to push the anger and confusion away. I did try.

I was curled up in a study nook, trying to memorize a conversation between two German students who meet in a school cafeteria. *Grüß dich, Michael. Wie schmeckt die Suppe heute? Sehr gut, danke. Was unternimmst du an diesem Wochenende? Wirst du zur Party gehen? Ich denke schon. Wahrscheinlich wird Jürgen auch hingehen. Wir treffen uns um halb Acht* ... I put the book down and picked up my little black dictionary. But not before glancing around nervously. I was still on the lookout for the jock with my sneaker print on his ribs.

"*Grüß dich, Michael...*" I repeated slowly, out loud, "*Wie schmeckt die Suppe heute?*"

"So now you're German?"

"*Nein,*" I said. My book fell to the carpet. "Uh, are you? Not German also, I mean?"

Halsey's hair hung over one shoulder. She was wearing an old pair of Levi's with a big hole worn in one thigh. The sliver of skin I could see in there, that same caramel color that had been haunting me since day one. She was holding a book in each hand.

"Mom's Turkish. Dad's American. What are you doing?"

"I don't know. But I'd better do it."

"Or else?"

"Long story. But the ending would feature me back behind bars."

"We already are, aren't we." She sat down in the chair next to me and crossed her legs. She was wearing the same rubberized boots she'd planted against that dude's chest a few days earlier. Boots that I'd heard people around here calling ducks.

"Ducks."

"What?"

"They used to call me Duckie back home. *Patico.*"

"Patico."

"Yeah. Cuz of the." I blew at my bangs.

"Where are you from, for real?"

"Camaroon."

"Really. That where you learned how to kick a guy when he's down?"

"Just following your lead."

"You really surprised me."

"Surprise is just about my only – "

There was a sentence in my head that wanted to get finished but there was also my heart that had just stopped. Speaking of surprises: Halsey was leaning over and pulling my empty sweatshirt sleeve from the pocket where I kept it tucked. Seemingly without any awareness that the gesture could be construed as invasive. Just inserting herself right into my whatever you call the space you no longer occupy but still claim rights to. My no-fly zone.

"If you ever need to find Cameroon on a map," she said, leaning back again, "I've got one." She held up one of her books: Deadly Designs: The Colonial Mapping of Africa. I just stared at her. First at her, then at my dangling sleeve. Impossibly, she leaned forward again. She furrowed her brow and took the sleeve and slid her hand up along it, squeezing it like milking a cow, until she struck stub. "There you are," she said. Luckily I was sitting. Only one other person, besides doctors, had ever touched the stump. She leaned back. "Sorry," she said. "Whenever there's an elephant in the room I just have to pinch it. It's a flaw of mine. One of many."

"Pinch the elephant," I said dumbly.

"I should have pinched it in your room. Sometimes I'm so

formal. I'm Halsey, in case you've forgotten."

"Formal?"

"Like the water fountain."

"Say whuh?"

"Halsey-Taylor. Satisfying Thirsts Since 1912? The water fountain manufacturer. Out of Oakbrook, Illinois."

"Where my parents are from, there are people named Usmail and Usnavy."

"It's my father's doing," Halsey said. "It was in his elementary school. For six years each time he took a drink he saw that name. Etched into the little metal ring around the water fountain drain? He ended up creating this character in his head. And then, like, after all that time he felt like he needed to meet his character. To bring her to life."

"Yeah well you and your character damn nearly beat that dude to into the infirmary the other day."

"I have some anger issues. Hahaha. 'Don't make me angry. You wouldn't like me when I'm angry.'"

"That makes you the second Hulk I've met since getting here."

"Who's the first?"

"Never mind," I said, pointing. "Did they send you? Like, on a dare?" Four rows into the reference section a group of preppily dressed girls was watching us.

"Ughh," Halsey said, lowering her voice. "If I'd known Wimple was going to be so bourgeois, I wouldn't have applied. And now I'm stuck here. I waited too long to transfer."

"Stuck is a relative term. No one's locking you in at night."

"It's like a frozen Alcatraz. No need."

She only asked me two more questions that night and neither had to do with what had happened to my arm or why I might just end up back in the pokey. Which I appreciated. The first question she asked as she put her books down.

"Do you mind if I sit here and study?"

"If I say no, you'll probably beat my ass with whatever's on hand. So please do. I don't mind."

The next question came ninety minutes later.

"Can I walk you to your room again?"

It was snowing hard. The only light was from the yellow faux-gas lamps that lined the campus walkways. Halsey jumped around to my right side and took my arm. At the dorm she opened the door and held it for me. Then she bound past me up the stairs.

"Which room again?"

When I reached the landing Halsey was leaning against the wall, breathing heavily.

"Good memory," I said, sticking my hand inside my shirt for the shoelace with the key. "Wimple's only single-occupancy triple."

"You've spruced up the place," she said, going in. She touched the sword of Ogún with two fingers. "This is definitely the most original boy's room I've been in on campus."

"You been in lots?"

I went and took the flask from my sock drawer, squeezed it between my knees, unscrewed the top, set the top on my pillow then held the flask out. Was my hand shaking a little? "Warms the bones," I said.

Halsey took a sip. "Do you do everything like a ritual?"

I shrugged. "Things get out of control quick."

"Oooh. A control freak."

She leaned against the windowsill. She drank again and passed me the flask. I sat down on the bed and looked around. I wished I'd had a radio or something. My eyes kept going back to the hole in her jeans.

"Don't you have a boyfriend?" I said.

"Does it matter?"

"To him, I'd guess."

"I don't."

"How is that possible?"

"Milo."

"First off you, you know, that first day. And you're so beautiful. I remembered your name. Of course I did. I remember everything. Your skirt, your pen. You beating a guy down like we was in the prison yard. Then you disappear like magic. Then you reappear. And you go squeezing my – "

"Here," she said, nearly whispering. She crossed from the window and she took my hand. She drew out my index finger and placed it right against the skin of her thigh, inside the rip. "If I can touch." She leaned into me. "You can too." She leaned even closer and I placed my cheek against her waist and inhaled and slid my hand entirely inside her ripped pants leg, ripping it more. She ran her hands through my hair.

"*Patito?*"

"*Patico.*"

She turned around. My face was against the small of her back. She undid her belt and I slid her jeans down. The radiator pipes pinged in the walls like prisoners tapping out messages after lockdown. She standing, me seated. Her back was hot like the sun was on it. The tiny hairs. No one could take that forever, no matter what his prior sex life looked like. Or lack of a sex life.

What I knew of sexual intimacy was pretty much this: dragging my ass once in a blue moon from Elder to Elm where some young West African girls I knew would take turns stroking the anomaly. Making little jokes about how pink it was, crowding around, looking at me with giggling curiosity or pitying, rolled eyes, walking away, then coming back to touch the blonde hairs again, and me always with my hand for balance against the cement stairwell wall, talking crazy dirty under my breath, my pants bunched below my trembling knees. If I'd been a summer movie you'd have called their laughter uproarious. Afterwards everyone would move away like from vomit on the sidewalk.

And now there was this. I stood, unable to bear a second more, hard as a wrench and already in love. I know that's how it was. Because the feeling has never left me.

After my mom, Miriam, died I never once dreamed of her. Which sucked because it was only through dreams that I thought she might reach out to me. To explain things. From the mystery lug nuts in the mail to why Hipólito had turned into someone else. By contrast Imaginary Mom, the mom who'd come to life in my head that day with the atlas? She'd developed the habit of showing up way too often. All up and down those years of nights when I couldn't really sleep. When she came all I could do was lie there. Eyes open or closed, lights on or off. Desperate, I brought toy store Kryptonite into my bed. A plastic sword. I knew she was really there because of the way the lights of the I-95 traffic whipped across her face like little pilot fish. "After what you did?" she'd say. "You're nobody's hero." She'd sit on the edge of my bed, like she was doing now. Her weight on the mattress, her hands reaching forward.

I woke sucking for air like someone who's barely found their way out of an underwater cave. Halsey spun in her chair. She was sitting cross-legged, wearing only my grey hoodie. Sipping tea from one of her Turkish bowls.

"You okay?"

"Nevah bettah. And you?"

No answer.

"And you?"

I opened my eyes. It was dark in my room but not so dark that I couldn't see I was alone. I stumbled out to the phone in the hallway.

"Could you wake up Halsey? It's okay. Tell her it's Milo."

"Hello?"

"Can you tell me something?"

"That it's two a.m.?"

"Why is it so frickin cold in these dorms? Who built them? Who's the architect?"

"It's cold because it's winter."

"That's the thing. It is not winter yet. Come over."

"Sorry. Bad timing."

"It's cool."

"Maybe tomorrow night?"

"Sure. All right then."

"All right. Night kiddo." She hung up.

I kept the phone pressed to my ear. Kiddo? What am I, your kid brother now? That was swell. A kid brother who you humped twice. I was thinking please, please come fuck me again. I walked to the window, looked out into the howling, crappola night. How could two in the morning be bad timing? Was she with someone else? I decided to go over there and knock to find out. And if it hadn't been so cold I really would have. Instead I ran back to bed and masturbated under my blankets.

The next night she did come over.

"You look like you barely slept," I said.

"I think it has to do with someone calling me last night at two in the morning."

"Funny how you were awake."

"Or maybe it was the cellular biology exam I had this morning. The one I was cramming for all last night."

"Yeah?"

"Have you even gotten out of bed today?"

"It's too cold."

"You're shivering like one of our lab mice. Let's go."

"Right now?"

"You need some warm clothes before the real winter. We mustn't tarry."

"Where do I get warm clothes? And why are you talking like Mary Poppins?"

"Come on ya big baby," she said. Jesus Christ. 'Kiddo', 'baby' – this was beginning to feel a little humiliating. We went outside. Snow tumbled inside my untied sneakers. "Where are we going?" I grumbled. "It's after midnight."

"B.C. Baileys!"

"The circus?"

"We're gonna get you nice and protected."

"What for?"

"For life," she said. "This is what I do." We piled into her car. "In Turkish families older sisters are like mothers. Even half-Turkish families. So - "

That was it. "Hold up," I said. "If you're looking to be someone's big sister? I mean big sisters oughtta keep their panties on, for starters."

"You're a little cranky for a guy being taken shopping. I have two little brothers. I wasn't referring to you."

"I don't need no babying."

"Some people would call it caring."

"I know that," I said, alarmed. "You think I don't know?" I said. But I did not know. This was caring? If so, then why did it feel like an assault? How ass-backwards was my head anyway? The alarms were still going off. In these matters I was moving blind. Let her lead, I thought. Let her take you wherever she wants this to go. And keep your damn mouth shut.

"Hey if you don't like it..."

"Just. Just keep doing whatever. I don't mind. I like it. This isn't how things normally play, that's all."

"Well, welcome to the upside-down world on Planet Prieto. Where's there's no air and ten times the gravity."

"There's air. I'm just gonna stop talking for a bit."

Half an hour later we pulled into B.C. Baileys' enormous parking lot. Not far up the coast a lighthouse light swirled in the fog like the cops were coming.

"On my three," she said. "You good?"

I nodded. We opened our doors and dashed across the lot.

"Holy shiiiiiiiiit!" I yelled over the wind. The gene-altering, flesh-thredding cold. I pulled up my hoodie with my hand, lowered my head and ran in an absolutely delighted panic toward the light.

VertiVille, The Bronx, 1979

"Last apple," said Ronny Linky, my friend, wiping his nose with the back of his hand. "Then we go in."

"Hurry the fuck up, I'm frozen solid."

"You're not even wearing a jacket."

"Next car then."

"Whatever it is?"

He waited.

I nodded.

Normally we were selective. The wrong car could produce the wrong outcome. The next car was a long dark Lincoln. Long dark Lincoln spelled backwards, for example, makes 'wrong.' Too late. As it passed there was a sound like two explosions, and then we were running again. Heads down, focused solely on escaping. I was twelve years old and I nearly left the ground I was moving so fast. Ronny, fourteen and getting really chubby, was puffing along right next to me — surprise, surprise what terror can do - when I lit headfirst, full canter, into a tree. I think it was a spruce.

When I came to I was lying under a car. It was still dark out. Ronny must have dragged my ass under there. He had his hand over my mouth. His faint eyes said what needed to be said: Shut the fuck up, dumb-ass. There were footsteps crossing this way and that in the dark around us. Some horrendous, lethal cussing. The cussing of honest, angry people with plans to kill you. Finally, what felt like hours later, we slipped out from beneath the car and headed home.

My head was killing me and I was cold. I had a raised, bark imprint like a peach pit on my forehead. A bunch of sticky anti-freeze had dripped from the car inside my shirt. Even so, we were already starting to giggle about the whole thing. The whole escaping death thing. The usual high you got from that. Too soon, it turned out. On a sidewalk a few blocks away four guys with pipes came out of the bushes along the water. They'd been hiding just like we'd been doing before we pelted their '72 Continental with crab apples as it sped up the Hutchinson River Parkway.

"Was it you, you little mothahfuckahs?" one of the guys said. He was wearing a dark suit and a tie. He set his cold length of pipe atop my shoulder. Not like he was knighting me.

"What?" I said.

"You little dweebs bust up my car with rocks?"

"What?"

"Did you muthahfuckin' mothahfuckahs fuck with my vehicle? I ain't gonna ask again. Piss-ant honky mothahfuckahs!"

"I'm a southpaw," I said quietly. "Or, was."

The guys looked at each other. One of them bent over and picked up a small stone and threw it to me. It hit me in the stomach and fell to my feet.

"Pick it up."

I picked it up.

"Throw it."

I threw it lamely into the bushes, trying to imitate the girls from school.

"And that's my fastball," I said.

"Whatchoo doin' out here?" said the guy in the suit.

"We're coming from the movies," I said.

"And what happened to your head?"

"I tripped at the movies."

"What movie you see?" said one of the other guys.

And this was what proved that Ronny was my friend. Silent, morose Ronny, who always looked like he was in the middle of being chastised for something. Who only ever really smiled when his dad was fucking with us. Right then, as I opened my twelve-year old mouth and said "The Champ," so did he. Directly on top of my words, like a choir that had rehearsed. Neither of us had seen the film or ever talked about seeing it. You couldn't plan for synchronicity like that. You couldn't plan to save each other's asses in the heat of some stupid event like that. But you were always trying. And sometimes it worked.

We ran up the pine stairs and ducked in the front doors. It was warm inside, and I instantly knew where every kid on campus bought their clothes. B.C. Baileys was preppy heaven. Earth-toned fleece vests and purposely-wrinkled button down shirts hung on racks set out across a huge wood-floored showroom. All that stuff, down to the last pair of socks, radiating security and privilege: whoever bought and wore this stuff would be safe in their never-changing, inheritance-secured New England futures. Wearing this shit to tatters then getting it replaced under lifetime warrantee. Despite how late it was there must have been fifty zombie-faced losers in there ogling themselves in mirrors.

Halsey took me by the arm. "The goal in Baileys is to leave not looking like Baileys." She led me along a flagstone path beneath sea kayaks suspended from the ceiling by rappelling ropes and around a rocky fishpond with real goldfish in it. To the left, a passage way led to hiking and mountain biking. To the right, casual senior-wear. I wondered what that even was. Then suddenly we were among men's coats.

"You ever watch Columbo?"

"Yeah."

"You like his coat?"

"I'm trying to lose the homeless look."

"You like peacoats?"

"Yeah. Real ones."

She pulled a navy blue one off its hanger. I put it on. It was really nice, much thicker than the one I used to have back home, with a silky, padded lining. I flipped the collar up. I looked at the price tag on the sleeve.

"Forget it."

"If you like it."

"I hate it."

"Done," she said.

She took my hand and pulled me away, towards camping. "They sell boots here too," she said. "No more Chucky-T's for you."

We got to the register where Halsey paid for it all with one of her like four credit cards. The peacoat made me feel so comfortable, inside and out. It made me think of my old bongos, because I had the same feeling as that Christmas. The joy and odd discomfort of someone giving you something without you having to ask for it. I promised myself, no matter what, that these presents would not suffer the same fate as my drums. Tossed from a window, lost forever.

VertiVille, July 1972

I suppose the day had to come sooner or later. The I-*really*-wish-it-hadn't-happened day. Was it inevitable or did I summon it? I still don't know and probably never will. Miriam stood in her underwear in front of the full-length mirror on her closet door, holding up different possibilities, frowning at each.

"You pick out my dress for tonight, Milo. I can't decide."

"Okay."

I wandered into her closet, slipping behind the hangered garments. The musty smell of shoe leather and fabric and Miriam herself. I stood there for a moment, my back against the wall, just watching how the slanted early morning sunlight from the street passed through each dress, or how the dresses blocked the light, depending. It was quiet and cozy and like being in a fort, but not a kid's fort. A more mysterious mom's fort.

"What are you doing in there?" Miriam said. "If you hurry up we can still go to the beach today."

"I'm choosing."

I moved my hands slowly along the fabrics, separating each dress, in a world of my own. Like an animal moving through foliage. Some of the dresses were scratchy and opaque, others just seemed to dull the light streaming through, or to turn it muddy. Then I reached the purple zebra dress and the light infusing it was like a soft lavender bath. I grabbed the hem and ducked back out of the closet.

"This one," I said.

"You know what?" Miriam said, smiling. "Hipólito bought that one for me in the city you're named after. Off the Piazza del Duomo. With the spending money Eleanor – they gave us, before we could get on our feet."

"Maybe I'm really Italian," I said, running past her and diving onto their bed.

"You know who's coming tonight?"

"No."

"Eddie Palmieri!" she said, taking the dress off its hanger.

"No way," I said, trying to feign excitement. To not feel the confusion again. It was the first time I'd ever heard the name - Eleanor, not Eddie - but I knew who she was.

"At least that's what Emérito says," Miriam said, smiling excitedly.

Emérito de la Garza was Los Balseros' timbales player. He was from Puerto Rico and played in lots of bands around the city, including with some big names. His claim to fame was that back home he'd done jail time for something Miriam tried to explain to me a couple of times: making fires so that Puerto Rico could be its own country.

Just as Miriam got the dress on Hipólito came home from the airport and his eyes went wide.

"*Muchacha.*"

"Your boy picked it out."

"*Bien hecho, chico,*" he said, winking at me. "Bought that for your mother in Italy." He headed for the bathroom to wash up.

"With the money Eleanor gave you," I said, bouncing on the bed.

Hipólito stopped. He looked back at Miriam like he needed help with something. She looked at herself in the mirror.

"You remember her?" she said. "With the tour group?"

"I do," Hipólito said.

"She gave us that money."

"Yes she did. I'd forgotten."

"So I'm Italian! That makes me Italian!" I yelled, still jumping up and down.

"Yeah," Hipólito said. "Sure you are, *chico*."

I kept jumping because, after all, we were playing a game, right? The game of discussing that woman and that other life, without admitting it. Imaginary Mom. Dodging very carefully what you might unearth if you started digging around: that mix of guilt and anger and confusion. All because of a dress that caught my eye in a closet full of light. Or because in the end all secrets move toward their own unraveling.

Later that morning I came into the kitchen with the snorkel and mask on. I watched Miriam spooning sugar into her little white coffee cup. She'd since taken off the zebra striped dress and laid it on the bed to change into later. When she saw me she shook her head.

"But you promised!"

"If you promised," Hipólito said, leaning against the sink.

"That was before those clouds. And before I realized there is not a single thing to eat in this apartment."

I wasn't about to give up. I started to feel mad. Because she'd said we were going to the beach. But also mad about the name behind the the money for the dress. About how terrible it made me feel.

"*Cariño*, it's supposed to rain. They said it on television."

"It's going to be sunny for a month!"

"How do you know that?"

"Because school is out!"

"You don't even go to school."

"Ronny does. And he's finished. He told me."

"Ronny's finished," Hipólito said. "That sounds about right."

"Okay," Miriam sighed. "But if it starts raining we turn around. And go to the A&P."

We went down to the garage and got into our funny old car. An apple-green, 1964 Cadillac Sixty Special. Hipólito had bought it second-hand with his and Miriam's share of the money they got from playing Carnegie Hall just after they'd arrived in New York. It was partly a celebratory splurge, partly an attempt to bring something solid from the old life in Cuba to America itself. And nothing was more solid than that beast. It weighed two thousand pounds and was an instant hit with everyone, even with Miriam, who was a saver and only ever flashy when on stage. The band was going to use the Caddy on its next album cover, with everyone seated in it and on it and around it. It exuded success, and fun, and just as important, Hipólito said, it would send a big fat fuck you to Fidel back home.

"You wanna curse?" he said to me one day while we wheeled our way up north through Westchester County, on a Sunday drive to nowhere, to other worlds built to other scales - that's to say, not vertically - along back roads and up culs-de-sac lined with mansions where just one family lived. "You wanna curse, you just yell Fuf!"

"Foof?"

"F-U-Fidel!"

"Muthafoofer!" I screamed out the window.

"Just fuf," Hipólito said. "Don't go crazy. Where did you learn that?"

"From Peñones!"

Peñones, aka Carlos the Cusser, was one of the trumpets in the Los Balseros horn section. Miriam had actually kicked him out of our house once for cursing too much in front of me. Peñones had left, bewildered, cursing.

Now Miriam and me were alone in the car, me jumping around on the back bench-seat, her pulling out of the parking garage beneath our building in VertiVille. Growling up the ramp into the bright light. I couldn't get the zebra dress out of my head.

"Fuf!" I yelled.

"*Siéntate*."

I sat down. For a few seconds.

"Mama, can we go to Eleanor Beach?"

"What?"

"To Orchard Beach."

"For a bit," she said, looking at me warily in the rearview mirror. "Then home and a nap."

"Ohhhh! Fuf!"

"It's that or *nada*," she said. "And stop that right now!" She was getting annoyed. Good.

We merged on to the Hutchinson River Parkway and got off and drove for a long time through neighborhoods I didn't know. But at each red light the street sign was the same. East 222nd Street.

"Is this the beach?" I said, talking through my snorkel. I'd put the mask back on, the breathing tube in, and was bouncing again.

"I have to make a quick stop," Miriam said.

"Where?" I said, jumping up and down some more, my hands holding to her headrest for balance.

"I forgot something," she said, pulling into the parking ramp off of a beige, 6-story apartment house, the tallest on a block of mostly two-story houses. She dropped the car into park and got out. The engine was still running. Purring, really.

"Sit down," she said sharply, through her open window. "I'll be right back."

I watched her through my facemask walk down the long, steep ramp to a set of closed garage doors. She took out a different set of keys and jiggled with the lock, then pushed one of the thick wooden door panels inward, accordion-like, and up against the cement wall of the garage. I watched this, boing boing boing, a peeved little seahorse in my fogged-in snorkel-world. Each time I came down I could see nearly all of Miriam's body through the front windshield. When I leapt up I could only see her feet. That made me imagine they were someone else's feet. And that got me more out-of-sorts. I watched those feet crossing now for the other half of the garage door. Eleanor Beach, I thought. Maybe that existed. An imaginary place like an imaginary mom. I bounced even harder. Today would be the day when I did everything Miriam said not to. I took my hands off the headrest. We weren't moving. So what was the fucking difference. On the next bounce I lost my balance and flipped over into the front bench seat, banging my head directly against the steering wheel, my arms splaying out in front of me. My right hand hit the stick on the steering column and I grabbed it and it slipped down a notch or two. Before I had even sat back up I knew the car was rolling. Slowly, but you could feel it. This part wasn't on purpose. Miriam had parked at the top of the ramp, where it looked flat. I scrambled to my knees and looked over the steering wheel like a kid strapped into the front car of a rollercoaster. Except I wasn't strapped to anything. The morning's anger gone. Miriam wasn't even looking. She was totally clueless, as if on a different plane of existence. She was pushing the other half of the garage door open and had her back to me. Almost immediately the car went from slow to very fast. I put my right hand on the dashboard and rose to my feet, somehow keeping my balance. I leaned out the window, tried to say something. To scream something. But I couldn't even remember how to make sounds. My mouth moved but the mouth alone is just a dumb hole. There wasn't the least bit of time for any other thing. I didn't know what a brake was, or even how to turn. All I could do was lean out the driver's side window farther, reach toward my mother with my left arm stretched out as far as possible, my fingers extended, as if I might have the time to tap her shoulder in warning, or to push her aside. But no matter what I dreamed of doing, the front of the car was going to get to her first. And that's how it went down. She heard something and turned and the car plowed into her and knocked her flat against the hood, her head smashing against it, arms out, like she was sunbathing face down, and at the same time we smashed through the half of the accordion garage door she'd only partly opened. It was made of some thick wood, painted black, and framed in iron but the impact of that huge car snapped it easily off its runners and sent one pleat of it slicing forward like a hatchet. I flinched and tried to duck back into the car and I mostly made it. Then there was a second crash that whipped me like a doll back against the steering wheel. This time the horn honked, and stayed honking.

I looked up, dazed, and I saw two things through my now-cracked diving mask. An arm at my side that I hadn't noticed before, bright red and at a weird angle, pinched between the car and a giant, jagged splinter of wood. Then, in front of me, just out the windshield, I saw Miriam. She was upright, her back straight against a concrete pillar, the pillar we'd slammed into, her hands on the hood of the car. One eye was puffed out like a ping-pong ball. Her top two front teeth were gone, her upper lip split and bleeding. The car was holding her there, trapped in the v-shape hollow of its grill, like a doll at somebody's tea party. We looked at each other like we'd both just time-traveled to another dimension. The diving mask was puddling with blood so I pushed it off. Now I could see her eyes clearly, the hidden one and the other one wide open and watching. The gravity in it. Then her head drooped over. Mine fell back, at the same moment, even though it felt so, so light. I rested it against the seat, looked up at the ceiling. There was a strange smell and I was aware that I was soaking wet. There was also a buzz growing in my ears, and some voices now, approaching but growing fainter at the same time. Even the blare of the horn was receding. My eyes got really heavy and began to shut. I didn't like it. Something was closing over me that I would have described as worse than and way beyond sleep and I could not fight it.

Bronx Memorial Hospital, July 1972

I woke for brief periods, like a sea turtle breeching for air. Each time I came to I struggled to stay awake. I didn't want to go back under, even though I recognized clearly and immediately that being awake sucked royally. For starters, I didn't know where I was. Occasionally, floating next to me, was Hipólito's thin face. But I couldn't remember his name or who he was. There was some strange, palpable anger behind the man's blank expression, that much was clear. This pain is for you, his eyes seemed to be saying, but I didn't know why. I sensed the aggression without any outward signs of it. Like his heart was linked directly into mine, same as the tubes that ran from the clear bottle hanging overhead and into my right arm. Except whatever was running from this guy into me was bilious. This was not a dream. I was hyper lucid in those waking moments, even if

I couldn't talk or get my bearings. Then inevitably the clarity would wane, and I would drift back to sleep, succumbing to the drugs and the constant pain humming through my body. The pain emerged from somewhere deep and it would not stop. Not for a split second. Like you'd been kicked hard in the balls and the zenith of that agony just hung there like a high picture on the wall, never taken down. As I said being awake sucked.

You'd think I'd have wanted to stay unconscious, oblivious to the fuck-awful state of affairs percolating in the woken world. The reason that was not the case was Miriam. I could see her face in my mind's eye and remember perfectly who she was. Where was she now? Where was she? I didn't know but I knew something was wrong. That was the terrible pressing mystery I needed solved before I'd slip willingly into that semi-coma of drugs and shock and exhaustion. During one waking spell I managed to work myself into enough of a panic to vomit on my own neck. The nurse on duty cleaned me up and turned the dial on the overhead bag of disappearing potion, and down I dove again.

One day I woke and saw Hipólito there and remembered him. I remembered the accident. Everything, just like that. For the first time I did want the drugs and the forgetting they brought on. I could remember how Miriam had looked in the wet, smelly stillness of the garage as we eyed each other from that close distance, through the blood and the blare of the horn. The tandem slumping liked we'd rehearsed it.

"*Mama?*" I whispered out loud. It felt like I hadn't spoken in years. It occurred to me that that was also the last word I'd said, or been trying to say, just before hitting her.

"*Ahora no puede,*" Hipólito said. His voice sounded strange too. "She's in a bed like yours, upstairs."

"Then... she's okay."

"I'm not a doctor," he said, rubbing his face. He looked really tired. His breath smelled terrible, like Skittles and shit. "You want," he said, "I'll get a doctor who can explain to you how fucked up she is." He got up and left the room. More than half an hour passed. Then an hour. My eyes started to go a little watery. I tried to raise my right hand to my face to wipe them. But I couldn't because moving it was the most painful thing I'd ever felt. I went to lift my left arm but it wouldn't move either. That's when I raised my head a little and looked. My eyes were playing a trick on me. I could feel it but not see it. How was that possible?

There was no one to ask.

In the evening a surgeon named Hotchkiss, a guy with thick blue glasses, sat down on the side of my bed. The nurse with the raccoon face who never once smiled stood in the doorway. "Where is your father?" he asked.

"Con mi mama."

"Do you speak English?"

"He's with my mom."

The doctor looked at the nurse. "I see," he said. "Milano. I heard your father call you Milo. Do you know the Venus de Milo? You're a smart boy, I hear. That's what your uncle says. That's good. You can never go wrong being smart."

My uncle? Someone on a speaker system started calling the doctor's name. "That's my life," he said quietly. "On call twenty-four hours a day." I wasn't sure who he was talking to. Me, himself or the nurse. He stood up in a hurry and left.

The next day Hipólito still hadn't come back. After lunch Hotchkiss popped in again. This time he was alone.

"Hello Milo. How are you feeling? I wanted to see if you had any questions. To see how you were."

"I have…a question," I whispered. Talking was still so strange and tiring. Hotchkiss slid a chair over and sat down next to me. He nodded kindly.

"Can I… have…a glass of water?"

The doctor filled a paper cup in my bathroom and held it for me while I took sips.

"Why can't I see my arm?" I whispered.

He looked at me steadily. "Has your dad talked to you?"

I shook my head, ever so slightly. He shook his head too.

"Milo. You're a very lucky boy."

I was looking up at him, wondering how he was going to make that one stick.

"You were hurt quite badly," he said, putting his hands on the rail of my bed. "Luckily there were people there right away who knew how to help you. It's a miracle you're with us. You lost a lot of blood." He scooted forward and blinked hard. "When you got here, we fixed you up. You had a big cut where your left arm and your shoulder meet. That's where we had the hardest work to do. And in the end we – "

"Turned it invisible," I whispered.

"Huh. Turned it invisible. Well, I'll be. No, little friend. I'm afraid that's not it. We couldn't put it back on."

"Where did you put it?"

"You still have your right arm."

"But I can still feel it."

"That's normal," he said.

That was normal. I was lucky. This guy said the most confusing things. Hipólito walked into the room with Chinese food.

"You can't bring that in here," Hotchkiss said sharply, turning in his chair.

Hipólito shrugged and turned to leave.

"A word," the doctor called out after him. Then he turned to me. "I'll be back," he said nicely. "I'll come in later today. We'll keep talking." He rubbed my head the way Three Bags did. Three Bags! Where was he? Why hadn't he come by to see me?

As the doctor went into the hall I heard him say something in a stern tone, then Hipólito responding that yes, yes, he had in fact told me. Yes, everything. If the boy couldn't remember it was probably because of all the drugs.

But like I said when I wasn't out cold I was as lucid as I'd ever been. Jacked alert on pain. And in all those moments Hipólito had barely spoken at all. Which meant that right now, for some reason, as I lay in that bed unable to move much except my toes and my head a tiny bit, my father was lying to my doctor. Why would he? Since I'd woken up it was like I didn't know him at all. Like he'd been switched out for some cold robot programmed to ignore and lie. Or hate. Or blame. I was really scared. Miriam, I cried, inside my own head. Mama. *Ven acá.* Come. Explain to me what's happening to our lives.

Miriam didn't come down to my room. But the nice doctor Hotchkiss came back a lot. A lot more than Hipólito, who was popping in once in the afternoon, before, I guessed, going home for the night. And in keeping with the new pattern he wasn't talking much. Basically not at all. So Hotchkiss set out to fill in the blanks for me. He explained how Miriam also wasn't talking, how she was resting as deeply as I'd been. He said she'd suffered a lot of "internal injuries" which he described as like what happens if you hit a bag of fruit against a wall.

"The bag might not break," he said, "but the fruit in the bag can get damaged."

"You fix… the fruit," I whispered.

"Or take some out. With your mom we did both."

"Why won't she wake up?"

"She will," Hotchkiss said, looking at his watch. "She's strong. Like her boy." He rushed out again, came back for his glasses, was gone.

The next time I came to Three Bags was sitting in the chair in the corner of my room, leafing through a guitar magazine. He was tanned but gaunt looking, like he hadn't been sleeping.

"Three," I whispered.

"Ja! Milo!" He was instantly on his feet, standing next to my bed. His brownish hair hung down around his face as he looked down at me, beaming. "That was a close one, that one," he said. "Oh brother."

"Crashed."

"I know. I've come nearly every day for the whole week."

"Are you my uncle?"

"I told the doctor that one. Otherwise the visiting hours are restricted."

"I can't remember... seeing you."

"Because every time I come, you are sleeping! Or faking!"

"*Y mi mama...*"

"She is resting. They won't let anyone see her. Only your father is allowed into intensive care."

"*Papá,*" I whispered.

"He's upstairs."

"Tell him I'm sorry."

"Everyone is sorry."

"I'm sorry," I whispered again.

Three Bags put one big hand on my head, brushed my bangs back. "It is not your fault."

"*Mi papá no está bien.*"

"He'll be okay. He is still in shock."

"He's not."

"He'll come around," Three Bags said. He seemed sure of it.

"Don't leave. I'm scared."

"I am not leaving."

"I'm afraid he might..."

The door opened and Hipólito walked in. To my relief several of the guys from Los Balseros were with him. Alex Quesada, the other trombonist, had a big brown stuffed animal dog under one arm.

"*Qué tal, m'ijo?*" he said.

I smiled.

"See, none of us is leaving," Three Bags said. "Are we?" He looked around at the band members but for some reason they didn't look at him much. There was a long moment of silence in which everyone except Hipólito came over and rubbed my head. This made me feel a little like Aladdin's lamp. That things were possibly going to be okay. Then, because it was late afternoon, a nurse came in and chased everyone but my father away. He sat down in a chair by the window and looked out of it, and the gloom resettled. After a little while he left too.

Nathan Hale Rehabilitation Center for Boys, The Bronx, May 1985

"You know what I like about you, Orphan?"

"Are you really starting? It's seven in the morning."

"Not one thing. I dislike every single thing about you."

"Whatever dude."

"I oughtta just kill you. My mom killed a boy like you. Almost."

"That's the crack talking. That towel's not folded properly."

"You think cuz you got that fucking stump you can just be the boss."

"It's a proven fact. One-armed people cannot fold shit."

"My mom folded shit for white folk. Probably folded your shit. Where you live? Mom used to take the bus to Rye. Take me with her if she had to. Town was so white up there even the grass was white. That last family she worked for, they didn't make her wear that slave outfit. Even let her use the car to get their groceries. One day - "

"So now this is story hour?"

Swope wrapped a pair of sweat pants around my neck and pulled the legs crosswise. I went from breathing to wheezing as fast as you could snap a picture. I grabbed his wrist but it was hard like bronze.

"Son, bad idea," said a guard. He jabbed my playmate in the back with his baton. Swope let go of the pants.

"You even got the man working for you."

"Isn't there like a three strikes law for causing me bodily harm?" I said rubbing my neck.

"I only stopped him," the guard said, "cuz I was lookin' right at him. I can't always be lookin right at him."

"That's your answer?"

"You shoulda thought about your particular circumstances before you did whatever you did to get incarcerated."

"Ha haha," said Swope, opening a dryer. "Ha haha." He had the all-time scariest fake smile on his face. "Guess the man ain't always on your side."

"See?" I said.

"I am still going to kill you."

There was nothing wrong with my legs except being bruised, and I had no "internal injuries," so within two weeks I was up and walking a little. Each day, after my physical and occupational therapy, which consisted in learning how to keep my balance now that I was four pounds lighter on the left side, the nurses let me push my metal IV gurney back and forth in the hall. First thing I did was figure out where the stairs were. I'd learned from Hipólito that Miriam was on the fifth floor, two floors above mine. The first chance I had I ducked into the stairwell, dragging the gurney with me, and carried the contraption up the two flights. It hurt a lot to climb like that. Like there were knives in my thighs. I rested on each landing, feeling like I might throw up. Finally I reached the fifth floor but I couldn't open the door. It was too heavy. Pulling with my right arm caused the muscles of my chest to flex, which in turn caused the muscles of my left shoulder to activate. And that felt like someone pouring acid on the sutures. So I knocked. And knocked again. After what seemed like an eternity, just as I was going to give up and hobble back downstairs, someone pushed the door open. It was a nurse, a man with a red goatee and a bald, freckly head. He looked down at me with wide eyes.

"What the?" he said. "Who are you? What are you doing out there?"

"I'm a visitor," I said. "Visiting my – Miriam. Miriam Prieto."

"Entonce' hablas español?" he said.

"Sí."

"Pasa, pasa," the nurse said, looking left, then right. Come on, come on.

He led me down a hall that was painted light green exactly like mine and into a small room. There were two beds, both with the curtains drawn around them. No windows, just the yellowish, wall-mounted fluorescent lights. He went to the far bed and opened the curtain partly. I stood there, thinking he was attending to another patient first. But he just stood there too, watching me.

"Well, you visiting?"

I walked over. Maybe it was because of her head, shaved like that, or because of the white gauze over her eye or the tube snaked into her nose. I let go of my gurney and reached out for balance against her bed rail. Then I touched her stomach. It was warm through her hospital gown.

"Don't touch anything," the nurse said to me, a note of urgency in his voice. I snatched my hand back. *"Nada.* You hear me? You got two minutes."

I nodded and he went and stood like a sentry outside the door.

I looked again. This was really Miriam. Her chest was rising and falling slowly.

"Mama," I said. "Wake up."

Nothing.

"Mama," I said. I stroked her belly like I could comfort her. "Wake up please," I whispered. "Something's wrong with papa."

"Ya está," the nurse said, startling me. "Time's up." It hadn't been two minutes but he was already pulling my gurney away from the bed and I followed it, afraid the IV might pull out of my arm. He shut the curtain again.

"You know you're not supposed to be up here," he said as we walked out of the room.

"Gracias."

"De nada, chiquillo. What are you, her kid?"

"Yeah."

"You sure about that?"

"I'm adopted."

"Got it. Listen now, go back down to your room this way. On the elevator. You're gonna kill yourself on the stairs."

I hadn't known there was an elevator. He watched me and smiled a little just as the doors shut. I must have been a sight. A few seconds later I was back on the third floor and wheeling my way toward my room. I was imagining going in and finding Hipólito seated there, sneaking himself a sandwich or something. He'd say, "Where you been?" And I'd say, "Nowhere. Visiting mama." And his face would get all twisted up, realizing that no matter how he might be changing he wasn't going to come between her and me. Because that's what my gut was saying he wanted to do. But when I got to my room he wasn't there. Hotchkiss and two nurses were though. They'd come to look at the 42 stitches in my shoulder, which were nearly ready to come out. Which meant it was nearly time for me to go home.

"That's good news," Hotchkiss said.

"Not without my mom," I said.

The next day after therapy - it is really hard to walk with one arm if you've never tried it, much less get dressed - I went for my little stroll near the elevators, hitting the up arrow each time I passed the doors. Eventually an elevator arrived with no one in it, coinciding with no one being in the hall, and I ducked inside. I went straight to Miriam's room, nearly colliding with the same nurse as I went in.

"Híjole!" he said. "I didn't see you!" He was pushing a cart filled with sheets.

"Como está mi mamá?" I said.

"She's out of it," he said. Then he put his hand on my shoulder, and whispered close my ear, "But she came to for a minute. She even spoke, you know."

"She did?"

"She said "Tell him it's okay."

"Who's 'him'? Is that me?"

"Yeah, I'd say so," the nurse said. "'Tell him it's okay,' she said."

I couldn't help but smile. "She said that?"

"Yeah."

"Can I go in again?"

The nurse looked around. "For one second. Then these visits gotta stop. I'm in deep shit if they catch us."

I wheeled over and put my hand on Miriam's belly again. "Mama," I said.

"Let's go," the nurse said.

As he led me to the elevator the same question I'd been asking Dr. Hotchkiss came rising up in my throat. "So then she's going to be okay?"

"Of course, of course - "

He stopped talking because two doctors came around the corner, women in green smocks with surgical masks hanging tightly at their necks. They looked at me, then at the nurse.

"What's this boy doing off the children's floor?" one of them said.

"He got lost."

"I was looking for my mama," I said.

The other doctor smiled.

"You're taking him back down?" the doctor said.

"Yes I am," the nurse said.

We both got on the elevator. The doors shut. The nurse cleared his throat.

"So you think you could get me her autograph?"

"What's an atagraf?"

"When you sign a piece of paper. You know your mom's famous, right?"

"Like when you go to jail," I said.

"*Órale*. No."

The doors opened on my floor. I wheeled my gurney off and turned around.

"Are you coming?" I said.

He shook his head, pointed up. "That was your last visit, okay."

"*Pues no.*"

"You got questions, you ask your doctor."

"You want her altagraf?"

"Not that bad."

"Milano?" One of my nurses was coming down the hall. "Where have you been?"

I spun around, nearly lost my balance. "I got lost," I said. My legs were shaking. She strode over and took my hand. I turned back to the elevator but the doors were closed again. I never saw that nurse again.

After that I badgered Hotchkiss about her incessantly. When was she going to be better? When would she come down to see me? When could I go up? He never seemed pessimistic talking about her but one day he sat me down.

"Little friend," he said. We were sitting on red plastic chairs in the kids' playroom off the main hall. There was another boy at the table there who'd suffered a concussion jumping garbage cans on his bike, imitating Evil Knievel. He was drawing a picture of a bicycle with wings.

"You're going to be going home before your mom," Hotchkiss said.

"No," I said. "I'm going to wait for her."

"You'll probably get to go home in a few days. Your mom is going to be here for a few more weeks at least."

"I want to stay."

"But we'll need your bed for any little boy or girl who is sick."

"I could hide under my mom's bed."

"I don't think she would like that," he said. "She'll get better faster if we let her rest. Very soon you'll be able to visit."

"What's taking so long?" I asked.

"Do you know what your liver is?"

The day came for Hipólito to take me home. It felt like being fed to the lions. But I had one last hope: that my release might somehow change him back.

"See you next Tuesday, *pequeño amigo*," said Hotchkiss, trying his best. He shook Hipólito's hand, expressionless.

"Thanks."

"You take care of your boy. Change his bandages each morning and evening."

Hipólito nodded. He had a hand on my shoulder, which was the first time he'd touched me since the accident. He was dressed all dapper today, wearing a pressed white *guayabera*. His shoes were polished. I wondered where he was coming from dressed like that. All I had on was a pair of old brown corduroys and a Tom Seaver T-shirt that Ronny Linky had brought me a few weeks earlier. His visit had been short and mostly silent, but he'd told me that I'd become a legend in his second-grade class. I hadn't seen him since.

The sun was low in the sky as we walked to the subway. Hipólito had taken his arm off me the moment we hit the sidewalk. He walked a step ahead, carrying a big bookbag with my stuff in it. Cars with dust and dirt on them drove by doing the speed limit. There was a black bicycle locked to a street sign, the seat missing. A man walked passed, looked at his watch, rubbed his ear. Everything was going along so normal, like I remembered, and it made me feel terrible. It's when I got that I was the one who'd been altered, that I was the thing that was no longer the same.

The subway ride was frightening enough for all the jostling. I clung to Hipólito's shirt and tried to keep my vulnerable shoulder away from the flow of pushy, oblivious people with their sharp elbows. For some reason we didn't get off at Pelham Bay but farther south at Hunts Point. Hipólito stepped off the train and stopped and turned to see if I was following him and I walked right into his legs.

I followed him up and onto the street. We jumped in a cab and drove another five minutes to the entrance of the big produce market. Trucks were coming and going. There were smashed heads of lettuce in the street with tire marks imprinted in them. We walked into the last brick high-rise before the market itself and took a very thin elevator up, getting off in a very thin hallway. Hipólito knocked at a door. I had no idea where we were, and when a fat lady in an African-looking dress opened the door I had less idea still.

"Hipo."

"Sara." They kissed each other on the cheek.

"Is Sixto here?"

"*Claro,*" the woman said, looking down at me. "He's expecting you."

We followed her into the apartment, walking slowly because that's how she walked. Her living room smelled of incense like the kind we sometimes burned at home. We sat down on a couch covered with a white sheet. Then a man appeared, fat but not as fat as Sara, dressed in white, with a white cabbie cap and shoes, and matching multicolored bracelets and necklace.

"*Hermano mio,*" he said.

"*Asere. Qué bolá?*"

"You tell me Hipo. Hello Milo. Eh? You proly don' member me. I 'aven't seen you since youze was a baby."

"*Hola,*" I said timidly, in Spanish. In that apartment I didn't feel like I was in America. The walls were covered in folkloric art from various Caribbean countries: two-dimensional, cartoon-like drawings of black figures farming, sculptures of pounded tin, dyed cotton tapestries. One corner of the living room was taken up by a huge wooden cabinet. Sixto went and opened it. Inside was a large terra cotta pot, draped in cowrie shells. Most of the shelves were covered in the melted wax of votive candles, dried now like lava. There was a small pair of crutches, a large piece of yellowish coral, a glass of clear liquid and various plates piled with different types of grains. It was the most elaborate Santería shrine I had ever seen.

"You know the Orishas?" the man called Sixto asked me.

"Of course he does," Hipólito said.

Sixto sat down cross-legged on the floor in front of me. "Den let's get started. Sometimes when sump'n difficult happens to us, we contact dem ta help out. Ta figure out howda get better. Dat's what weeze is gonna do today. You cool widdat?"

"Okay."

"Okay. Say hello ta Babaluaye."

"Who?"

"San Lazaro. You're gonna get a formal introduction later."

"I know San Lazaro."

"Good, kid. Sit tight." Sixto and Hipólito disappeared into another room. Then Sixto yelled out, "Sara, get da kid sumpin' ta eat!"

"*Por favor.*"

"*Por favor, mujer!*"

Soon enough Sara came around the corner, as slow as a bank vault door, with a plate with two slices of white bread and pieces of sliced cucumber on it. She set it down on the little table by the couch and made a sandwich, then flattened it hard with the palm of her hand. For a moment you couldn't see the sandwich at all.

"You've got to get some good food in you," she said. She went back slowly and silently the way she'd come, into the kitchen. I could hear Hipólito's voice rising and falling through the closed door of the other room. I picked up the sandwich and walked over. The door must have been made of cardboard because up close you could hear everything.

"*Vamo', Hipólito,*" Sixto was saying. "You really think that's the problem?" I didn't remember Sixto but what I knew about him for sure was that he was a Santería priest - a *babalawo*, you call them. I knew it because of the way he was dressed, and because of his demeanor. I'd met plenty of *babalawos* before. Sometimes at our apartment, sometimes at the *bembés*, the music events. They were a part of the community. People went to them in private when they had problems. The *babalawo's* job was to get you back on the right track. He might toss his cowrie shells and though not exactly see the future, at least get indications from your people about your situation, based on a bunch of yes or no questions. That was one of the cool things about our religion; your dead relatives were still on your side, routing for you and, if you knew how to reach them, sending advice. The *babalawo* passed on that advice. If you were sick he or she could use these same divinations to help you heal. This was what I thought Sixto was going to do for me. For all of us actually, since we'd all gone ill in our own ways. But Hipólito wasn't seeing things the way I was.

"It's the boy," I heard him say. "I'm sure." I froze in mid-bite, the cucumber sandwich jutting from my mouth. I could hear Sixto moving things around, then the light, papery clacking of the shells. "I had a bad feeling," Hipólito was saying. "Ever since we took him in something's been wrong. She never used to look at other men, much less..." his voice trailed off for a moment. "Lately, things weren't getting better, but they weren't getting worse. You know she's not the easiest woman to live with. And now this. The kid is cursed, Sixto. Somebody cursed him. You've got to help."

"Who is his real mother?" Sixto said gravely. "His real father?"

My knees nearly gave out. I knew that I shouldn't have been listening but I couldn't pull myself away now.

"His mother was some crazy *yanqui*. His papa..."

A hand came down on my good shoulder. "That's no place to eat a sandwich," Sara said quietly. Somehow she'd drifted back, silent as an iceberg. She steered me back toward the coffee table. I craned my neck back toward the door but the voices of my father and the babalawo had been reduced again to murmurs. There was the faint clatter of shells, then silence, then shells then the voices. Sara sat with me so I finished the sandwich. It was like eating wet paper now. My tongue had stopped working. I wiped my mouth on the back of my hand.

"You must be happy to be out of the hospital," Sara said.

The door opened, and my father and Sixto came out. My father looked very serious. Sixto sat on the floor in front of me.

"Member weez was talkin' about Balaluaye?"

"Yeah."

"Forget im," he said. "He's for healin' diaper rashes."

"Okay."

"Milo, you know how some kids lack iron?"

"No."

"Well some kids lack iron. It's in da blood." He glanced at Hipólito, then Sara. "You lack iron," he said. "Without it you're weak. An when you're weak you can accidenally, well, have accidents. Think of it like a curse dat weez is gonna cure you of. Like in da movies." I'd never seen a movie like that. He put his hand on mine, and it was like my sandwich under Sara's. He looked me in the eyes. "All weeze gotta do is get da iron back. Some doctors give you a vitamin. But me, I'm better." Now he grinned for real. "I'm gonna give you to Ogún."

And that's how I got accepted into the pantheon, initiated into the four warriors, the gatekeepers Elleggua, Osún, Oshosi and Ogún.

On the subway after Sixto's I was thinking how I was going to get better, now that the warrior Orishas were protecting me. It was like I had just joined a superhero alliance. But then Hipólito put together the longest string of words he'd directed at me since before the accident.

"Whatever happened to you, happened before you were born," he said, "We didn't do it to you."

"Do what?"

"That's one thing the shells said. The other is that the warriors are going to hold that evil off. Otherwise no one around you is going to be safe."

"I just need iron," I said.

"Iron doesn't matter."

"Sixto initiated me."

"To protect us from you."

"Okay."

We walked the couple of miles to the overpass connecting the Bronx to VertiVille. My shoulder was aching a lot. From the bridge over I-95 those round buildings rose up before us, a circle of dark grey silos, something you needed to observe from space for it to make any sense. We climbed across and down to the expansive treeless, grassless lots. There were tons of other people crossing too, people coming home from work, but I didn't recognize anyone. I wondered if Kaylie and Mrs. Potter were in the beauty salon. I really wanted to see them. But Hipólito took me straight up to our apartment.

"Nothing's changed," he sighed, holding the door for me. "You know your way." He held out my backpack and I took it. Then he went to the kitchen and opened a beer and stared out the small window. He didn't seem like he was going to speak more, so after a minute I padded down the hall to my room. Things, as Hipólito had said, were exactly the same. Except for the spirit of the place. A terrible feeling came over me, but I didn't dare run to Hipólito for comfort. If I was cursed, I didn't want to harm him. I set the bag down on my plastic handicrafts table and laid myself gently on my bed. In the kitchen the phone rang. My scar was itching like crazy. I tried not to scratch at it since it was all scabby still, but I couldn't help myself. I took a T-shirt from my chest of drawers, balled it up, and rolled it gently back and forth over the tender, inflamed skin. Later I used it to daub up the droplets of blood, which caused it to itch more. There was some medicine for this in the kitchen, in a plastic bag, but I didn't know which bottle it was and didn't want to ask.

To take my mind off the agonizing irritation I tried to figure out exactly how much time had passed since the accident. It had been a hot summer morning the day we'd set out for the beach. But now the evening was cool, the air crisp. Ronny was already back in school, I think for like a week. Which meant I'd missed a week of kindergarten. I thought to ask Hipólito about it but again my gut said bad idea. I'd just get up in the morning, I thought, go by Ronny's, tag along with him. He could show me where to go.

When I woke it was still dark. I washed my face then tried to brush my teeth. I put the toothbrush on the edge of the sink. When I tried to squeeze some toothpaste on to it I knocked it into the open toilet. I had just peed. I fished it out with my hand and dropped it in the sink. I washed my hand under cold water, gently palming the bar of soap.

For clothes I chose the largest T-shirt I could find and a pair of shorts with a snap instead of a button. I wanted a big shirt because I figured it'd be easier to get on, and would better hide my injury. It hurt like hell anyway pulling it over my head. I slipped my feet into a pair of flip-flops.

In the kitchen there was the bag with the bottles of medicine I was supposed to take. But I didn't know how or how much and I couldn't read to figure it out. I got a chair and pulled it over to the refrigerator and opened the door. For breakfast I had a glass of water and two cold chicken wings. I was staring out the window, trying to decide when it would be light enough to go get Ronny. Better early than late, I thought. I undid the chain and opened the front door.

"Wait," came Hipólito's voice from down the hall. He came shuffling out of his room in his underwear.

"*Adónde vas?*"

"School," I said.

"You take your medicine?"

I shook my head.

"This is what you need to stay on top of."

He went and grabbed the bag and shook out two different pills, then consulted a sheet of green paper. He handed the pills to me.

"The little white one, you can't forget to take it. Every eight hours. It's so you don't get sick. The other one is if it starts hurting."

"Okay."

"Don't forget," he said.

"Okay, I won't," I said quietly. I put the pills in my pocket.

"You end up back in the hospital and I'm gonna have problems."

I nodded and left, walked down the hall of my building. I needed not to get sick to keep my dad out of trouble. I needed iron to keep the world safe from me. I got off the elevator on the 32nd floor and walked once past Ronny's door, listening for sounds of movement, breakfast dishes, voices, anything, then sat down on the floor by the emergency staircase and waited.

I woke up at the sound of a door opening. But it was the door next door to Ronny's. "Whachoo doin sittin out here all by yourself, young man?" the woman said as she passed.

"Waiting for a friend, to go to school."

"On a Sunday?"

When she was gone I took the elevator back down to our floor. But I couldn't get back in to our apartment because the front door was locked. So I sat down and tried to fall asleep again. From someone's apartment I could hear a radio. There was singing and then a preacher. He talked about an original sin and how man must spend his time asking God to forgive him for it. When Hipólito finally opened the door it wasn't because he was looking for me. He was going somewhere. He had his coat on. When he saw me his eyes went wide.

"We've got to get you some keys," he said. He held the door for me so I could go inside. Then he shut it. I just stood there in the entryway for a while. Everything was so quiet. It was definitely a strange feeling to be alone in the house. But less strange than being there with my dad.

I watched TV and dozed until Hipólito came home, in time to cook us an early dinner – pancakes from a box of powder. Without thinking he told me to do the dishes, then said forget it. The next day I got up early again and ate something out of the fridge, then took the elevator up to Ronny's floor and waited. He came out pretty soon after, carrying a Jets bookbag. He was moving quickly and the door shut behind him even quicker. He'd gotten his head shaved, which made his round face seem rounder.

"Hello," he said.

"I like the Giants," I said.

"You're home."

"Yeah."

"That was a very long time."

"It was summer," I said. "Now it's Fall."

"You look all right."

"I'm okay."

"Well, I have to go to school."

"Wanna see it again?" I said

"Yeah."

I reached across with my right arm and lifted up my T-shirt. I pulled the loose gauze to one side.

"Snap," he said. "It's so red. Like a tuna. Is that bone? How many stitches was it again?"

"42. That's more than you've had."

"I've never had any stitches," Ronny said, staring. I pushed the damp, sagging gauze more or less back into place, then lowered my shirt.

"Well, I gotta go," he said again.

"Me too. I'm going to school too."

"Okay. Come on."

"What floor is it on?"

"4th."

In the elevator he said, "Something's really stinky."

"No it isn't."

At the school I followed him into his class.

"Who are you?" his teacher asked me.

"Milano Prieto," I said. "I go to kindergarten."

"Who is your teacher?"

"I don't know."

"What is that odor? Have you been hurt?"

"No," I said, instinctively turning away from her.

The woman slipped on her reading glasses and lifted my shirt.

"Well that's just terrible. When was the last time you went to a doctor?"

"I came home two days ago."

"And when was the last time someone changed this dressing?"

"I don't know. At the hospital."

"Pat," the teacher said to a younger woman by the windows. "I'm going to take this boy down to the office."

After that Hipólito made sure to wash my wound and change my bandages every night. He also went shopping, bought some juice and milk and some bread and jam. Once a week some lady started stopping by to check in on us. She was Puerto Rican, and actually lived in VertiVille herself, although in Elm, two towers away. We always told her the same thing, that everything was fine. Once she asked me if Hipólito was treating me okay, if he was hurting me. Everything was fine, I said. Hipólito was sitting next to me when she asked me that.

He never did hurt me physically. It sounds strange to say, but somehow that was part of the problem. If he'd been smacking me around there'd at least have been bruises, something tangible, something that might have forced this nice lady's hand, compelled her to intervene. But what he was doing was the psychological equivalent of beating me with a phone book, which if you do it right doesn't leave marks. Dr. Hotchkiss may have been right when he said he was sending me home with no internal injuries, but I was sustaining them now.

In the face of Hipólito's efforts to unknow me I adapted as I could. Hanging in there became the focus of all my will. Part of me even began to feel better. We had thrown up an altar to Ogún, and I was saying my prayers, lighting the candles at night, topping off the little glass of rum, setting out rice and other grains on a plate, burning incense. Maybe if I did everything right the warrior-saints would forgive me. Help me get my strength back. Hipólito had said it was impossible, but I would go on eating, bathing, taking my medicines, going to school. Because this was all temporary. Miriam was coming home. Sometime. And when she did I'd be safe again. I'd tell her about the curse or whatever it was, about what the babalawo Sixto had said, and she'd cure it herself. Or at least send it into remission.

Two weeks after I'd gotten home myself Hipólito took me back to the hospital to see her. And I knew there would be no such talk. At least not for a long time. Miriam was too weak. She could barely speak.

"*Hijo mio,*" she said, looking up at me with her good eye.

"*Cuantos tubos,*" I said, my voice nearly a whisper. I counted four different tubes or wires running from machines into her. "I'm sorry."

"How is school, *m'ijo?*"

"I like it. One girl teases me."

"Why?"

I wiggled my shoulder.

"And what do you do?"

"Nothing. I don't care."

Miriam signaled for me to give her my hand. "Look at how strong you are," she said. "You know what all this proves, right?"

I shook my head.

"That you can take anything." She lifted my hand to her mouth and kind of kissed it with her cracked lips. "Now, let me see."

I wanted to tell her then, to tell her about the damage I'd caused, about how damaged I myself was, but I couldn't. I didn't want to scare her, or scare her off. Instead I slipped off my denim jacket and lifted up the left side of my T-shirt. She looked like she would cry. She touched the scar tissue gently with her fingertips, sliding them along the reddish, mottled lines like someone reading Braille. I thought I would faint.

"*Voy para un café*," Hipólito said, leaving for the cafeteria downstairs.

When he was gone she said, "You looking after your papa?"

I nodded. "Can you come home today?"

"Not yet. Soon."

I felt the lump in my throat. I tried to swallow. Then I said, "I'm sorry mama."

"I heard you the first time," Miriam said, looking serious. "And I don't want to hear it again."

"Okay."

"Do you know why?"

"No."

"Because it's not your fault. I left you in the car. I forgot the brake. I'm the one who's sorry."

I nodded.

She started to say something, then stopped, and said, "And Ronny?"

"We take the elevator to school together."

"You must be a hero in your class."

I tried to hide my smile. "No," I said.

"You're one of mine," she said. "I want you to do two things. Never say sorry to me again about this." She waited. I nodded again. "And I want you to listen to your father."

The second request was going to be easy, since there was basically nothing to listen to. And at that very moment, at least, it seemed the first part would be possible too, as I stood there being smiled at, and touched, and absolved.

That afternoon after seeing my mom I went up to Ronny's apartment. There were three guys in the first elevator that came, smoking something in a pipe and laughing. One of them pointed at me. "That is fucked up!" he said coughing. The next elevator was empty. At Ronny's apartment Mr. Linky opened the door. "Hey, hey." He was holding a beer. "If it isn't Houdini himself!" He stepped to the side and I was surprised to see Ronny lying on his stomach on the floor. There was a green nylon rope wrapped around both ankles that ran to his wrists, which were behind his back, then to a slipknot around his neck. He looked up at me.

"Hi."

"Hi."

"Come on in, Houdini," Mr. Linky said. "Let's see if you can squirm out of this one."

He put down his beer and walked over to Ronny and pulled a second slipknot near his son's left foot. The whole complicated binding went slack, and Ronny lowered his feet to the floor and rolled on to his back.

"It's impossible," he said, smiling apologetically, rubbing his wrists. "I've never gotten out of the Black Widow."

"I said, come in," Mr. Linky said. I took a step into the apartment and he shut the door behind me.

"What's the black widow?"

"Lie down, Houdini."

I shook my head.

"You're tellin me you're afraid of a little rope?"

"What's up?" Ronny said. But I couldn't have said. I wondered where Ronny's mom was. Sleeping, I guessed. She worked at an all-night market, one of those places that competed against the bodegas. Not that she was any nicer. I was going to just leave. I was actually turning to go.

"You've got luck on your side, kid."

I stopped. Again that word.

"Not everyone would have walked away from a wreck like that. A little lighter for the effort, but still. Come on, show us your magic. Show us how you escaped the last trap. I'll time you. It'll be a competition."

"Yeah!" Ronny said.

I lay down on my stomach and submitted myself to the Black Widow. Nobody had called me lucky in a long time, except for Hotchkiss. The word ignited this irrational hope inside me. Maybe it could be true. Ronny's dad rigged me up but couldn't get the choke line to work right; with my arm gone it was like a chair without a leg. Everything he tied I got right out of. Each time he'd laugh. He said, "Damn, you are a little Houdini." I ate dinner there too. Ronny's dad had us do the dishes then start cleaning the whole kitchen. When he was passed out in his chair I closed the oven door. Ronny was already asleep, right there on the linoleum. I went home. I had my own key now so I could get into the apartment by myself. I hadn't seen Hipólito since the morning but I knew he was gone because there were no new dirty dishes in the sink. Sometimes he was out of town for several days at a time. Touring maybe.

One day in late October, just before Halloween, I came home from school and there was Miriam sitting on the couch in the living room. She was wearing a big brown cardigan sweater exactly the color of her skin. Hipólito hadn't told me when she was coming home. She was reading a magazine. When she heard the door open she looked up.

"What on earth are you wearing?" she said.

"The boy dresses himself," Hipólito said from the kitchen. "He's done a lot of growing up."

I ran down the dim hall toward the living room, ignoring this latest petty betrayal. Her smile. That was the real door opening. I was running but before I reached her I knew I had to slow down. She was not better. She was pole thin. Her neck especially. Sitting like that, she reminded me of an insect, a praying mantis or something, with her arms half folded at her chest and her head now so disproportionately large. Her one good eye sunken like a dark gem into her face. The other still patched over with white gauze. Her hair still not all grown back. For some reason she hadn't looked nearly this bad when she was lying down.

"*Despacito*," she said. *Easy.*

"Mama."

Her teeth. Her voice. I went and sat down next to her on the couch and took her right hand in mine and lay my head gently against her shoulder. This was the exact same way we used to sit when we watched TV. Except now the full extent of the damage I'd caused had me shaking. Even though I'd been absolved. Guilt, I was learning, didn't wash off so easily. Hipólito came over and handed her a glass of water and a little blue pill. She swallowed it, dribbling some water on her sweater. She winced.

"You okay, baby?"

"Are you better, mama?"

"I moved around a lot today. I just need to sit still."

"You sit still," I said.

"As soon as I can get around," Miriam said, "We'll go shopping. We'll get you some clothes. And a ham for Thanksgiving."

"The boy will go shopping," Hipólito said, coming into the living room. "You just give him a list." He'd made a sandwich for himself. I looked at it, then tried not to look at it.

"You hungry, *hijo*?" Miriam said.

I shook my head.

"What's that behind your ear?" she said. She pushed my ear forward and scraped at its base.

"Ow!"

"You're all scabby back there." She glanced at Hipólito.

"I brush my own teeth," I said. "I learned how."

"What you need is a total scrub down."

"I've been working a lot," Hipólito said.

Miriam was looking at me. I was looking over her shoulder, then at the ceiling, then at my hand. I covered my eyes.

"What's wrong? she said.

I fell back against her, heard her gasp a little and go tense, then her right arm pulled me close. So much for me staying strong.

"Why are you crying? I'm home. I'm going to be okay."

Hipólito got up and took his plate and headed for the kitchen.

"He's been like that," he said. "It's why I took him to see Sixto."

"Sixto?"

"To cheer him up. To show him things will get better."

That was it. I stood up and wiped my eyes and screamed toward the kitchen, "Liar!!! Liar!!! Liar!!! Liar!!!" I swung my hand slowly through the air, then faster, like I was punching at someone.

"What's wrong with you?" Miriam said.

Hipólito came out, drying his hands on a towel, and stood in front of me.

"You don't want to do that," he said.

I hesitated, my fist in the air.

"What is going on?" Miriam said.

Hipólito shrugged.

"Liar!" I yelled one last time, swinging my fist at his balls but hitting his thigh. I ran to my room, slamming the door. The anger took me over completely. I punched my pillow again and again. I was screaming. I didn't hear Miriam come in. She was in a wheelchair, which I hadn't even noticed was in the living room.

"Hey," she said. "Sixto is our friend. Don't be afaid of him."

"Not him," I said. "Him. Somebody switched papá."

Feast of Babalu Aye (San Lazaro), December 1972

My uncle Three Bags could not only play the most monstrous bone. The man could cook. Today he was making us something that in Norwegian sounded like guts splayed on a cutting block but turned out to be roast ham. It smelled delicious. From where I sat on the couch, next to my dad, I watched him move around our kitchen with his perpetual stoop, a man grown too tall, sliding open this drawer and that with his long arms. Moving along right beside him was Consuela, a freckled, green-eyed Cuban who we called La China. La China was the daughter of a Cuban diplomat and had been living in Mexico with her family when she'd decided to come north and never go back. She seemed very old to me, but she was only twenty. She sang back-up for my mom in the band.

Hipólito hiccupped. He was with me on the orange couch in one of his sleeveless undershirts, staring at a football game on the television, beer in hand. He normally didn't watch football but this season he'd taken a liking to it. Or to just staring at the television. It was hard to tell since the accident.

Miriam was in her room, resting.

Three Bags opened the oven door. "This ham is ready!" he said.

I slipped off the couch, adjusted my shirt over my bandages and went to help Miriam. When I got there she was already seated in the old metal chair.

"I can push you."

"Help me out of here."

I wheeled her with difficulty to the table in the living room. Everyone was watching us. There, where her normal chair used to be, she locked herself down. When Three Bags saw her he got a sad look. He had set the ham out and was shuttling platters of yucca and plates of pineapple rings and bread to the table. Hipólito came over and put his beer on his paper napkin and we sat. It was clear he wasn't going to do much else so Three Bags started talking.

"Well," he said in his messed-up English, "Here we sit together. We are thankful that both Miriam and Milo are back with us. If Babalu Aye had a hand in that one, thank you. San Lazaro. Please watch after all the sick beings of the past, present and future. And may you be free of suffering yourself. From the drawings it looks like you are suffering too. We offer this ham so that all sentient beings may be liberated from samsara." He cut a piece from the ham and set it on a small empty plate at the center of the table where it steamed, unaccompanied. We all stared at it.

"Nobody can touch that one," he said.

"Who's it for?" I asked.

"It's for all the hungry beings in the world. And if they don't eat it, it's for Babalu Aye's dogs." He stood and grinned and leaned back over the ham. "Now this we can eat!"

"Who's Sam Sara?" I asked.

Three Bags laughed. So I laughed. "That's good! Samsara's not a person! It's all people. It's the whole world of actions and reactions, the endless wheel of cause and effect which leads us to misery."

"*Está' loco*, Gunnar," Hipólito interrupted. It was just three words but you didn't need more. The heaviness intruding. The heaviness that had moved in with us and stayed. Even with Miriam home from the hospital. "You and your crazy talk," he said.

"He understands," Three Bags said, winking at me. "I just use the wrong words maybe. But anyway you're right," he said, shaking his head. "It is time for me to shut up!" He raised his can of beer and drank. "Eh Milo?" he said. "You're like me. You have your feet in two worlds. That's why we understand each other. But you are luckier than me," he said, pointing with his fork. "Me, I never had anyone like me to guide me!"

Miriam smiled weakly, silently. She looked happy herself for a second, watching Three Bags insist that happiness was okay. When Miriam spoke these days you could barely hear her. Her singing was finished. That was sinking in hard. But at least now she seemed cheered. I was giggling too and nodding my head. Normally it wasn't what Three Bags said that made me laugh – not at that age, not that day – but the way he said it.

"Take love," he went on, despite himself, tapping his temple. "I am Norwegian. Norwegian girls are extremely crazy. Did you know? When they love you it is always like a project. Like rescuing a cat from a tree or stacking wood. It is very enjoyable but it is serious business, with a goal. But Cuban girls, just for example? They are not trying to save anyone, achieve something, to construct some larger meaning out of the moment. They are in the moment with you and then you watch the moment slip away together. It is very Zen. Altogether, completely without sense. I recommend it. One day."

La China smirked. "I'm with you, Hipo, Who is this *loco*? *Cuidado*, Papi. You're starting to sound senile. Enough to drive a girl like me into the arms of a young man like Patico here. Who's closer in age, by the way."

"Now that would not be Zen," Three Bags said. "That would be cradle robbing. And that never works out." When he said that he wasn't looking at La China. He was looking at Miriam. Hipólito was staring at his beer.

"Hey, Three Bags," I said, "*Tú eres* Zen!"

"If I'm Zen, you are Zenner!" he said, stabbing his ham.

The love he'd just been rattling on about was a mystery, and I wanted him to explain it more. But he was passing the plates around now, loading them with ham and the golden, slightly burned yucca, humming, then pursing his lips without realizing it, the way horn players did. I watched him from behind my long bangs.

"You'll see. You'll see, Patico. You are also of two worlds. Maybe three!"

Hipólito nudged me. "There is only one world. And in it the food grows cold. Eat."

I picked up my fork, humming to get out from under that, ate some yucca, then tried to cut the meat. The ham was tender but it was too thick for me to work the fork through. Before Miriam got home I would have picked it up with my fingers. She was sitting across from me, glaring at Hipólito.

"*Qué?*"

"Help the boy."

"He can cut his own meat," Hipólito said, sipping his beer. "He's been getting along just fine. He's big enough to push you in that chair."

"Are you going to take that back? Or do I need to wheel over there?"

I wiped at my eyes with my napkin.

Hipólito put his hand on my good shoulder.

"I'm teasing. Sit up. Eat."

I would have given my other arm for him to not be lying. Since the accident Hipólito was always doing this, then lying about the lying. The tears kept falling and I could feel Three Bags' eyes on me. If only he could offset what my dad had become. I needed him to come over more and watch TV with me. I needed him to take me out of the house sometimes, maybe back to Botnitz's some Saturday even though my music days were finished too.

He was shaking his head now, cutting through his ham with his little knife like it were paper. "Is what you are serving more appropriate for a five-year-old?" he said. "Cut the boy's meat already."

"He's old enough! *Coño.* And if he isn't, the sooner he grows up the better." Hipólito stood abruptly and took his beer and disappeared into his bedroom.

Miriam watched him pass. When he was gone she set her napkin down and flipped off the lock on her chair. I thought she was going to go after him but she swiveled around and wheeled over to me. She picked up my knife and grabbed the fork from my right hand.

"You *are* getting to be a big boy," she said quietly. Two ideas occurred to me then. First, I would never do that, never cry, in front of Hipólito again. This was more than an idea. It was an oath and a commitment. The second was that Hipólito would no longer be my father. I wouldn't let him. Now that Miriam was home. He was forfeiting his rights through meanness and negligence. Which may have been exactly what he was after. Either way, with my mom back the idea didn't scare me anymore. My mom, who'd said she'd forgiven me. For whom it had all been an accident, one-hundred percent.

I wiped my eyes again and took the fork back from her.

"This way," I said, sticking the fork into the ham. She thought I meant this was the way we could cut the meat. Me holding the ham down, her cutting it with the knife. But I was thinking, this is how everything will work. The two of us getting whatever it is we need to get done. Dragging ourselves back towards normal. Like the devotees of San Lazaro. The way Miriam had explained it. On hands and knees, tethered to cement blocks, moving inch by inch, leaving behind trails of blood and skin on the streets, some with their eyes to the heavens, sliding on their backs, or crawling, day after day. What kept them going was that final destination, the arriving, and beyond that the hope that this year or the next their healing might begin.

I brought the first piece of ham to my mouth. It was hot and sweet with the pineapple juice. I was mulling over Three Bags' weird ideas on love again and I thought, what's wrong with the way the Norwegian girls do it? Loving to rebuild what's been broken. Babalu Aye would approve. I promised myself to love Miriam that way for the rest of my life. To love her and to push her chair, to complete her wherever I could, until she was restored.

Orchard Beach Cemetery, The Bronx. March 11th, 1973

On the day of the funeral it was so warm and sunny, which made
no sense unless it was part of some larger insult. Where were the sad
clouds? The heat and the glare had everyone on edge and fidgety.
Also there was the issue of that deep, dark rectangular in front of us.
Three Bags was especially out of sorts. He was crying like crazy.
Hipólito was looking at him funny. He didn't give you the feeling that
he was about to get up and hug his friend. My dad just sat next to the
grave, on a brown metal folding chair, rolling his thumbs, as silent
and grim-faced as he'd been for the better part of the six months
since the accident. Nothing about him had changed at all in that time.
It made me think that he'd been mourning from day one, before the
doctors had even begun replacing their optimism with neutral
platitudes, with the possibility of bad news, with the certainty of it.
As for me, I never saw that certainty coming, or hadn't wanted to.

I was sitting on the far side of the hole, trying not to look back across at my father, trying to keep my mind on the mundane details. They could distract me from this ending. There was an old RC Cola pop-top sticking out of the high mound of dirt, the sun making half of it glitter. There was the dirt itself. When the wind blew you could see the tiniest amount of it slip loose and avalanche into the hole. How many years would it take for the wind to fill it in? The men with shovels would be faster, of course. I was dismayed to see them arriving. I'd never thought about how you lowered caskets into the ground, but when the ceremony was nearly over I learned that it required six men struggling with dirty ropes, slipping in the loose dirt in dress shoes. Our little corner of the Orchard Beach Cemetery was packed with mourners and they all rose to their feet as Miriam went in. So many friends and so many of the players had come around to say goodbye. Reporters, even, from the music magazines and radio. *Adió' bonita!*, they called out - *Cuídate mi amor! Nos vemos muchacha!* They'd all come out to see off their friend and colleague. This woman who'd never changed on the inside despite the hardships but whose insides could not be coaxed back from their own set of difficulties. The blunt trauma of the accident, on top of the earlier trauma of her year in prison, had finally conspired to send her liver a cold directive: power down. And there she was now, listing and swaying into the hollow, the guys lowering her like they were docking a boat for the first time, quarrelsome, somewhat panicked. I stood up because I couldn't find another thing to think about except that, and kicked furiously at the mountain of loose dirt with my leather shoe, sending dirt showering over the grave and onto the laps of all those friends seated on the far side. La China stood and came and kicked the dirt with me once, as if to say I understand, which was all it took to get me in a rage. She led me against my will back behind the white plastic awning that hid the whole thing from the nearby road. When she tried to hug me it just made me panic. I started screaming.

"*Mama!!! Mama!! ! Mama!!!*"

"*Patico,* la China whispered, "calm down, calm down."

Goodbye mama, I tried to scream. Goodbye. This was not mourning. Not yet. This was the terror that Miriam wasn't going to hear me say it. That it was too late. I pushed La China away and ran back around to the hole. How I wanted to be the one lowering her in. So that I could break ranks and pull her back up. Get her out of there. No, I wanted to shimmy down one of those ropes and join her directly. *"Mama!"* I shouted, cupping my hand around one side of my mouth and leaning out over the edge. *"Mama, mama, mama..."* My voice was going hoarse. I stamped my feet. Say it. Say it. I saw Three Bags stand up and move toward me, waving at me with his hand, passing Hipólito, who was still sitting and staring downward, but now with his hands covering his ears, the heartless fuck I think now although then it seemed fair. Say it. I would have right then and there but I lost my footing and fell in after her, faster than her, rope-less. I could hear a collective gasp from above and then I landed face-first on top of the hard casket. The impact spit my lip and knocked one of my lower teeth out, and it tore the ropes out the hands of the grave workers. The casket fell the last foot or so and hit the dirt with a loud bang. I thought the whole thing would split apart but it didn't. The pain in my shoulder was like a forest fire. No matter, this was my chance. This was it. Everyone was just standing over me, still and slack-jawed, like they were staring at some rat who'd swum up the toilet pipes. Three Bags, the pallbearers and, to my horror, imaginary mom, as serene and witch-like as ever. I turned away from her, from everyone and everything up there, pressed my face against the cold smooth wood.

Up close, at last. As close as I'd ever, ever get again. Goodbye Mama were the words. The words that hadn't come when they should have. But when I opened my mouth to say them now only blood and vomit came out.

After that, nearly everyone was even gentler with me than usual. I was in somebody or another's arms all that day and deep into the *descarga,* the final fairwell party, that night. My passing out in Miriam's open grave had everyone pretty freaked, I think. Three Bags told me that evening, at the Elder Tower community center, as the opening *toque* to Eleggua began, how he'd jumped in and scooped me out of there. How they'd carried me to the cemetery administration building and laid me on a couch. La China stayed by my side fanning my face with a magazine and singing quietly to me as they finished the ceremony. That's the first thing I saw when I opened my eyes and for the cruelest moment I was certain that Miriam was not dead. Later, La China carried me to the bus stop. My head lay against her chest as she walked. She stroked my hair softly, but all I could feel was who she wasn't.

That night at the party everyone, from the Cuban guys crushing ice and *hierba buena* at the bar to the famous radio disc jockey with the two girlfriends, Al Something, came around to ask about my sutures even though they were long out, to admire my swollen lip, maybe to mention the tooth fairy, some to say they remembered how I used to play and then try to segue out of that one. No one mentioned Miriam directly, but everyone said that it was not my fault. After hearing that like ten times it was more than clear to me that someone must have been saying that it was.

I didn't have to look very far to figure it out. Only toward the music. That night the players were on fire. Hipólito sat front and center, his grey cabbie-cap pulled down low over his eyes, his sleeveless white undershirt tight-fitting as his skin, his sinewy charcoal arms flailing like the limbs of some lost, spastic alien signaling to the stars, hands cracking and booming against the double-headed drum on his lap, the lead of the sacred *batá* and the biggest. *Iyá*, the drum of Yemayá, the Goddess of his lost wife. The Orisha who was supposed to have protected her. His left hand smacking the small goatskin *cha-cha* head in those staccato patterns, unpredictable to those who didn't know them, his right hand improvising thunderous calls against the deep *enú*, calling out to the *itótole* and the *okónkolo*, as the cowrie shells around the drum's hourglass body jangled like hail against the hood of a car...*boo-dagga boo dak! boo-dagga boo dak!*...signalling the changes in direction, the roads the songs travelled, searching desperately for a way, it seemed, to close that new distance, that new darkness that separated him from her. Yemayá had let him down but maybe she could now be a bridge back. She owed him that much. His grey dress slacks covered in cigar ash and spittle and sweat and droplets of dribbled and spilled rum. He nearly standing from his chair as he played, out of his depression for the first time in months, as far as I knew, his whole heart pumping into this, given over to this, his eyes burning ahead like the forward lights of some ship lost in fog, obliged to shine into the nothingness until something, anything, could be found. Any sort of clue as to how to survive this. And when I stood and those lights swept over me without stopping I knew once again I was not that clue, that I was as lost in the nothingness as Miriam was, as he was, or the nothingness itself.

"I'm not telling you again. *Suelta mi pierna, ya!*" Let go of my leg, now!
"No, *no no no no!!!!!*"

I was sitting on Hipólito's foot, my legs wrapped around his
ankle, my cheek pressed against his knee, my arm around his shin in a
perverse but effective half-hug. He was moving slowly, taking one
step with his free leg, then dragging me, a sniveling sloth, along with
the other. Shut up, he said, but I wouldn't. We were in their
bedroom, for one full week now his alone, moving in this agonizing
way toward the open front door of our apartment. Both of us were
sweating for our stubbornness. Both of us were in the same pain. But
we were looking for opposite remedies. I was trying to cling to life.
To *a* life. Hipólito was trying to let one go. Or so he thought. He was
holding a big cardboard box against his chest with a photo of home
stereo speakers on it. Now it was stuffed with clothes. Overflowing
with skirts, blouses, dresses, shoes, panties, shawls, T-shirts. And the
purple dress with black jagged stripes like some Warhol zebra. It was

hanging out over the side and fell to the floor as we slouched along. That very one. Chosen by me for the show I'd pulled the curtains on.

Hipólito kicked it with his free foot across the room, like a cleaning rag. It had been her favorite. You couldn't undo something being a favorite. You couldn't really undo someone, for that matter. She had to be here, somewhere. I could feel it. Lingering in the air between that dress and the box and the foot of her husband where I clung with everything my little arm could give. But when I tried to explain this to Hipólito only one word came out - 'no, no, no' - over and over. Finally he smacked me. That was a first. He set the box down and cuffed me on the back of the head hard enough for me to bite my tongue. I hung on, stunned. Were these the new rules? *"Suéltame de una puta vez!"* he growled. He drove his other knee into the side of my head. This time I did let go. I fell over.

"Eh," he grunted at me, picking up the dress. "Get up. You're not hurt." He was putting the dress back in the box but he hesitated. He went to the window and stared down at the street, toward the garbage containers by the curb. He raised the dress to his mouth. He wiped his brow with it. He buried his face in it and stood there for a second. Then he picked up the box again and walked to the door. "Get up," he said.

I didn't move.

"This house is not going to be a museum," he said from the hall.

He did make sure of that. By the end of the day there wasn't a single reminder of Miriam left inside. None of the obvious ones, anyway. From my room I could hear him throwing everything away: all of the black-and-white photos from Cuba that had stood on the false mantel: the two of them with the original orchestra outside the Copacabana Hotel in Havana; some drab street corner in Matanzas, Miriam seated on a Russian scooter, sunglasses on, a loaf of ration bread in one hand; the three of us at Orchard Beach the summer before, me holding both their hands, balanced on a chunk of concrete. Hipólito carted all of this to the trash out front, and more, and more. The coffee mug she used, her Yemayá deity and altar relics, the myriad *ofrendas* of now-dry flowers, sugary treats, photos, candles and other things, the refrigerator magnets, two big plastic bags filled with toiletries from the bathroom, her pillow off the bed. He even tossed out things that he himself would need, like her set of keys to the house and the car. By nightfall what had been distinctly hers, or of her in any way, was gone. All of it piled lifelessly by the curbside.

Just before dinner I came out of my room, took a lone tour of the apartment. In the living room I noticed that another photo was missing. The color one, taken at one of the many anti-Castro marches Hipólito had been to. For years now it had stood on the small plastic table next to the couch. In it, I was sitting on his shoulders, fist in the air, politically oblivious, deeply happy. Miriam had not been in the photo. Just him and me together.

The night of that purging I lay awake in my bed, in a state of raw, unrelenting pain. I was actually whimpering. Like a dog, to my own ears. But no one else was around so I didn't care. Was this my fault? Was it? Oh God. The answer was yes, it was. Hipólito was making that clear with his silence. I had taken from him the woman who'd taken me in. The love of his life, his reason for even being in the U.S. So far from his real home. She'd been gone a week and in that time he'd barely said three sentences to me. He seemed hardly able to function except when he was focused on erasing her. I brought my fingers to my head where he'd kneed me. Each time I touched the welt it caused a pain behind my left eye. My heart writhed like a fish in a boat bottom, over her, over him, over all the photos whisked in a fit into the trash. Hipólito said he didn't want the house to be a museum, but now it would be a den of eternal mourning. Obliterating reminders of Miriam only made her absence harder to bear. To move on from. By removing the sight of her he had to have known he was anchoring us to her. I couldn't take her total disappearance like that. I needed something of her in order to keep going. I felt that I could never let her go. I felt so alone. I wished Three Bags would come around. But though I didn't know why, I knew that he wouldn't. I turned, rolled from one side to the other, trying to fall asleep and escape, whispering 'no' again and again into my pillow. This was the grief that had not arrived in time for the funeral. I was learning quickly, lying there with my Speed Racer bedspread kicked to the floor, the precise way in which love's loss frothed in your guts, and that it did not abate.

I got up and went into the bathroom and blew my nose directly into the sink, holding one nostril closed, then the other, then washed my hand and face. All was quiet as I padded back down the dark hall to my room. But my heart was racing because of what had happened the night after the toque for my mom. Hipólito had been on the phone in the kitchen, just around the corner. His voice was so calm and quiet. I was supposedly asleep, not in this very same spot going for a glass of water.

"'scúchame una cosa," he was saying, "If you ever come around here again? Eh? You are listening? Three Bags. Hold on. Listen. I will cut your balls off."

I froze. Three Bags must have been responding because my dad didn't hang up. But whatever Three Bags was saying it didn't matter.

"Sí, sí, okay. Three Bags. Three - I understand. Listen. Your balls, eh? Then your head." He put the phone down on its cradle. Again, silence. Then he came quickly into the hall, bearing down me, a great flat shadow in the darkness. I nearly buckled with fear. After everything else now here I was listening in on his conversations. But he strode past without the slightest hesitation and went into his room and shut the door. I'd stood there for a moment, still as a houseplant, then slipped back to bed, my thirst forgotten.

Since Hipólito wasn't really talking to me, everything I'd learned about what was happening I'd been gleaning from Kaylie at Afro Solutions. I'd wandered in to her salon a couple of days after the funeral, still not back in school, desperately searching for something normal to do. I didn't need a haircut. I sat in a chair and looked absently at the magazines.

"You should be at home," Kaylie said. "You're not in school so that you can be with family." She was sweeping the floor but mostly watching me.

I nodded. There were no customers in the salon.

"I miss him," I said, sitting.

"Your daddy'll snap out of it."

"Three Bags."

"Ah?"

"He's my uncle. This one time, he took me to Botnitz Music and we played the drums."

Kaylie didn't say anything, but she set the broom aside and sat like a queen in one of her black swivel chairs.

"Do you know where he is?" I asked.

"No, Patico." She rested her big doughy elbows on her thighs.

"But don't you worry," she said. "You know he cares about you."

"I wish he'd come over," I said, tearing up. "But he can't."

"Has your dad talked to you?"

I shook my head.

"You know," she said. "Three Bags cared about your mom too."

"I know."

"They used to hold hands. Did you know that?"

"No."

"Your dad, he didn't like that."

"How come?"

"I guess he wanted her just to hold his hand, and nobody else's."

I looked down at the magazine on my lap. Some tears fell onto a photo of a tennis player leaping over the net. The headline: "Ashe!" Kaylie stood and came over and scooped me up effortlessly, like I was made of hay. I buried my face in her neck.

"Sometimes people just can't be friends anymore," she said, rocking me.

"But what about…what …?" I couldn't formulate the question. I couldn't bring myself to ask about me. Because I suspected I already had the answer: 'me' had no more place in the scheme of things.

"Hang in there, Patico," Kaylie said. "He'll come around. Everyone's just in a lot of pain."

I raised my head. "Three Bags?"

"Your father."

I climbed back into bed, my nose already running again. There was a distant clang: a cat knocking the lid off one of the garbage cans on the corner, outside. Then more clatter. I stood and went to the window. I rubbed my eyes to make sure.

I could see him under the streetlights, bent over behind one of the trash containers. If I wasn't mistaken he was fishing through the trash. Our trash. Miriam's things. His hands were rifling around in the box with the speakers on it. Like a homeless man foraging. What was he looking for? I knocked quietly on my window, afraid to rouse Hipólito whose room was next to mine. I had every reason to believe what he'd said on the phone. I was imagining him darting out the front door, a pair of insanely long silver scissors glistening in his hand, to snip Three Bags between the legs. I went and turned on my bedroom light, then ran back to the window and waved my arm frantically. The problem was that with the light on I couldn't see anything outside. So I ran back to my door and switched the light off, then ran back to the window. Three Bags was standing up now, motionless, staring right at me. I pressed my face to the window. He tilted his head a tiny bit. I guessed that now he couldn't see me. I tapped again, this time pretty hard. Fuck it. He couldn't be that close and not come see me. I unlocked the latch on the window but couldn't budge it with my one hand. I rapped on the glass again and saw Three Bags put his finger to his mouth. So he knew I was there! The light came on in Hipólito's room. Oh shit, no. A second later his window shot up and he stuck his head outside. Three Bags froze. Hipólito let loose a whole long machine gun barrage of insults. More lights came on in other apartments. Three Bags said something back. He stooped and scooped up a box of who knows what and turned to go. No, no no. In a panic I grabbed my bongos from the floor under my bed and swung the cha cha up against the glass. It shattered loudly and gave way easier than I thought. So easily that I lost my grip on my drums and they went crashing down to the sidewalk below.

"Uncle Threebs!" I screamed.

Hipólito disappeared for a second then reappeared, leaning far out the window with something in his hand. It was his little plastic alarm clock. He threw it down at Three Bags, hitting him in the back, which set the alarm bell off. Buzzing like a metallic cicada there on the sidewalk. Three Bags screamed. I screamed.

"*Métete en la puta cama, pinga!*" Hipólito yelled at me from his window. "Get the fuck back in bed now!"

Terrified, I stepped back from the hole in the glass, losing sight of Three Bags.

"Milo!" he yelled. He sounded so far away. "I'll call!" I ran back to the window. He was striding away from us down the street. He stopped once, turning around and staring back at the tower. He held up his hand like he was telephoning. I couldn't bring myself to scream again, much less to get dressed and go after him. But that's what I wanted to do. If you defined family by caring - or at least as someone who would talk to you - then I was watching the closest thing I'd had to family in nearly a year disappear. So what if he'd held Miriam's hand. So had I, probably every day. I stood there in the cool breeze coming through the window until Hipólito came in and turned my light on. I ran to my bed and climbed in.

He was panting. He looked at the window and at the broken glass on the floor.

"You think he's your friend but he isn't," he said, pointing out the window. Maybe he'd been crying. "The day he fucked your mother he stopped being friends to any of us."

"He held her hand!" I yelled. "He held her hand!"

"You and him," Hipólito said. "Go on with him, if you want to. Go on, eh? Get your stuff and go."

A moment ago I'd really wanted to. But now the suggestion, coming from him, was like another knee to the head. Miriam was still somewhere in the house, I was sure of it. If I left I'd never see her again. Never feel her again. And I'd never see my father again. He'd become like this but still he was my dad. I couldn't just leave him. How does a five-year-old leave his father? He doesn't. Besides, I didn't even know if Three Bags would take me. And he was probably already long gone, five miles down the sidewalk and fading fast.

"I don't want to."

"What?" Hipólito yelled.

"I don't want to go," I said, a little louder.

"You don't want to," Hipólito said, imitating me. "You say that now." He shut the door.

So you learn to dress yourself. To make your own sandwiches. To wash your plate, to wash yourself. You can match socks, connect on the buses, read library bedtime stories, take phone messages from concert bookers, change the batteries on the TV remote, sign for mail, order the worst possible pizzas over the phone then wait till closing for the kid to throw them in the dumpster, unsold, then have Ronny Linky climb in and get them. You get very good at some things and good enough at others so as to not draw attention to yourself. From the authorities, whether that be teachers or parents or the police or social services. On the street, the key is pretending that you live a normal life with your father. At home, you pretend you live alone, since that's what your father is doing, and because you are no match against that. In Spanish the verb is to *ningunear*. It means to render someone who is there not-there, to reduce them to none or no-thing at all. It is worse than ignoring, and it is worse than any of our language's baroque and much celebrated insults. Insults at least have a target. They hit something.

Hipólito no longer really saw me. I became a ghost, the ghost of VertiVille, whether roaming through the apartment or outside, wherever I wanted, without particularly wanting to, and usually with my friend Ronny who was my friend because for the longest time he was the same. He was alcohol's ghost, living with parents who treated booze like their first-born and him like trash.

We spent a lot of time just wandering, harmlessly, aimlessly, passing the time, the years passing, up onto the I-95 overpass, out to the dusty, pebble-strewn ball field behind Elm, into the tall reeds along the Hutch river to chuck rocks at the rats, or into the Towers where we didn't live, which meant they were like separate towns. But never so far that we couldn't find our way home. At least not at first. Because at five, six or seven years old you still do want to go home. You still hold out hope.

Then one day our wanderings changed. They took on a purpose. We were around eleven. The aimlessness and the harmlessness went out of them, replaced by an infectious focus and excitement. They became an outlet for our unnamed rage. It was the bad turn we were bound to take at some point, and the person who set it off was a man who showed up at VertiVille one late Saturday afternoon in the Fall of 1978 wearing a camel-hair coat and acting like the mayor of everything.

Ronny and I were playing Star Ship Elevators in Redwood. It was a race we'd invented. You each took an elevator and raced the other to the top floor of the Tower and back. 34 flights up, 34 down. That day luck was mine in Elevator B. I made it to the top with only one other passenger getting on, and came all the way down in a free fall like Captain Kirk rushing to the bridge, the floor numbers on the wall panel lighting and going dark like dominos falling. The door opened on the lobby.

"Yo kid, come here."

Standing there in the lobby was this camel-hair coat guy, this tall, scary white dude with bad skin, rough and red, a high forehead and the tight, uniform-blonde curls he could only have gotten with a salon permanent. He had one hand in a front pocket of his grey slacks and was jingling change loudly, or keys. He was smoking.

"I didn't do anything."

"Do me a favor, kid," he said, looking left and right, squinting through his own smoke like Steve McQueen in the movies. "Watch that car out front for me. Huh? Be a good kid and there'll be somethin' in it for ya." He grabbed me by my fake-leather Fonzie bomber and dragged me toward the door, flicking his cigarette butt to the lobby floor. "See it out there?" he said. "The only car out there worth watching? You watch that car, hear me?"

"I can hear you."

"I gotta visit a lady friend for a while, and when I come down I don't want the smile on my face to vanish, got it? I wanna go home smiling. If something happens to that car I will lose my smile, you understand me?" His voice was loud and it scared me.

"Yes, sir," I said, "I can stay till –"

"You can stay till I get back," the man said. "Don't worry about it. What are you worried about? Your mama spankin' your bottom? Don't worry about her. I'll talk to her if there's a problem. There won't be. I won't be long." The elevator doors opened and he disappeared inside.

"Who won't be long?" Ronny said, coming out of his elevator, panting.

"How are you panting?"

"It's a race. When you race you pant. Who was that?"

"Some giant guy."

Ronny shoved his hands deep into his front pockets, his default posture. He looked over his shoulders. "Well, you won, Scotty."

"Not so sure, Uhura."

Ronny hung around the lobby with me for an hour or so, picking sullenly at his fingernails, then said he was going home. He left, then came back for his New York Jets coat that he'd left by the lobby water fountain. I sat down just outside the door in the cool air. People were coming and going. A half-moon was coming up over the guy's car, the sky violet around it. The car was a convertible and it was red, but that's all I can remember. I was going to go home, but then I fell asleep. When I woke it was the fastest I ever had; someone was lifting me clear off the ground.

"Is that watching?" Camel-Hair said through his teeth, pulling me over to his car. "I was so happy just now," he said "I was smiling the whole way down in the elevator, you know that? Guy comes and has a nice visit with a lady friend. Then he has to come down and be freakin' dis-a-ppointed!" He circled the car, still pulling me along, looking for scratches like I was some chump from a rental car agency. "You were supposed to watch the car," he said, looking down at me. "How did you not understand 'watch that car'?"

"I did," I said. "I was." He cuffed me on the back of my head. Once. Twice. It hurt like hell because of his rings. "Ow!" I yelled. Then, "Papi!" against my will.

"Go on, cry for your mama," the man said, nuggying my head with his knuckles. "I'm gonna tell you something now, you little douche. You lost your chance. From now on when you hear the name Tommy Fizzio, you just stay inside."

Tommy Fizzio?

"Yeah, that's right. Fuckin' kid. You had your one chance to get in good with the Tommy and you blew it. So now, you hear I'm comin' around, my advice is you stay the fuck away. Cuz the Tommy ain't gonna wanna see your scrawny one-arm ass again." He walked me back across the parking area to the Tower and pushed me down against the wall where he'd found me sleeping. "Go back to your nap, gimp," he said. Who was this guy? He'd said Tommy fucking Fizzio like I couldn't not know the name. I slumped to the pavement, looking up at that red, messed up face and his blonde perfect curls and I knew that there was not one kind blood vessel in him. I didn't care if he had a lady friend upstairs or wherever. He was the sort of guy who'd run someone down in that car of his without thinking twice if it meant not having to stress his brake plates. I wanted to get mad but he'd hit me already and I was more scared of a second beating than anything else.

"Sayonara," he said, walking away. "Go run to your mama if you're gonna cry." He started his car and came out of his parking spot so fast in reverse I believed he was going to crush me into the wall. I covered my eyes with my hand. As he sped away the fear broke, just like that, and the rage came. I stood up and screamed after him, my head swimming with fury.

"A gimp is someone with a limp, dumb-shit!" I yelled, my voice breaking. I knew that because I'd been called it enough times by dickheads to look it up in the dictionary. I wiped the spit from my lips with the back of my hand. I thought, don't worry, you dickhead fucking asshole, you won't ever see me again. I was four towers from home anyway, and there was no particular reason I had to wander back over here. Ronny and I could fuck around anywhere. The Tommy was just one of like ten thousand weirdo wiseguys wandering the North Bronx. The chances of crossing paths with him again were minimal.

Several weeks later we did wander back. How could we not? When I saw his car in nearly the exact same spot my legs went weak.

"He's back," I said, spinning on my heels and hiding my face. "I don't believe it."

"No, wait." Ronny grabbed my arm.

"I'm not waiting to get smacked around again. That's his car."

"But no one's around. Come on!" He ran to the side of Redwood Tower, by the drains, and picked up a piece of a broken, dark green beer bottle. "Watch the elevators," he said, slinking across the road.

"What are you doing?"

"Watch the stupid elevators!"

I ran into the lobby despite the rising panic in my gut. Maybe this was a bad idea. One of the elevators was arriving. I nearly fainted with fear. My mouth went dry. I turned around and literally pulled my t-shirt up over my head. The doors opened but I didn't hear any footsteps. I turned back around. No one was there. I looked out through the glass doors to Camel Hair's car; Ronny's legs were sticking up out of it, kicking like someone practicing swimming. I ran outside.

"What do you think you're doin'?" I hissed. These were the days before car alarms but I was scared someone would happen by. Before I saw what he was doing I heard it: the ripping. Then I was gazing upon the tattered leather seats, the gashes in the leather on the doors and backrests. The white stuffing bulging out like pig guts.

"You just did all that?"

"Your turn," Ronny said, grinning, panting. He held out the piece of glass.

"Nuh uh."

"This dick punched you, right?"

"Yeah, so?" I probably sounded like a chicken. But it wasn't that. I remembered what he'd said about my mama spanking my bottom. How I oughtta run home to mama, even as I was yelling papi. Did he somehow know? Did he know and was just being a sick fuck about that? Ronny was still holding out the piece of glass.

"Nah, man," I said. "Just back away from the car." There was a curbstone by the front left tire, an extra one from the construction. I walked over and picked it up. I could barely keep a hold on it with one hand. But I managed to raise it up over my head. I stepped forward and smashed it against the front windshield. It left the tiniest nick in the glass. My hand hurt from the impact. Motherfucker was going to talk shit about my mother. I lifted it and hit the windshield again and a host of cracks shot out in every direction, like the roads leading from Rome. On the third try the stone passed through like the glass wasn't even there; it all just rained down in clear, blue-green chunks all over the hood and the dash and the ripped-up bucket seats.

"Holy cow!" Ronny yelled. His eyes were full of surprise. I'd never seen him much surprised by anything. "That was cool!"

"We should go," I said. We went sprinting around the corner. I had to go a little slow for Ronny, who was already huffing. "Hey," he gasped. "Hold on."

"No way! Hurry up!"

"Wait," Ronny insisted. "What if Camel-Hair had someone else watching his car?"

"He didn't. I didn't see anyone." I had not thought of the possibility. If someone had seen us then we were dead meat.

"He made *you* do it the other day," Ronny said.

"There was no one there."

"We gotta go back!"

"No way! If there was someone there he would have said something."

"To who?" Ronny gasped. "Would you have really said something the other day if some guys had started smashing up his car?"

"I'm not going back."

"We gotta tell him not to say anything."

"Why would he listen to us?"

We had no leverage whatsoever, nothing to offer. But Ronny was already looping back. Sometimes my best friend was not that bright.

"Stop!" I yelled. "You idiot!" But he just waved an arm in the air. As in, follow me. He disappeared around the corner of Redwood. I stopped running, bent over and put my hand on my knee to catch my breath. That's when the bellowing started. I couldn't make out the words but I recognized the voice. Ronny came right back around the corner, the way he'd gone, like a movie in reverse, moving faster than I had ever seen. He was pointing for me to beat it. I ducked around Maple Tower, but not before I glimpsed the coat. And the hair. I wondered if that giant man could run. How far and for how long. And worse, if he'd seen me. Don't let him catch me. Don't let him catch me. This was one of those moments in your childhood where a monster is chasing you and it's not a bad dream, or a book, and you have no real place to hide and you know you can't just turn the page or wake up and have it all worked out. And that scares the living lights out of you. It fills you with an unnamable despair and regret and panic that causes you to promise a lot of things. You swear anything to anyone if only you can get out of that mess. I was doing that now. I was swearing I'd be a good kid, that I'd make things up with Hipólito. Even though I didn't have the first clue how. I bolted straight into Maple and hit the elevator button in the lobby. None of the lights above the doors was working so I couldn't tell how far away they were. My bladder was about to give out. Camel-Hair would kill me, I was sure of it. Out the glass doors I saw Ronny fly past, heading across the central dirt park that had been seeded in the

spring but was still brown. He was going to try to make it to Willow
Tower, or the one next to ours, Spruce. But he had something like a
hundred yards to cross. He was halfway there when Camel-Hair came
huffing past, going very fast himself. I crouched low and pushed
myself up against the wall. But he was yelling after Ronny. His coat
tails flapping behind him like a heavy curtain in wind. Ronny looked
back once, then put his head down and pumped his arms. I had to
pee, but bad. It was out of fear and because I hadn't gone in hours. I
went slowly, painfully, to the glass doors, holding myself. Ronny
made it across and disappeared inside Willow; a full 30 seconds later
Camel-Hair reached the doors and was gone inside too.

I ran out and ducked back around to Redwood. My heart was
pounding, but my insides were worse. Where to pee? Camel-Hair's
fucked up car was still there, and it being mid-afternoon no one was
around, at least that I could see. I looked left then right then ran over
and scrambled up on the hood and rose to my feet. I could see
Willow from where I stood and there was no movement at all by the
doors. Camel-Hair must have been racing after Ronny in the
elevators, as futile as that would be. I fumbled with my fly and with a
few adjustments began making a splattery pool on the driver's seat.
Peeing right through where the windshield had been.

And as I was peeing I began to feel such relief. It made me
tremble. Cuff me motherfucker but you can't talk about her.
Motherfucker with your car that's more important than anything or
anyone except your own acne-ass self. I was getting angrier and
angrier, but the anger wasn't dragging me down, as it usually did. It
was causing something to split open inside me. That's what it felt
like. Who oughtta take the cuff to the back of the head, anyway? The
boy? Each time the boy? Or the owner of the machine like this one
that destroyed this boy's life? Or, second best, the machine itself?
This was the first time I'd thought about it in this way. What I'd done
to Miriam had been an accident. If only she'd put on the brake. If
only she hadn't mentioned that name. Maybe things would have
happened differently. Maybe I would have sat down when she asked
me to. Instead of defying her. How long would I have to pay? A
mom dies but the son has lost as much as anyone. The real danger
was the two-ton vanity rides like Hipólito's Cadillac. Which out of all
of us had suffered the least damage. A wrecked grill, smashed
sideview mirror, a slew of dings and scratches. As I peed on this one

I was starting to think that possibly, just possibly, there might be gestures I could make to neutralize them, to even the score, or at least to feel better. I realized this because it was already working. My spirits rose higher than they had in years. I could show Miriam in this concrete way how sorry I was. She'd always been trying to help. To make me see that it made sense for me to be with her, with them. Now the broken glass and the slashed seats made their own sort of sense. They could be an offering to her, a way of acknowledging her good heart, my sorrow and my debt.

Hipólito could search for the link to his lost wife in the language of the *batá*, but my path started there, on the hood of Camel-Hair's car. As vandal, mercenary and penitent. Let's see who finds her first, I thought. When I finished peeing I shook and zipped and leapt from the hood as high as I could into the air. As I fell I said to Miriam, as loud as I could in my head, I am not a ghost. I hit the ground and twisted my ankle.

"You bring a screwdriver?"

"Yeah."

"Flathead?"

"Flathead," I said.

We came out of the elevators, pulled up the hoods on our sweatshirts and climbed the clanky metal steps of the I-95 overpass, stopping for a moment to take in that whump of metallic energy and compressed air as cars hurled past below us.

Tonight was going to be a first. Leaving VertiVille after dark. Without adult supervision. Really leaving. Not just to hang at Afro Solutions or to buy a nickel-bag. We were going far afield, into the quiet streets of the northeast Bronx. We were going scalping.

"Ponce from my class told me how to do it," Ronny said, his round face lit up by the highway lights. I wondered if was ever he was going to shave that wispy pubescent mustache off. "You just slide the screwdriver under the nameplate and lift, and pop. They come right off."

"All right."

It didn't work on the first one, a 1975 Chevy Nova. The nameplate snapped in two, between the 'o' and the 'v'.

"It's made a plastic!" I said, picking up the pieces from the street.

"What'd you think they were made of?"

"Chrome."

"This ain't the 1950s."

We moved on down a dark, one-way street. I dropped down behind a brown, two-door Volkswagon Rabbit and slid my screwdriver under the plate. "They're attached in more than one place. You gotta wiggle one side, then the other, little by little. Otherwise they break." That's what I did, and that's how I got my first scalp. A grey plastic 'Rabbit' plate, slightly scuffed up but intact. I put it in my back pocket, then thought better and pulled my hood down and hid it inside.

We were working our way down a little residential street called Wickham Avenue, past the two-story houses and the tiny neat lawns with the cars parked out front. Families were inside watching TV or eating dinner probably. Or the kids were going to bed. Whatever. The only thing we cared about was that people didn't come outside. On Wickham alone we got seven nameplates. Me five, Ronny two. He kept breaking them. We headed west on Mace and down Gunther, strolling along like two guys going to the movies or something. Then stop, drop and pop. The most expensive car Ronny got to first, a 1967 Mustang Fastback convertible. The least cool was mine, an orange AMC Pacer. It was thrilling to be on a street so close to home, and yet totally unknown to me. It was also thrilling to be getting away with our piddly misdemeanor, to feel my hood getting bulky with trophies. To know that in the morning, or someday soon, the owners of all these cars were going to discover that someone had stolen something from them, however small. That they'd have that feeling of injustice, and anger. That they'd invariably glance up the street and down as if they might really find the thief. And feel the disappointment when he wasn't.

But after serpentining up and down four more streets I realized we were going about this wrong.

"Yo," I said.

"What?"

"In the movies, when do Indians scalp people?"

"I dunno."

"After they kill 'em," I said.

"I seen a movie where they scalped a whole family when they were still alive."

"If they scalped you alive they killed you right after," I said. "The point is we can't just scalp nameplates and walk away."

"Totally, right? You're sayin' we gotta – what?"

"Kill the cars. Otherwise the scalp doesn't mean nothin'. It ain't really a trophy."

"How do you kill a car?"

"A dead car is a car that can't roll," I said, kneeling next to a Dodge Dart with worn old tires. I jabbed my screwdriver as hard as I could into the side of the rubber. On the third try I punctured it. The air hissing out was like a last breath. After that we started stabbing out tires on every car we scalped, leaving the vehicles to list. This was the real deal. This had meaning. And when you did it, I swear, sticking the tire like that, it was like you'd stuck yourself, shooting adreneline into your own veins.

Adreneline meant you were doing things right.

But on our walk back home down Astor Avenue a cop car pulled up onto the sidewalk in front of us. I pulled my lifeless sleeve from my pocket and wiggled it like bait, the idea being that the police wouldn't harass a cripple. Or suspect him of vandalism. When that didn't cause the two officers to stop their advance we ran.

Hipólito took me and the two cops in as if nothing had happened at all.

"Hipólito Prieto Vazquez?" one of the officers said.

"Yes."

"You've come to pick up your son."

"Yes."

"He get inta trouble like this much?"

"No."

"His name's not in our system anywhere. Neither is the other kid's. No one's ever even seen 'em. But I gotta tell ya, they had a damaging debut. Like I told that other kid's father, you're on the hook for it."

"For what?"

"For poppin' nameplates off 27 cars that we know of. And popping the tires on 19 of 'em."

"But he's only, what, uh."

"Your son is twelve," the officer said.

"I don't have that kinda money. He's just a kid."

"You got no choice," the officer said, signaling for me to stand up and go with my dad. "Precisely because he is a kid."

My dad filled out all the papers, the release form and so on. He had no expression on his face. When we got home I knew what was going to happen. I was cringing. We'd been living together now, just the two of us, for coming on eight years. The weirdo father and son in 402. The ones the neighbors gave sideways glances to. We walked in the front door and Hipólito made himself a sandwich and opened a beer. He took his sandwich to the couch and turned the TV on. I made my own sandwich and went to my room. Eventually I fell asleep.

In the morning he did not ask me for money, and he never did. He never told me I had to get a job, he didn't ground me or hit me or explain to me how what I'd done was wrong or make me go personally apologize to all those people. Ronny eventually came back to school and as the days passed the bruises on his back diminished, the swelling at the back of his leg disappeared. As twisted as it was I wished I'd gotten what he'd gotten. One of those secret beatings that teachers never see. Because then at least you had something to heal from.

My dad must have paid the money for those new tires, for the nameplates. He and Mr. Linky must have gone to those houses or hired a lawyer to do it. But he never brought it up and I never heard him on the phone talking about it or anything. My response was to do it all again. And again. So was Ronny's. Like I said earlier, we were real friends. Pretty soon though scalping got old, and not only because a lot of guys were starting to do it. It was just too dangerous, because if the cops stopped you with all the nameplates stuffed in your pants or sweat socks you were guaranteed to be the laughingstock of the precinct that night. So we gave up on the trophies and focused solely on the kills. We didn't carry screwdrivers or nails or bricks or anything. We used whatever was on hand to do whatever damage we could. A curbside garbage can to smash a front windshield on an ambulance. An old umbrella stuffed perfectly up inside the exhaust pipe of a Celica two-door with Minnesota plates. A smallish rock to scratch the paint off a 280-Z. We started doing shit like that, being resourceful. But the problem was that that got boring too after a while.

So we started hanging around to witness the owners' reactions if possible. This kept the adrenaline pumping. We circled the block after breaking the side-view mirror off a Chevy Impala parked outside a White Castle until the woman came out, keys in hand. We saw her face. That look of hatred toward the whole goddamn world. The impotence. The world has just shit on your head, and you've got nothing to clean it off with. You are going home without your mirror or justice or faith in humanity. We got more brazen, sometimes even stopping to commiserate with our victims. The only thing between you and getting busted was your shit-ass lying face. A man with a cane that you could tell he didn't really need finds the back windshield of his Nissan minivan punched in, a heavy manhole cover lying on the backseat next to a baby seat.

"You kids see anything?"

"No, sir."

"Some assholes," he said. "Can you believe that?"

"We're just comin' from AstroArcade," says Ronny. "There was some young guys comin from this direction, laughing, high-fivin.' Who knows." And the guy goes speeding off down Waring Ave like he's gonna find them, the heavy iron cover still in his car.

And then, I should have known, this got old too. As we started talking more and more to the suckers we'd just fucked, I kept feeling the urge to give the whole thing away. To go along all nice and then say, wait, oh yeah, I saw the guys. You're lookin at 'em. And then just belt the guy in the face and run. Get the adrenaline bats all flapping up through my chest again. It was crazy how we had to top each outing to get the same feeling. We hardly ever did the same thing twice. We started throwing shit at moving cars, which was a huge leap forward in both risk and reward.

That's how we found ourselves that night having to prove to four guys with pipes that we were incapable of having pelted their Continental with crab apples. After my pathetic girlish throw, and showing them the arm I didn't have, we were a half-step from free.

"Now you," the same guy said to Ronny.

"Now me what?"

"Throw a rock."

"We're comin from the movies, y'all."

"Throw."

Ronny picked up a little rock. And instead of being smart about it, he threw it exactly like I did. What are the chances of that? That two teenage boys walking together down the street both throw like the same girl? Zero. I've gone over this a thousand times since. We went from pitiable to like we were making fun of them. Also because Ronny let out a little giggle. The guy with the pipe who'd been acting like he might let us go wacked him straight up in the back of his round head. He did it with one hand, like he was prepared to be grossed out, leaping back, I guess not to get blood on his suit. But I didn't see any blood. Ronny dropped to his knees and fell forward like a narcoleptic. Then you could see the blood. One of the other guys walked up to me and kicked me in the stomach. But not before I punched him weakly in his surprised face. His shoe in my gut took my breath away. I collapsed, got kicked a few more times. Took a pipe to my shoulder, my back. I lay there, still as possible, my hand over my head, until it stopped. Then I heard them walk off and the car driving away.

"Ronny! Yo!" I hissed. I sat up heavily. But he didn't respond, not even to me talking directly into his ear. His arms and legs didn't move if you touched them. The blood was making a little pool as it ran around his neck and dribbled from his adam's apple to the asphalt. And that's when something finally dawned on me. That all this shit we were getting into, from The Tommy's car forward, was pure bullshit pretense. It wasn't adrenaline I was after. I wanted that pipe. To the head. I wanted to be dead. I knew because I actually felt jealous watching Ronny out cold. It was just a matter of provoking the right crazy person at the right time. Of stumbling upon my own killer. I stood, clutching my stomach, and stumbled away as fast as my trembling legs would carry me.

Since we were friends, each other's only friends, the whole idea was always that we would fight our enemies together or perish. That had been the very first thing Ronny'd told me. You stick together. Well, it turned out that from pretty much the beginning our Number One Enemy wasn't other kids from the other towers, like Ronny had warned. It was our dads. Mine and Ronny's dad, Paul Linky. Paul Linky hated us. He hated us so much he tricked us into thinking he liked us. His sadism worked like that experiment with the frog in water where the temperature rises so slowly it doesn't notice. Until it's too late and he croaks. Cooked unaware. Mr. Linky controlled the water temperature. The water was their apartment. He would start out tepid whenever I popped up.

"Is Ronny home?"

"Ehpp." A sluggish nod toward his bedroom. No eye contact.

Later, from tepid to warm, popping his head in to Ronny's room: "There's bologna in the fridge that's gonna go bad. If you kids are hungry."

Then warmer still, from the living room:

"Hey, get your asses out here. I got something for ya."

Sometimes Mr. Linky would have two folding chairs set out for us. It meant a competition was about to start. He'd sit back with a beer in his Barkalounge.

"Siddown, tough guys. You too, Houdini. Okay, so you're gonna hold your legs straight out. First one to lower them shall be crowned the Supreme Pussy of Vertiville."

We sat as he'd said, our stick legs sticking straight out, giggling at first, then trembling. Him watching the ball game like we weren't there.

"Owwwww," Ronny began. Which was when you knew he was going to lose again.

"You kids are tough," Mr. Linky said. "A lot tougher than them chinks and blacks you're always running from. You just don't know it yet." Well-timed little crumbs like that gave us a second wind, got us to push ourselves a little further, extending the cruelty. They made us want to prove him right. Until finally we just couldn't. Ronny usually gave in first and was met the derision his dad held only for him.

"You little fucking pansy. I did not, I honestly did not think – You are truly a pussy. That's the crux of it. If your mother was home I'd have you pull your pants down and show her your vagina."

Poor Ronny. Meanwhile I'd be holding my legs out still, red in my six- or seven- or eight-year-old face, trying not to show the strain, holding out for something less scalding, like:

"Look at your pussy friend Houdini. And with one arm."

Which was enough to make me feel perversely okay. My opioid was attention, no matter how lame. Though I was still a pussy, and the Houdini nickname had nothing but meanness behind it, I'd done better than Ronny. This was as close to adult male positive reinforcement as I was getting and I'd take it. But then I'd look at Ronny and feel rotten because I'd realize the whole fighting the enemy together thing was just absolute bullshit. If it meant getting a crumb from his douchebag dad I'd beat him at just about anything. To make up for it, I'd bad-mouth his dad when we were alone again.

"Your dad is totally stupid, if you think about it."

"You think?"

"When you're like twelve you'll be able to punch his fucking face in."

"That I don't know."

Ronny never seemed to hold a grudge against me. The bastard. On some visits we'd have to hold those same chairs over our heads for as long as we could. Contests involving the arms would generally go to Ronny, who had the natural advantage. Or we'd run in circles into one of us collapsed to the floor. Or there was the time I spent the weekend – Hipólito was playing out of town - and we couldn't eat or drink anything. You know, because that's fun. And because Ronny's mom was at work. It wasn't the dehydration that landed Ronny in the hospital. It was his head hitting the coffee table when he fainted. Which reminds me of the night we played who could stand the longest. One time we were going to see who could keep their hand on the electric stove longer, but Mr. Linky thought better of that at the last minute: the winner would have some damning evidence charred into their skin. Who could hold a match the longest was ruled out too. But cold was okay. Cold was really fun. One Sunday during a Harlem Globe Trotters game on CBS we pulled our pants down and sat on ice trays. I won that one too.

Then all those years later Ronny loses yet another contest, the final one, the who-can-throw-a-rock-most-like-a-girl derby. His consolation prize, getting dinged by the Pipe Guy into another dimension. When I ran off I ran to get his dad. Probably I saved his life. But after that, when he came home from the hospital, it was clear how impossible it would be to call him my best friend ever again. Or even to show that I cared. I wanted to but I didn't have the slightest strength for it. Caring would have involved feeling remorse, and letting in remorse required cozying up to a whole lifetime of missteps and regret. Either you were all in or you were all out, and I was choosing out.

"Hey Milo. Milo. Hey Milo. Hey."

"Oh, hey Ronny," I said, stone cold. "Wussup man."

"Gonna get us. Right into a tree. Uh. Keep runnin. They're comin."

"That's about right. That's how it went down, didn't it."

"Yo, Ronny, *hermano*! Ronny the Rocket Scientist!" That was Hector Rodriguez butting in. He was part of a new crew I was trying out. Five or six dimwits who thought they were funny. But not really, deep down.

"Milo. Milo," Ronny said, touching my elbow. "Head up, Milo."

"Damn," Hector said, "this boy has a serious crush on you." Everyone laughed at that, which was a perfect example of unfunny. Today we were just lurking in the Elder underpass. Passing spliffs around, getting up in anyone's face. I hadn't expected that to include Ronny and I was mortified inside. One thing was to *ningunear* him. Another was to have him stumble right into this band of knuckleheads. He'd shuffled up out of nowhere. Not only had I not been caring, I'd barely seen him since he'd gotten out of the hospital a couple of months earlier. It was too much. You could see your old friend was gone even as you were looking right at him. And you'd had a hand in that.

Ronny's right hand was where it always was now, worrying the back of his head. Like he could still feel something there. Like he was stuffing something back. This is what remained. His hair had come back where the stitches were. But little else.

"We gotta get em Milo. Run run. One more apple. Come on. Hmmm."

That set off another round of laughs.

"Ronny the Rock Thrower," Hector said, putting his arm around his shoulder. By then everyone knew the story. Ronny flinched. Hector took off his Yankees cap and set it on Ronny's head backwards. "You ain't gonna catch no one with your motor half burned out, *compadre*. Tell him, Patico."

Patico, now completely rotted out on the inside, the king asshole who in that moment would confirm that he'd accept even the worst company over being alone, smiled corpse-like at his pals.

"That's right, Ronny," the King of assholes said. "Hey Ronny," he said. "Throw me the hat. Give us your best pitch."

"Milo Milo."

"Watch this, *vatos*," said the Asshole King, so clearly enjoying himself. So at ease and unconflicted. "Come on, Ronny," he said, louder. "Throw the hat! Like you did the night you got your candles blown out. Come on!"

The funniest part wasn't that Ronny did it, but how; he threw the hat slowly and deliberately straight up, like an old man graduating from Slow Motion College. We nearly died from laughing. That's how it felt, anyway. Death and laughter together. A real shit cocktail. Somebody give me a gun.

That night the hollowness had engulfed me entirely. What the fuck was I? I felt so shitty and desperate. Finally I worked up the balls to go up to his apartment. Mr. Linky opened the door.

"Um, is Ron —"

"You don't come around here."

"I just thought -"

"No you didn't. You didn't just think anything."

"Please. If I can do— "

"Do? Do us one last trick, Houdini. Dis-a-fuckin-ppear forever."

Disappearing wasn't that hard because it was already the natural course of things. At home I was long invisible, and pretty much in school too. Breaking with my new crew turned out to be as easy as saying once, the next day, "You guys are lame." Nothing like a little honesty to stop the bong in mid-gurgle. Afro-Solutions had since closed shop, Kaylie moved away and Mrs. Potter retired, so that was a wrap. There was not a single thing tethering me to the ground.

Two more years went by like steam into the sky. I was a specter moving from one disappointment to the next and then barely moving at all. Stoned most all of the days. Miriam was so long gone I could sometimes not remember what she looked like. Hipólito was as checked out as ever and on the road even more. Only Imaginary Mom remained, more vivid and intimate with me than any physical person. I was still going out destroying stuff, for something to do, or maybe for hope's sake. Maybe with the idea of being caught, then forgiven. To have someone say just once okay so you fucked up. Or maybe I could still get my own head cracked and be freed forever. In school recently they'd been talking about the Vandals sacking Rome. I wished I'd been alive then. Back then you were rewarded for breaking shit. There'd even been a Vandal King, a kid named Genseric. An actual gimp. Guy had Spain and North Africa in his hand. What could his cunning and viciousness get him today? Probably 15-to-life. He wouldn't fit here, just as I didn't fit and wasn't ever meant to. One morning when I was seventeen I was thinking about this while I walked by myself to the bus. And again I ran into Ronny, who was getting out more and more. Even if he wasn't going anywhere in particular.

"Today's the day we get 'em," I said, before he could speak. It threw him off. "Into a tree," I said. "Under a truck. We'll get 'em. We'll finish this now."

"Run run," Ronny said. "Under a – a truck? Not a truck, Milo."

"It's time to end this."

"Under a car, Milo. You're safe under the car."

"Okay, Ronny," I said. "Okay. Listen up now. You take care."

On the bus to school I wished I'd hugged him. It dawned on me that I'd been picked up by the cops exactly seventeen times since the night Ronny had gotten his senses knocked sideways. In a way that made the number seventeen sort of magical. Another indication that this was my year. Not to win the lottery but to go down for good. Up till now it had all been kid stuff. Vandalism which, thanks to experience and luck, the police could almost never pin on me. Only twice had they caught me red-handed: once because I keyed a car without seeing the guy inside it, and the other that first night with Ronny and the car name-plates. This was all before the three-strikes laws started causing jails to overflow, but it didn't change the fact that I had two against me. And at seventeen I was going to be eligible for a good old-fashioned adult spanking if I wasn't careful. Jail time. In some ways Ronny was luckier than me. Maybe we'd both been destined to self-destruct or at least dead-end, but he'd been taken out of the game. The doctors said his brain wasn't going to heal more, that his voice would stay all weird. But at least he had the freedom to walk around outside without looking over his shoulder. He didn't have to worry about getting locked up, and nobody thumped on a retard. It had been nearly five years now since he'd last led us on one of our incursions. His life was stunted but also stabilized. Whenever I saw him with his parents it was like they'd taken an interest in him. It had taken a tragedy for them to step up but at least they had. They looked at me like I was the Antichrist.

All that day, the more I thought about that, and my future in general, the better I started to feel. I was thinking, why not make today the day of my parting commentary? Hipólito could wake up from one of his tours or binges and say to himself, I lost the wife and now the son. Maybe he'd lose some sleep over it.

That night over at Elm I convinced one of the girls, Chrissy, to send me off one last time out on the stairwell. Maybe because we were alone her gaze was kinda friendly.

"Who's gonna get your rocks off," she said, "when the race wars begin?"

"You think there's gonna be race wars?" I whispered.

"We're hardly growing closer."

"I hope you win."

She clicked her teeth. "Black folk are never gonna come out on top."

"Can we talk dirty and not about that?"

"Suit yourself, Patico."

I let loose a litany of things I might like to do to her. Her mouth half open in surprise. The tremble. I looked at the scene at my feet then surprised her further with a kiss on her soft lips. Then I zipped up and slinked over the I-95 overpass for the final hurrah. This is where'd I'd jump from, on my way home. I would like to be able to explain how the idea of cracking your head on a highway only to be hit by trucks can lift your spirits. But I can't. It's just what I felt.

I took a bus this time to Riverdale, where things could get really quiet at night, and wandered. First item of business, a tool. I took a terracotta planter off a brownstone stoop. The sides of it were slippery and I had trouble at first carrying it. I don't know what the flowers were but they had thorns that pricked at my face. Next, a target. I needed to find something quick. Then I had the best idea of all. Of course. I put the plant back where I'd found it, took the bus home and ran out to the parking lot behind Elder. I needed a tool for this too. By the garbage bins I found an old brass floor lamp with a weighty circular base. A neighbor named Menendez walked by and called out. *Qué pasó, Milo?* What are you doing? Looking for something, I said, just standing there with the lamp like that farmer with the pitchfork in the painting. Minus the wife. After he'd gone I felt an itching on my cheek and wiped at my face with the back of my dirty hand. It came away bloody. Damn prickers. I lifted the lamp and set it over my shoulder and began walking the lot, looking for it. It took me a full ten minutes in the dim light. First I smashed a window on the Chrysler next to it, for practice. An alarm started whooping. Shit shit shit. I balanced the stem of the lamp against my body, base in the air over my head, and brought it down on the Cadillac by bending quickly at the waist, using my shoulder for torque. The base dinged against the hood, just below the front windshield. Shit. One or two more tries and it would be time to scram for the overpass. I got the lamp positioned again against my body, gripping the stem to steady it.

"*Híjole! Está loco!*"

"*Chinga su madre. Es ese, el hijo del congero!*"

It was Menendez again. He was with someone I didn't know but who apparently knew who I was: the son of the conga player, he'd shouted. Turned out this other guy owned the Chrysler. Of all the bad luck. Try fighting off two stocky Mexicans with one arm and a broken floor lamp.

What Hipólito said to me as we waited for the police out there in the parking lot:

"This time you're going to jail. And if you ever get out, you do not come back here."

He was wearing a bathrobe and drinking a beer, leaning against his car, not looking at it on purpose. I imagined him weeping over the dents later. Everyone fell silent. After a few minutes of me not struggling Menendez and his smelly friend stopped restraining me. It wasn't like I was gonna run away. But I managed to take a step forward and punch Hipólito in the beer can, which was pressed to his mouth. Mainly it just made him wet. For the first time he really started to let loose on me with his fists. His ropy, animal strength. But the cops showed up then and started taking pictures and interviewing everyone. Then they took me to the precinct house where I was booked and told I was welcome to legal representation. I was going to be charged with destruction of property, a felony, and since Hipólito wouldn't hear any talk of bail or whatnot I was sent to a juvenile facility on the East Side of Manhattan until a trial date could be set. While there I got a near daily taste of my own blood. What is so fucking fun about pounding on a cripple? Somebody please tell me. A couple of weeks later I told everyone I would just plead guilty. The public defender told me I was one stupid shit. They held a sentencing hearing in court. There the judge called me youthful. As in, a Youthful Offender. On my way out of the courtroom the uniformed goon escorting me told me I was one lucky stupid shit: if you're a YO you can get sent to the kiddie pool, even if you're over 18, to serve your sentence. It's up to the judge. I guess that's what happened, on account of my arm and the forgone conclusion that in Big Boy Prison I would have been made into a bologna sandwich on day one.

I got driven in a police van to a big brick complex back in the Bronx, near Riverdale ironically. The Nathan Hale Rehabilitation Center for Boys. It looked like some old factory, with lots of tiny little windows on the street-side façade all covered with metal mesh. I got my own blue uniform and was put in a room with like 20 bunkbeds bolted to the floor. It's where I had the honor of meeting Swope. Whose real name was Gerald but you didn't dare. Between the beds and the reinforced entry door there was just enough space for Swope and the guys to hold me by my hand and spin me in circles. That was great fun. All I had to do was close my eyes till they'd gotten their thrill. Once my ankle clipped a steel bedpost and broke. That was fun too, judging by the laughing. At Christmas I got a really bad case of strep throat and nearly went from the infirmary to the hospital. When I got out Swope took my meds, said he was gonna sell them.

"What is wrong with you?" I whispered

"I don't know, Orphan Boy. Some people just inspire the rage. And you one a them."

"Well please find another outlet for your savagery. Like, ballet."

"Who you callin' a pussy?"

Wham wham wham. Wham wham wham.

Outside, there was a dirt courtyard where the guys could throw softballs around. No bats or gloves though. School was easier than real school and not every day, even though I think it was supposed to be. One day I got a letter forwarded to me by the New York State Department of Education, from the SAT's. I'd forgotten I'd even taken them. I opened it. Math, 680. English, 740. There had to have been some mistake. My regular grades were just average.

But several weeks later a woman came to see me. Her name was Lois Haver.

"Prieto! Visitor! To the library!" a guard called out.

"Hey," yelled Swope. "Hey, how can the orphan have family?"

"I ain't an orphan," I said, walking over to him. But instead of throwing my typical telegraphed hook I just stood next to him and stared out the window. He didn't seem to get it, which allowed me time to elbow him in the throat. That's when I learned about throats. Swope's pal Richie stepped in and hammered the top of my head with the bottom of his fist. Like he was literally pounding a nail. My teeth snapped shut and things went fuzzy for a couple of seconds. I got up off the floor to try to elbow him too, amazed by what jackasses these guys were and me the even bigger one for taking the bait. One of these days, I thought, maybe just maybe some other loser in there was going to look at this picture and say, this is wrong. Like, you can't keep drop-kicking a skinny dude with one arm who refuses to stay down. But so far none of my chums had stepped forward. Except of course to join in.

When the guard unlocked the door I was on all fours, with blood coming out of my nose. Swope was busy tying a scary loop out of a bedsheet.

"Prieto," the guard said. "You want I send the lady away? Look at you for Christ's sake."

I followed after him down the hall with its seven turns before you reached the cafeteria, the infirmary or the library itself which doubled as a visitor's center. He buzzed the door and I went in.

"Milano Prieto?" said this short, skinny, curly haired lady, standing up from a chair. She was kinda foxy in an older way.

"The man, the myth, the meatball."

"Would you like a tissue for that?"

"Nah."

"Would you like to get out of here?" She smiled mischievously. She handed me a tissue.

"I love it here," I said.

"I can see you're making all kinds of friends."

I liked this lady right away so I talked seriously after that. "Yeah, I would like to get out of here," I told her. "I'd leave with you this very moment. I'll hide under your skirt."

"No can do," she said. "But there's a chance you can be out of here before the end of the month. In time for the start of college in September. College. Would you like that?"

"Whose college?"

"Do you know who Cal Joiner is?"

Suddenly you could hear some hollering. A bunch of the inmates from my floor were walking past on their way to lunch and were laughing at me through the window on the door. There was Swope making like he planned to cut my throat.

"I don't know Cal whoever," I said. Lois Haver explained that he was rich and wanted to do right by fuck-ups like me. I kept my mouth shut because I was surer than ever that there was some mistake. I just kept nodding.

"Your SAT's," Haver said. "That's how you got on Mr. Joiner's radar. That and your police record. Bad but not too bad. He thinks you and a handful of carefully selected boys might get things right with a second opportunity."

"He can do that?"

"For the most part Cal Joiner can do what he pleases. Especially if it makes politicians look good. You'd have to behave, of course, get good grades. And I'd need your father's signature."

"I'm eighteen tomorrow," I said.

Haver reached into a leather briefcase and took out a clipboard with a form on it. "Then just sign here," she said. "I'll fiddle with the date."

Haver advised me not to say anything about the program, which seemed like good advice. But pretty soon the boys on my block caught wind of my luck. They did not bake me a cake.

"Why the fuck does the white orphan get to walk?" Swope said. He threw a softball at my head. We were out on the patio. A guard stepped forward. "Easy, there." Swope ignored him. He seemed very worked up by the news.

"I am gonna show this motherless motherfucker orphan shit-ass white piece of cracker trash what's easy," he said. He was right up in my face. "You ain't going nowhere, you fucking ghost faggot. Not before me. And that's on principle."

Now I was scared. I thought, he is planning to kill me. And while death held a certain special appeal, my idea had always been death by my own hand, thank you very much. So I rushed to the guard who'd heard the whole thing. A real pussy hustling across the yard I was. I think because of my new celebrity stature with AIM the guard went to the warden who had me transferred right then and there to a holding cell by the front doors. When it opened I could see puddles on the sidewalk from the summer rain. I could smell them. I didn't see Swope or any of the other boys again.

Three weeks later I was on a bus to Maine. Where I might Achieve something. I didn't care whatsoever about school or what direction the bus was headed. I'd signed on to get out of that nightclub of Neanderthals. To get out of my dead-end life or end it period. This was my crossroads: grow up or find a way to die again. The problem all along was that growing up required some ritual. And a guide. That's what my estranged religion taught and promised, even if that same religion had fenced me out and posted a warrior god as sentry. And then I met Halsey and thought she might be that guide. That my rite of passage could be just loving her. If only I could figure out how.

Wimple College, November 1985

It was a snowy Saturday and Julien had gotten us together for a jam session in his dorm room. Us being me and Massachusetts. I was about to do something I'd been sure since age five that I'd never do again.

"Do you know Dust in the Wind?" Julien said.

I pulled the bongos over. Where had Julien found bongos on campus?

"We'll get together each Saturday," Julien said. "The more the merrier. Bring your god-buddy next time."

"We've kinda had a falling out."

"You had a falling out with a statue," Massachusetts said. He was holding a tambourine in one hand and a three-hole recorder in the other.

"Hey, that reminds me," said Julien, stopping. "Have you thought

144

more about Hallersdorf?"

He was referring to a new semester-abroad program being organized by our German professor, Dr. Tobias Uwingen. He and Massachusetts and me were all in German 101 together. At Wimple, and apparently at most liberal arts colleges, you had to study two years of a foreign language. One you didn't already speak. Which meant Spanish was out for me, and French out for Julien. Massacusetts, you could have argued, barely spoke English. But he'd opted into German too.

"Of course," I said, "Hallersdorf," as I tapped out the first quiet triplet in 14 years on the smaller drumhead. That sound. So taught and charged. The rough, cool cow-skin under my fingers.

"It has beautiful beaches," Massachusetts said. "I seen pictures."

"So now you're in?"

"We ain't exactly getting voted most likely to succeed here. Why not?"

"Why would you go to the other side of the world to learn a language they only speak on the other side of the world?"

"Because," Julien said slyly. "Right next to the other side of the world, in Spain, my parents happen to have a coastal villa just waiting for us. And I just happen to have my Spanish girlfriend waiting there too."

"You?" Massachusetts said. "What's her name?"

"Lola," Julien sang. "L-O L-A Lola! She has friends too. So you in?"

I was torn. My gut had been screaming bolt since we'd first arrived at Wimple. And then came the slight twist to things that was Halsey. There had been so many moments - for example, with her lips pinching the edge of my ear - where she had my brain so scrambled I couldn't have added two and two. At those moments I would have chosen life in a cell with her all riled up like that over freedom all on my own.

There was an urgent knock at the door.

"Gents!" It was Don.

"Where's your tuba?" Massachusetts said.

He was all red in the face. "Milo. Don't go to your room."

"I wasn't planning on it."

"There's a dude there says he needs to see you. I swang by for the weed money. This guy is seriously scary, man. I'm gonna call the

Staties."

"What's he look like?"

"Older. Black. Like, African American."

"I get it."

"Big puffy coat. Stomping his feet all over the place, saying he has unfinished business with you."

"Hipólito," I said. The old bastard must have found out I'd been sprung.

"No. He said something like 'soap.'"

I tore out the door. No coat. Boots untied. It took me three minutes to reach my dorm. There he was, just sitting there. Leaning casually against my door. I walked over and stood right over him. The hall was empty, thank god.

"Story hour."

"What are you doing here?" I said.

"Ha haha. Ha haha. So the orphan found a home after all."

"This is invitation only, jackass. You can't just come waltzing in here. And anyway why the fuck would you?" Swope was dressed for the arctic. His eyes like always.

"Because I'm out now too, motherfucker. And I need me a home. Was thinkin we'd room together like old times."

"I'm here because I did good in school," I said. "Sort of. They picked me. They didn't pick you." Even to my own ears I sounded like a pleading ass. I should have manned up right then. But who was I kidding? The last time he'd seen me I was running like a pussy for my life. From him.

"People like you," Swope said, pointing up at my chest. "You only realize you're not better than others when you realize you've been bested yourself." He pulled a small silver nine-millimeter from his parka. My mouth went dry.

"Maybe you can explain something to me first, Orphan. Hmm? Listen up. As I was saying, there was my mom, driving the Vorheese's Mercedes, me in the back, running some errand."

"What are you talking about?"

"The story you so rudely did not allow me to finish in Nathan Hale. About my mother. Your black-ass maid. Or your neighbor's. So we're driving through Whitieville, running some kind of errand for the Vorheese Family, when this white boy all of five pedals out of nowhere right into the road. We dinged him good. He stops skidding

146

like 40 feet away. I'm the same age as him but that's the only thing we had in common. I thought. I never had seen my mom so crazy. She and me was running to that kid. His bike was stuck up under the car still. I am not sure where white people hide in the suburbs but before we reached the boy there was a big crowd around him. Came outta nowhere. And of course one of them is a doctor. One of them is a nurse. And one of them sees me and picks me up. Not like a kid wants to get picked up.

"My mom sees that and she's no longer thinking about any accident. 'Put my boy down,' she says.

"Not so fast," this man says. He's hefting me for who knows why. But it isn't to give me a lollipop or to ask me who my favorite second-baseman is. It's like he's taking a hostage. Or collateral. There are sirens and I am thinking they're coming for me. I can tell you that that's as scary as it gets. To be held by a white stranger like that. In my whole life, the worst. Meanwhile that boy? Turns out he ain't even that hurt. A miracle. The doctor has him standing up. He's all burned down one arm and bruised but besides that he's pink and crying and his mom has him.

"What are you even doing here?" his mama hisses at my mom. "Running over children playing in the street. How dare you come here!"

"You had better put my boy down," my mom says to the man. He's trying to slip deeper into the crowd.

"Not until the police arrive," he says.

"That man musta never watched Mutual of Omaha's Wild Kingdom. He didn't know what a bear does when you take its cub. When the cops finally did arrive I was back on the ground. So was that man. And so was my mom, laid out with a broke jaw and a bunch of that man's hair still in her hand. At the trial I found out no one talked about the little boy jaywalking on his bike, or how the man sure seemed like he was aiming for some strange-fruit vigilante justice with me. It was only about what my mom did to that man's face and hair, that's all. I didn't see her for five years. Now how is that fair. You need to tell me, Orphan. How is it fair that you end up here?"

"But that wasn't me."

"There you go talking down to me again."

You could hear sirens approaching at a distance. Don or someone must have called the cops. I held a finger up

147

"That sounds….kinda familiar."

Swope stood and cocked the gun.

"What are you gonna do?" I said quickly. "What your mom did? Maximum damage before the cops pull up?"

"Why not? Except my mama surrendered. I won't."

"Your mom went away for a long time. You're either gonna be dead or locked away for life."

Swope raised the pistol and cocked me in the head with it. I fell back against the wall. "Well," he said, "we'll have to wait for another day then." He stashed the gun. "I'm not in a rush. Next time I will blow your white egg of a head off," he said. "The very next time. Which will be soon Mr. better-than-everyone gimp-ass bitch. Enough now of white people takin' everything and havin' their cake too."

He darted for the stairs.

"Don't you dare come back," I said weakly.

"Ha haha!"

I heard a car moving away quickly.

I counted to ten then ran out.

Back in Julien's room everyone was still just sitting there. Don was clacking two spoons against his thigh.

"Way to have my back, guys."

"I called campus security," said Don. "Did he do that to you?"

"You are campus security," Julien said.

"It's nothing," I said.

"You got blood on half your head."

"Man, was he crazy. Homeless, I'd guess. Must have seen my name on the ink board outside my door. I think the cops are already arresting him."

"That doesn't add up," Julien said. "Who's soap?"

"I'm in," I said.

"What?"

"Hallersdorf. It'll be like The Great Escape, but backwards."

"Awesome," said Massachusetts.

"Well that sucks," said Don. "You guys are the only fun event around here."

There was a knock at the door. Halsey came in. Julien and Massachusetts exchanged a glance.

"Princess Half-a-Turk," I said.

"Jesus, what happened to you?" she said, touching my hair. "You get in a fight?"

"Nah. Hit my head on a thingie."

"On what? You need to go to the infirmary."

"Hey hey. This is a club," I said. "What's the secret question?"

"What is the sound of one hand spanking?"

"There are shakers in the bag," said Julien.

"One hand spanking?"

"You're so good at it," she whispered. "What happened? Why are you so on edge? Would you go to the infirmary already?"

"One song first," Julien said. He passed a hand along his ponytail. "I just close my eyes/Noting for a moment that the moment's wrong/I say slip away/and all your troubles won't another visit buy/Dust in the wind…"

I scootched the bongos closer. Julien's fucked up lyrics made me suddenly feel like I could tap out some sort of pathetic little rhythm. They reminded me that I was not the only loser in the room. Maybe also playing would clear my head, which I needed to do fast. Swope had gotten back inside it. That crazy crack-head wasn't gonna go away until he'd whacked me. Unless I went away first. Massachusetts lost the beat on the tambourine. A drop of blood fell on to the bongos. The song train-wrecked.

"Are you ever gonna tell us what happened to your, uh, body?" Massachusetts said. "I mean, your little flipper is all wagging like a puppy tail. Like it wants to play along."

"I need to go to the infirmary," I said. Now was not the time for tales. Now was the time to figure out how to dodge a madman. "Anyway who cares?"

"Me," Halsey said. That caught me off guard. She may have pinched the elephant that day in the library, but she'd never pushed me for an explanation afterwards. At first I thought she just couldn't be bothered to wonder. What with her busy life and her pre-med crazy studying. But lately I'd been thinking she was just letting me be, well, me. She seemed to be good at that. Even if she was also good at not popping by or even calling for 2 or 3 days at a time. Or disappearing over an entire weekend with those friends her age. Then absolutely refusing to apologize for it.

"I'll tell you at intermission," I said.

"Intermission," Julien announced.

"I was stealing a car."

"How'd you get into that racket anyway?" Massachusetts said.

"Out of revenge."

"Against who?"

"If I knew that," I said, my mind racing. Think, I thought. Live up to your name. Milano. Milan. City of second chances. Then boom, genius struck: "I started stealing cars from people because a person in a car stole my mom from me."

There was real poetry to that. Plus it was nearly true, which made it easy to get creative fast. I told them how the whole thing started, one humid summer night when I was ten years old. How Miriam put on her pink bathroom slippers and went out to buy yucca and black tobacco at Janski's Produce on the far side of the I-95 bridge.

I told them how it had been just like any night where you know nothing much of interest is going to happen. How me and Hipólito were sitting on the couch watching *The Waltons* figure things out, when we heard a screech of car tires through the open windows, four floors below, and a dull sound, the short flight and thump of something soft, then a second screech as someone drove away at high speed. Then screaming. Hipólito and I looked at each other. His arms had already gone tense and cord-like.

"*Dio' mío.*"

We both jumped up and ran to the elevators. Going down, neither of us said anything. The beginning of how things would be. My stomach turning. The noise could have been any number of things. On the street we couldn't see what had happened because of the small crowd. I saw the pink slipper near the curb before Hipólito did. But he saw her body, and slumped to the ground. Kaylie from Afro Solutions was there in the gathering crowd. She tried to take me back inside.

"Come with me, child."

I fought her hard but she was big and strong. She couldn't get me in through Elder's metal doors so we ended up falling back on the cement entry ramp. Me making a high anxious sound against her big chest. "The doctors are coming," she was saying, rocking me in her tight grip. "Don't you worry."

"So that's how it started," I told them. "I can still see every detail from that night. Except for the identity of the driver. He got away. Hit and run. No witnesses. And I could never let it go."

"So?" said Massachusetts.

"So a couple a years ago, I came across the most guilty looking car you could imagine. A big old 1973 Fleetwood Brougham Cadillac. Apple green, tan interior, whitewalls. Unlocked. I got it running in under a minute. But unfortunately in under a minute I had the cops on my tail."

"Why was it unlocked?" Ron said. "In New York City and all."

"Because the world is filled with dumb-asses," I said. "That thing was a tank. The steering all out of alignment. Cops didn't have to do much except watch me bounce off a bunch of parked vehicles until I skipped a curb and crashed through a wrought-iron cemetery gate. Up there at Woodlawn. Just before the crash I stuck my arm out the window to flip the cops off. Too cocky. That was my mistake. Next thing I know part of the iron gate has snapped off and sheared my shoulder to the bone."

"And they couldn't sew it back on," Halsey said.

"I nearly ended up parked in that graveyard for good."

"Holy," said Don.

"*Putain.*"

"So, you fucked up your body and your life taking revenge on...a car?" Massachusetts said.

"I destroy inanimate objects. Apparently, you destroy faces. What's the fucking difference? We both ended up here."

As I was boogeying out of there Halsey stopped me in the hall. "I'm sorry."

"Yeah, well, whaddaya gonna do?"

I was glancing around, checking the stairwell, avoiding the windows. My heart was pounding. Screw the infirmary. I had to go back to my room to pack for the Big Scram. If necessary, I'd tell the police what I'd told these guys: some crazy homeless *loco* had shown up on campus randomly, crossed my path. No past between us whatsoever.

"Hey, relax. You don't have to talk about all that if you don't want."

Halsey put her head against my chest. I thought, all I had to do was make it to Christmas break. Damn it. I was so screwed. Then I had an idea. "Let's move in together," I said.

"Woah, really?"

"I do like your room more."

"Mine? But it's so much smaller. Anyway what - "

Julien opened his door. "Hallersdorf," he said, winking. "Woohoo brother. You're gonna love it. You'll see." He disappeared back inside.

"What's that?"

"That," I said. "That's the other thing I wanted to... We're going abroad."

"Who? Like, to live?"

"After Christmas break."

"When were you going to tell me?"

"Just now. I just decided. It's only for a semester."

"But you just this second asked to move in with me. For three weeks? And then, you're leaving? Are you nuts?"

"Hold up. You're the one who called this place Alcatraz. Like you, leaving has been my plan since before - " I gagged. Halsey's hand on my throat was strong. Her other was cocked back in a fist, ready to punch me in the eye. Fuck, I thought. I was playing this badly.

"You do not just sneak off," she hissed.

"I'd come back," I gasped. "In the Fall."

"Sneaks don't sneak back." She rapped me hard on the forehead with her knuckles. Harder the second time. "What am I doing anyway? Always getting mixed up with boys like you? Maybe my mother was right. Maybe I should just. Wait. For a nice. Turkish. Man." After the sixth ding on my skull I started to get pissed. I grabbed her hand and pulled it off my throat and twisted it. You could say too hard, looking back on it.

"For the last time I am not a boy - "

She went to her knees. "Let go of me!" she screamed. But you still heard the light snapping sound. "Owww! Owwww!"

"Shit! Are you okay? What'd I do? Did I do that?"

Julien and Massachusetts and Don were watching us from the doorway.

"She hit me first," I said.

Later that night – after walking behind Halsey to the campus infirmary, after watching silently as they put a brace on her sprained wrist, after following her and her upperclass girlfriends home and then her door closing in my face – I found myself alone in the deserted parking lot of Arsenault's Lobster House. I knew it was a step backward but I hadn't been able to stop myself. I was feeling ever so slightly unhinged. I lowered the rock and tried to catch my breath. I'd cut one of my fingers a little and was bleeding on the snow.

Arsenault's was about a mile from campus on the edge of town. It was beyond freezing and I was shivering in the silence with just that one mute car frozen there in its parking spot. Everything was glowing red from the neon lobster claws humming on the closed restaurant's roof. Even my breath. The little Mazda 626's windshield and side windows were gone. I'd just smashed the living shit out of them, trying for the ten millionth time in this way to strike and arrive at some other, faceless culprit, a man to call my mother's murderer. A rock in the face for wrecking our entire lives, then and to this day.

But the car of course was empty. I stood there, panting. Shit, I thought. Were you really flirting with sticking around? Starting to believe this second-chance would actually change things? Erase everything that came before? The hottest second-chance of your lifetime had already walked right up and kissed you repeatedly on the mouth. And yet here you were, slipping back into the sewers. Your natural habitat.

I slunk back to campus and crashed on Massachusetts' floor.

That Monday I put the final bullet in the Era of Wimple. "*Lasst uns nach Deutschland gehen!*" I said, walking into German 101. Let's go to Germany.

"About time," Julien said.

"On one condition. That we go to France for a long weekend. There's an architect I need to punch."

"*Wie toll!*" said professor Uwingen. The good *Herr Doktor* was standing behind his desk munching on his morning Kit Kat. "That's fantastic news," he said. Dr. Uwingen was a friendly, high-energy guy who developed frothy white gobs of spit at the corners of his mouth when he spoke. He knew this and was always wiping at his mouth with his fingers, even when he was saliva free. We'd taken to calling him Chewy Uwy, or just Chewy. He was tall and closing in on 60 but his skin was almost like a baby's. His hair was unkempt and white.

"Now we will be 17 students," he said, rocking on his heels. "*Wie toll."* He was so clearly pleased. This semester abroad was his baby. Normally freshman didn't go overseas. We – me now, included – were going to be his guinea pigs on this first ever freshman-year program. It was the kind of thing that could make or break a professor's career.

"Direktor Vietz doubted I could pull it off."

"Director Feets?"

"An old childhood friend. He runs the school where we'll be studying."

"Cool. A sort of homecoming for you."

"I do also have family nearby." Chewy's face got distracted for a second. Then he arced his eyebrows, feigning suspicion "What convinced you to come?"

"Love," I said. "Of language."

He smiled. Ever the optimist, despite the crappola cards he'd been dealt. Professor Uwingen had been one of those few Germans who'd had time to leap from their low Berlin apartment windows in 1961 when, one morning, a wall was suddenly seen to be rising from nothing. That leap, from two stories up, was why Dr. Uwi walked with a limp. His sister, he told us once after class, had also jumped but had lacked his physical strength. She'd landed okay but still on the eastern side, and was dragged off by soldiers of a different loyalty. Chewy never saw her again. He'd eventually ended up in Britain and stayed there for many years, which explained his accent.

Maybe because of his own tough beginnings I'd taken a shine to him. Despite losing everything, he didn't seem to have any worries about anything, not even taking three certified fuck-ups on an extended vacation to the Baltic. He was watching us now, beaming. "I'm still so glad your father could convince the school," he said to Julien.

"We're students like everyone else," Julien said. "Same rights, same responsibilities."

"Same semesters abroad," Massachusetts said, without looking up from his newspaper.

Weeks earlier Wimple had raised a holy stink when Julien had signed up for this semester abroad. Dean Florestine, the same guy who'd said I couldn't take Spanish, had had the nerve to object on the grounds that the AIM students had been freed under certain conditions.

But Julien's hotshot lawyer dad looked into it. He pointed out on fancy letterhead that "those certain conditions" were not specified in the AIM agreements with the State of Maine, except to the extent that we couldn't get into trouble. But "equal to all other students, in all respects" was written right there in black ink. Wimple could either let us go or find itself in court, for discrimination. And that most likely would have displeased *Herr* Joiner, our benefactor. So the trustees had conceded.

"I'm glad to be going," I said to Chewy. "Hey, no comment?"

Massachusetts looked up from his newspaper and smiled broadly. "Goddamn. I was starting to think Mr. Whipped was staying put."

"Yeah, well that kinda went to hell, didn't it." I hadn't seen Halsey since the sprain. I'd swung by twice and called but she was never in. Thinking about her made me feel panicked and depressed and ashamed. I hadn't slept much.

"Hey," Massachusetts said. "We've got a whodunit on our hands."

"What is that?" Julien said.

"Someone smashed the hell out of the mayor's ride couple a nights ago." Massachusetts held up the weekly newspaper. The headline read, Vandals Target Mayor Chussey's Car. There was a picture of his car, windowless in a restaurant parking lot.

"There's a trail of blood and everything," Massachusetts said, looking at me. "And it heads from the scene of the crime towards a certain college."

Later that day I was walking back from the library when I heard a hissing sound. I looked toward Togan Pond, the frozen puddle ringed by willows on the edge of campus. Leaning against a tree, half hidden behind the hanging branches, I saw Don, our faithful pot-supplying security guard. He waved me over with a nod of his head.

"Donny boy!"

"Would you?..." He held a finger to this lips.

We hurried to the road and climbed into his car.

"Shut the door," he said.

"You in trouble?"

"Me."

"Me?"

"Bigelot's on his way."

"Here? Why?"

Don looked out the window. "I know why you were in juvi."

"It's not a secret."

"Cuz Bigelot knows and he told me."

"I don't know what you're talking about."

"You can't let him see that finger."

"I cut it on a beer bottle."

"You can't let Bigelot see you at all. I felt it was fair to warn you."

"What am I supposed to do? Build an igloo?"

"It don't matter. Just don't go to your room till he's gone. He ain't gonna sleep here. He just wants to ask you about it. But his curiosity is piqued."

"I've been crashing at Massachusetts' anyway."

"Too close for comfort."

"Can you drop me off on the other side of campus then?"

Don started the car. "Wherever you go, go there till Sunday."

"Don, thanks man," I said. "I appreciate the heads up."

"Not a problem. You guys have been cool with me."

"And I'd appreciate it if you kept all this between us."

"That is not a problem either."

"Julien and Massachusetts don't know. Not about the mayor's car. Or why I ended up, you know."

Don pulled over. I stepped to the street and pulled up the collar of my Peacoat.

"Milo," Don said, leaning toward the passenger side window. "Why did you do it anyway? Just wrecking them? No stealing, no joyrides. Just parked cars. What's the point?"

The point? I opened my mouth to speak, to say some wise-guy thing, then to say that I didn't know. But all I said was, "I owe you one."

I walked looking down, my Peacoat collar up and my hat pulled down low over my ears, until I was inside Halsey's dorm. When I knocked on her door my heart raced again but still there was no answer. I let myself in with the key she'd given me and lay down on her bed.

"Milo."

"Oh, shit."

I must have fallen asleep.

"What are you doing here?"

"There's a cop from our program looking for me," I said. I thought it best not to mention my other suitor. Swope.

"Well I didn't call him. Though I should have."

"Listen. I got a little wound up the other night."

"Really. I didn't notice. I have to wear this brace for three weeks."

"I'm sorry. Beyond sorry."

"Why's the policeman after you?"

"He thinks I smashed up the mayor's car."

"Did you?"

"I don't know what I'm doing. I just need to lay low for the weekend."

Halsey grabbed a bag and stuffed some clothes in it. "I'll be back on Monday then." She left. Which she did on some weekends anyway.

Standing on the ice only added to my sense of insecurity. But I was the one who'd asked her to meet me out here, on the center of Togan Pond. Where no one could overhear us. Where I could see the long road climbing from Wimple to campus. I had one eye out for a squad car, the other for anyone black and packing. I'd spent the last two and half weeks on Massachusetts' floor and now there were just a couple of hours left for me on the Wimple campus. The final stretch. Seeing Halsey again was ripping my heart down the center but I couldn't not see her.

"What are we doing out here?"

"I wanted to explain," I said lamely. "These things just have their momentum."

"And ours?"

"I never knew I was going to meet you. Much less that you'd give someone like me the time of day."

Across the pond the firs at the forest's edge stood like great racks of dresses, their sleeves gathering snow.

"Well I did, didn't I."

"But why? You're a year older. Your friends are older. You act older. Sometimes on the weekends you go off who knows where. To some mountain resort owned by the Kennedy's or something."

"The Kennedy's," she said. "Who do you think I am? And why this need to control me? My grandfather? He was a Turkish guest worker in Germany, I'll have you know. My mother came to the U.S. when she was 16, with nothing. My dad's a schoolteacher. I think you're a bit confused."

"Where in Germany?"

"It doesn't matter. Hannover. The point is, I'm as far from high society as you."

"Huh. Well you fake it well."

"I'm not faking anything. I just don't give a shit."

"I do. I don't belong here," I said. "Not even close."

"Clearly you've convinced yourself of that. But that's where you're screwed up, Milo. You do belong here. You're different. This place needs you. I need you. I don't want you to go." She raised her fist in the air. She was clutching a chunk of metal. "But here you are, going."

"Wait," I said. Oh shit, I thought, she is going to crack my nose.

"Close your eyes."

"Don't –"

I felt her slip the metal thing into my coat pocket.

"What is that?"

"The beginning of me," she said. "Now you have to come back."

She punched my chest and started walking. Fast. I kept my eyes closed. Do not open them. If you do you won't leave. And if you don't leave you'll be jailed again or killed. Or if by some miracle neither of those then just plain lost. You will watch yourself wreck everything. Because you're in love but loving lies beyond your range of possibilities.

The footfalls crunching through the snow. Softer, softer, silence. I let a long moment pass and I knew she was gone. I opened my eyes, scanned the road again. I put my hand in my pocket and pulled the object out. It was a ring. Or more precisely, the circular metal fitting of a sink drain. So she hadn't made her story up. There was her name, inscribed on it like runes.

I walked to the edge of the pond, following what I imagined to be Halsey's trail. Then I walked back out to the middle. I stood there for a long time, until it was pretty dark and the cold began to seep up through my boots. I ran in place, pumping my legs up and down without actually going anywhere. Occasionally some straggling student or professor walked by and stared and continued on. I headed for the student union building.

After a cup of coffee I felt better. I paid for it and told the guy at the bar to have a merry Christmas then headed out into the night walking and walking until I found myself under a spruce. There was no snow under its boughs and I sat down on the dry needles beneath it. The campus was nearly deserted. I was going to need more than coffee to make it in that cold. It was only seven o'clock.

When she came out of the dorm she was wearing a big green backpack on her back. I ducked behind the trunk. She'd changed coats. Somehow that bothered me. But what bothered me more was the four-by-four filled with boisterous classmates that pulled up in front to pick her up. So this was her ride down to the airport in Portland. She jumped in through the door behind the driver. I could hear music and laughing in the moment before she pulled the door shut. The vehicle slid a bit as it moved from the curb, then got stuck.

A couple of boys I didn't know jumped out and started pushing. I nearly ran out to help. But how would I have explained me under the tree? Then three more guys came to lend a hand. What the hell. I pulled up my hood. Under cover of the crowd I jogged over and threw my arm into the mix. Hoping to catch a last glimpse of Halsey even as I pushed. I could see the back of her head through the back windshield. When the car rolled free it was like my intestines were tied to the bumper.

After the engine faded away I collapsed under the tree again. For like six minutes. Then I hoofed it back to the student union. It was after seven-thirty now and the doors were locked. A young girl inside shook a finger at me through the window. I hugged myself twisting from side to side and made brrrrrr'ing noises but she just turned back to her mopping. I tried to get inside a couple of dormitories, to buy some time to think, but those doors were now locked too. For fuck's sake. So this is what being literally the last person on campus feels like. Or what it feels like to be any animal that actually lives outside.

Another reason to hate nature. I walked back to my dorm, but pulled back around the corner.

Turns out I wasn't the last person on campus. There were four others. Guys outside my dorm door, tugging on it. Talking trash.

"You mean you dragged our asses all the way up here and he's gone?"

"I don't get it," said the voice I knew. "It ain't Christmas yet."

"We oughtta shoot his windows out."

"Fool. Put that away."

I ran as fast as I could, cutting across campus to the road where it looped back around toward town. I didn't hear the car approaching until it was too late. I tried to scramble over the ploughed embankment but slipped and fell. The car stopped.

"Get in dummy it's minus 4 degrees out."

"Fuckin' A. Don!"

I jumped in.

"You nervous or just frozen solid?"

"How do animals do it?"

"Do what?"

"Not die out here," I said.

"Where you goin?"

"I was thinking Burt's Coffee."

"But you gotta ticket to somewhere, right?"

"To Germany."

"But between now and January?"

"Was thinking of hibernating. Making me an igloo."

"Yeah well tell you what," Don said, leaning away from me a bit, which was his way of showing intimacy. "You can hibernate at my house if you want. I got a sofa in the living room."

"Really? Thanks man. Maybe I'll do that for a couple of days."

"You'd be dead before sunrise in any igloo."

We were rolling through Wimple now. The town was Christmas itself. All the antique shops and the hardware store and even the gas station were gussied up with tinsel. It made you feel like you couldn't possibly get shot. Ah the magic of Christmas. Don pulled into the gas station.

"What are you doing?!"

"Fueling up."

"Now?" I said, getting out the passenger side, scanning the street.

"We could wait if you want. But then we'd be out of gas."

A car appeared at the far end of Main Street, a Buick with tell-tale yellow New York plates. Swope was in the passenger seat staring out the window like he'd torch the town down. I dove back into the car and sunk into my seat, counted backwards slowly from ten.

"That Skylark gone?" I said, unmoving, when I reached zero.

"It's right behind us," Don said. "In line."

"Shut my damn door!" I hissed, slipping to the floor.

Don stepped forward as he pumped the gas and kicked it closed just as one of Swope's pals walked past. No questions asked. Saved my life. Made possible all that was to come.

PART TWO

Hallersdorf, West Germany, January, 1986

There was the bar at Logan where the guy wouldn't serve us, then the KLM flight to Amsterdam with the flight attendants who kept the Heinekens coming. I was drunk, and high; Don, who'd driven me down from Wimple, had gotten the three of us stoned in the parking lot one last time before we went into the airport to join Chewy and the other Wimple students.

"Happy trails, gents."

"Later Don," I said. "Thanks for everything."

We crossed the bus and taxi lanes, hefting our bags and packs.

"Y'all come back!" Don called from his smoke-filled car.

Now we were somewhere over Novia Scotia. It was dark outside the window. It was my first time on a plane.

"Thanks," Julien said, taking three more beers from a woman whose wing-tag read "Anne."

"*Danke*, Anne," I said, sitting up and taking her hand.

"They're Dutch," Julien said.

"We say Dank," she said. "*Dank u wel.*"

"Dang thee well, Anne," I said. "I like the way you Dank. Wonerful people, the Dutch. Anne von Dankuwel." I sipped more and smiled dumbly. I was liking these strange foreign women. From our height high above the world I could imagine many more like them waiting below. Entirely new characters ice-skating to school across frozen ponds on long pale legs. And if you were lucky enough to say the right thing, that is, whatever it was they wanted to hear, it would surely be enough to make a whole new life there among them. I could nearly hear their odd names all choked with unexpected k's, structures that forced you to make new sounds with your throat and which were unrelated to anything ever having to do with, say, water fountains. You would never stare down at a drain and find their names staring back at you…

"How long have we been on this plane?" Julien said.

I looked up. I glanced over at Massachusetts. Fast asleep. Then I was asleep. Imaginary Mom came out of the cockpit, dressed as some sort of hybrid Mother Teresa-flight attendant pushing a rattan cart, her face plasticky and half-hidden behind a white veil. The incomplete face I'd invented for her. The best I could do. She stopped at our row, smiled at my friends. She handed each of them a mesh bag tied with ribbon. Inside, lugnuts and washers identical to the ones I'd been getting each Christmas, one at a time, in the unmarked envelopes. My puzzle pieces from Miriam. Those were not hers to give. Where had I hidden my own bag? They were with me always. I felt around and realized they'd been falling out of my front pocket and slipping to the floor. Rolling all over the plane. I tried to stand but my seatbelt had no buckle to unbuckle. I pressed the panic button in the center of my left hand. So the hand was back. But the thumb was on the wrong side. Now I.M. was looking at me. She was about to say it again. How had she gotten on this plane? My idea had been to leave everyone behind, including her. Maybe, deep down, especially her. And then I was being shaken awake.

I held to the back of Massachusetts' shirt as we filed through a checkpoint, then another — wait, where was Dank u Anne? - and then into a bar to wait for our flight to Hamburg. At some point I dropped a huge beer glass called a Stein. Pronounced 'shtein'. The other Wimple students swayed like sea grass. Or I did. The rising turbine roar as we lifted off again. I don't remember anything in a concrete way after that. There was something at baggage claim, something funny there, then a bus and a crowd by a yellow school building and the looks before Julien and a blonde boy helped me into a boxy green Mercedes like I was some government official who'd been shot.

I woke the next morning alone in a bed with a pillow as long as the bed's width. My head was killing me. There was a window letting in too much light. Below the window I saw my duffle and my pack. I went back to sleep to escape the pain and awoke at some point and stood and went to the window. The old Mercedes in the driveway brought back more images from the night before. I could remember getting out of the car, the awkward silence as the blonde boy and a man with grey bangs in a tennis sweater helped me up the stairs of a house. This house. Me repeating over and over *Dank u wel, dank u wel...* and had I heard a whole bunch of screeching monkeys?

There was a knock at the door.

I turned from the window, my heart racing. "Just a minute!" I called.

"Here we eat the breakfast at eight thirty," came a woman's deep voice, in English. "It is now ten-eighteen."

"It is too late for breakfast." This time a man's voice. "You will have to wait until tomorrow morning."

"Uh, sorry!" I called, dressing hastily. *"Entschuldigung!" Excuse me!*

"Now we'll work in the garden."

"Okay! Just a minute!" Jesus, who are these nut jobs? I had a class to get to. And I was really late. Shit shit shit. I went to the door and opened it. It was the man from the night before, I was sure of it. He was tall and had straight blonde-gray hair that hung into his eyes and down around his big ears. The woman was tall too, with fine mousey hair to her shoulders. They wore matching gray house slippers. They were watching me sternly.

"I am...I am...*fertig*," I said. *Ready.*

"*Gut.* Then we'll go to the garden," the man said, in English.

"*Schule?*," I said, in German.

"The garden shall be your school."

"But I am student. Studying… is, uh, is pleasing to me." With that I'd exhausted my feeble Deutsch. "Listen," I said, rubbing my temple with my thumb, trying to snuff the pain out. "I'm sorry about last night. But I think there's a misunderstanding. I've come to Germany to study. We're college students? I have classes…"

My host-parents looked at each other. The man laughed and doubled over and put his hands on his knees. The woman lay her elbows on his back and cupped her face.

"Hoo hoo," the man said. "Hee. Oh."

The woman held out her hand. "Halo Milano. I am called Anja. Anja Wartemann."

"And I am Wolf."

"I'm sorry about last night."

"*Ne, ne*. There's no problem."

"So, the gardening thing…?"

"We have made a joke," Wolf said.

"A couple of jokesters."

"We love the jokes," Wolf said. "We have a son not much younger than you. Together we are always joking."

"The blonde kid."

"Jan," said Anja. "Our only child."

"Don't worry. I normally don't drink - "

"Jan is shy," Anja said. "But he has the humour too. Once he opens up."

"If there are girls on your program, maybe you could introduce him."

Anja elbowed him. "Wolf."

"Really? Sure. Where is he?"

"At school," Wolf said. "Where we need to get you. Your Doktor Uwingen will be wondering what kind of parents we are!"

Wolf and Anja led me down the front stairs and I started wondering the same thing. At the base of the stairs was this long, wood-paneled post-and-beam living room, lit by skylights set in the high ceiling. Beyond it there was a doorway and you could see a kitchen with a bar and stools. It was uncomfortably warm in there, and it was decorated with a half dozen hammocks strung between posts like some Indian longhouse. There was no other furniture. The floor was polished concrete speckled with white, brown and green shit stains. And seed. Overhead a whole bunch of green parakeets and other exotic birds flew freely among the rafters, swinging on tiny wooden trapezes, clinging to knotted ropes dangling from the ceiling, swooping and winging around erratically. Their flapping was like someone fluffing pillows. When they saw us they perched where they could and began to whistle and caw.

I flinched. "Jesus. Do they bite?"

"Most definitely," Anja said.

"Do not let them land on you," Wolf said.

"Do not look at them in the eyes."

"Right right," I said. "I'm catching on to you guys. So, what are these, pets?"

"*Ne, ne*," Wolf said seriously, taking Anja's hand in his. "They are orphans."

When I got to class I knew something was different. It was the look on Chewy's face. No light-hearted smile. No frothy spittle. How weird. He held a wooden pointer and was tapping it against one palm. It was already eleven o'clock. "You missed the morning reception in the gym," he said sullenly. "With the students and faculty. There was marzipan."

"Sorry Dr. Uwingen. I. Well, you were there." The Wimpletons laughed. "Won't happen again."

Massachusetts also looked serious, as did Julien, come to think of it. I sat down behind him.

"Hey," I whispered.

"Let him sulk," Massachusetts said.

"About what?"

"Apparently, not everyone's living accommodations are equal in every way," Chewy said quietly. "At any rate we are here to learn German. No matter what your new home is like. No matter what they might serve you for breakfast. Shall we continue?"

At noon that day we had our first break. The school we were at was a high school, not a university as I'd thought. Turns out Germans went to high school until they were 19, one year more than us.

"That's why they're so smart," Massachusetts said as we headed outside.

The school itself was striking, a high, yellow rectangular block that looked like it was made from a series of stacked cubes. All the windows and doors were oval shaped. The locals called it *der Käsebunker* - the Cheese Bunker. We shuffled out the front door into the windy, cloudy afternoon, unsure how to kill the half hour before our next class. The school stood on a promontory at the juncture where the white-capped Baltic Sea met the Trave River, a tranquil waterway lined with old wooden sailing ships. There was a constant flow of boats. Tugboats, ferries big and small, gargling barges carrying containers with Chinese names on them.

And there was the East German border, right there, just a little ways across the river. I thought, are you kidding me? Can that be real? The grey DDR gunboats motoring along the far shoreline. The barbed wire, the watch towers. Everything that was built was built from cement and nothing was painted. There wasn't a tree within a mile of the line, just bare brown fields, patches of snow. Two soldiers watched us with binoculars from behind a green and white car parked on a road behind the fencing. I waved.

"Move over."

"What?" I said. "You're really gonna play?"

"Well waving didn't work," Julien said, opening his guitar case. He frowned at the sky, then slid the strap over his shoulder and jumped up on a low wall by a staircase that led to a rocky beach. He started to sing Blowin' in the Wind at the East Germans, at the top of his lungs.

"How many boats must a man sail on/Before he can fall to the sea/Yes and how many years can a white dove exist/before he is forced to be free…"

The guards had stopped watching us. I looked in the other direction, along our side of the line, down the empty beach with its boarded-up snack stands and small wooden cabanas, dormant in winter, toward the neat streets inland, the smart houses with their charcoal slate roofs, the manicured gardens, the pruned, leafless lime trees lining the sidewalks. Sober, bourgeois Hallersdorf was like carnival in Rio compared to the drabness in the East. And the Cheese Bunker itself was the lead float in the samba parade.

"Kind of an eyesore, isn't it?" I said, gesturing back with my thumb.

"Compared to where Julien and I are living," Massachusetts said, "this is eye candy."

"What'd you get?"

"Fat soup. Warmed on the radiator. That's what our host parents gave us for breakfast."

Julien jumped down from the wall.

"How'd you do?" he said, out of breath.

"I think good. My host parents are wack. Most of the downstairs part of the house is like this giant tropical bird sanctuary."

Julien and Massachusetts looked at each other.

"You don't believe me? The house is just around the corner. Come on!" I said, jogging backwards along the boardwalk. When we got to the house I knocked, but no one answered.

"You hear em?"

"Those are not parrots," Julien said.

"Not parrots." We waited a little longer. Then I remembered the shoelaced key around my neck. I opened the door. "*Hallo?*" I yelled, "Anyone home?"

We went into the longhouse. Julien crouched like a guy getting off a helicopter, then threw himself into an orange and red nylon hammock. His put his hands behind his head and closed his eyes. Massachusetts stretched out on another.

"Anything to say now, folks?"

At first the birds cawed and fussed from on high, but after a minute there were two dozen of them climbing on and jumping between my pals. I guessed they were looking for food. Julien opened his eyes and startled a parrot from his knee.

"Ow," he said. "The bastard clawed me. I wonder how hard it would be to smuggle drugs in them."

"In the birds?"

"This is where you live," Massachusetts said, swinging himself gently. "I don't fuckin believe it."

"Would you like to switch with me? Massachusetts and I live next door to each other," Julien said, trying to shoo a bird from his hair. It had leapt from the hammock rope onto his head and one of its feet was tangled in his ponytail. He sat up abruptly, swinging his arms.

"Putain!"

The parrot was flapping its wings like crazy, making it look, as Julien rose, like bird lifting man. It freed itself and went squawking up into the rafters.

"There was a bird stuck in my hair."

"Where are you guys living, anyway?"

"In rowhouses in a village called Knöbnitz. Half an hour south of school. Basically the slums, but with – "

Julien screamed like a baby.

"Oiseau de merde!"

Another parrot had come back to mess with his hair. This time it got both its feet caught in his frizzy black locks. It was screeching like a cat on fire, trying to fly away, pecking at Julien's scalp and his hands when he tried to grab it. He stood and flailed his arms in the air. He spun around, accidentally backhanded the thing to the skull with a fist. Just like that it went quiet, free-fell backwards. But its feet were still stuck in Julien's hair so it ended up hanging there upside down like a sleeping bat, its beak nestling against Julien's ear.

"Get it off me!" Julien shouted. He bent over, shaking his head.

Massachusetts poked at the bird with his finger. It didn't move.

"What the fuck, Julien!"

"What?"

"What, what? You're gonna get me kicked out of my house on my second day. You killed it."

"There is a dead bird in my hair!"

"Don't move," Massachusetts said slowly. He gripped the bird where its feathery thighs disappeared into its torso and yanked hard.

"Ow!"

"Hold still. Milo, get me a knife."

"Oh, no, no. You're not going to cut my hair."

"The bird's feet. Relax."

"It will bleed all over me!"

"It's dead," Massachusetts said. "It can't bleed."

I found scissors in the kitchen and handed them to Massachusetts. Up in the rafters the other parrots perched silently. Masachusetts slipped the scissors through Julien's hair and snipped.

The parrot fell heavily to the floor and lay there face up, its wings spread open. Julien looked at it.

"You cut my hair," he said, touching his head.

"Holy shit, folks, it's way after break," I said. "Chewy's gonna kill us."

I found a plastic bag in the kitchen and scooped up the bird and all the loose feathers I could find, and we were running out the door.

"They won't notice one bird gone," Julien said as we jogged along the boardwalk.

"I really fuckin hope not," I said. I'm finished, I thought. I was casting around for a garbage can. When we reached the Cheese Bunker I still hadn't found one. But there was also no litter anywhere. I was about to just throw the bag out onto the beach when a voice called out to us.

"Hello American boys!"

I spun around. On the steps of the school there was a group of maybe 8 or 10 Germans, about our age, smoking cigarettes, shoulders hunched against the wind. One of them was smiling at us. He flicked his cigarette to the ground and came down the stairs.

"I am called Michael!" he called. "But that has no importance. We must establish the rules."

"Only English," Massachusetts said, pointing to his ear.

"*Nichts da! Ihr seid jetzt in Westdeutschland!*"

"What is he saying?"

"And we don't want commies here in the West living. You should have stayed with your friend Fidel. But since you here are, we are happy to show you Honecker's gate!" The boy called Michael pointed toward the river and the border beyond.

Massachusetts, Julien and I all looked at each other, then at this guy jabbering. He was plump and tall. What kind of a teenaged douchebag dressed entirely in black and carried a square black briefcase?

"What's he saying?" Massachusetts repeated.

"All I got was commie and Fidel," I said.

"Okay, no problem," the German boy said. "I will speak in English. So that we understand each other from the start." He came down the cement stairs. "I bring you something," he said, giggling, looking at his friends, then at Massachusetts. He walked up to him and stopped and reached into his coat pocket, pulling out a green apple. He tossed it once in the air, then wung it right at Massachusett's face. Massachusetts did not flinch. The apple hit him above his right ear and exploded into bits. Of all the ways to commit suicide.

"A green apple" Michael barked, "for a red Cuban!" He turned and laughed to his friends. Massachusetts wiped at his head with his coat sleeve, picked some apple out of his hair.

"Yo, bro!" I yelled. "Right back at ya!" I ran up and hit Michael square in the face with the bag. "Eat parrot motherfucker!" The bird turned out to be a pretty good weapon – light but stiff, with the little claws and the beak. A thin line of blood ran down one of Michael's cheeks.

"Commie bastards!" Michael yelled, stumbling backward, a hand to his face.

"Still hungry, douchebag?" I said, raising the bag again.

Michael's friends were already down the stairs. I browbeat one of them as fast as I could swing my arm. Julien charged into their midst with his guitar case held like a battering ram. Everyone was screaming. Someone clocked me in the jaw and I thought it broke. Then my bag broke open and the green parrot spun out and tumbled limply to the sidewalk. It was in much worse shape than in the house. Both wings were bent funny and there was blood on its face. Michael's or its own. Everyone stopped fighting to look at it. Except Massachusetts.

He had eyes only for this Michael. He was watching that asshole like a linebacker. Michael must have decided his best play was backwards, toward the school, because he was backpedaling. He looked about to poop himself.

"I am bleeding," he said weakly, holding up his briefcase like a shield. "We –"

Massachusetts swatted it aside. It flew from the boy's hand, spilling open next to the bird on the pavement.

"Easy Massachusetts," I said.

"Do not kill him," Julien said, reading my mind.

But Massachusetts was not going to listen to us. He strode like a robot up to Michael, arms stiff at his side, fists clenched, his huge head slightly down. Then he pulled his head back and snapped it forward like one of those piston-guns they use to kill cattle. Right against Michael's chest.

The German boy crumpled like a sheet from a clothesline. To my surprise his friends just scattered. We must have taken out their king. I ran over and kicked his briefcase for good measure, then bent over and snatched a fancy monikered pen from the ground and shoved it in my coat pocket. We bolted up the stairs of the school.

"I think you just took an apple for me," I said to Massachusetts breathlessly. I was on fire with the adrenaline. "He called you a Cuban commie. What the?"

"He fucked up," Massachusetts said. "You're the only commie here."

"Fidel Castro put my mother in prison," I said, rubbing my jaw, walking as fast as I could to keep up with him. Julien was way ahead of us, his guitar in hand.

"Hurry up, gentlemen!" he called. We hustled back into Chewy's classroom. Our professor looked as dismayed as ever. We took our seats. He turned his back to us to continue mapping out something he'd labeled "genitive case" on the chalkboard.

"Milo!" Julien said. "The bird!"

"Gentlemen!" Chewy said, his voice rising, his back still to us.

Holy shit. The bird. The evidence. I needed to destroy it. I started to stand but somehow Chewy sensed it.

"*Überhaupt nicht*, Prieto. You were late this morning. You were late after break. You will not be leaving early this afternoon."

"I gotta use the bathroom."

"Not now."

I sank back down, anxious. If that dead parrot fell into the wrong hands, I thought, I could end up falling back into the long arms of a certain size-extra-large police captain. Go straight to jail. Do not pass Wimple. Never see Halsey again. The person I was fleeing from to begin with. Although now, faced with the dawning possibility that she might be out of my life forever, I was beginning to think no frickin' way. I cannot let that happen.

The Cheesebunker's *Direktor*, Herr Vietz, came into the classroom. Chewy looked surprised. I felt bad right away. It didn't take a genius to know that he was getting in trouble with his old friend. Over our little rumble with Michael-in-Black and his boys. Vietz spoke slowly but he was red in the face. Chewy said something to him quietly, deflated, then turned to the class and said, "Sullivan. Bowles. Prieto." Just like Powders on the bus in September, except without the enthusiasm.

Vietz marched us out of the classroom and up two flights of yellow cement stairs to his office overlooking the frozen sea. Chewy came in behind us. From up here you could see several more lines of barbed wire defenses running deep into East German territory. You could see the beach where I'd hoped to do away with Anja and Wolf's sorry dead boarder. I peeked quickly down to the sidewalk below to see if the creature was still there. It wasn't. My stomach sank. Then Michael himself came into the room with a man who I assumed was his father. The only difference between them, besides twenty years, was the older man's clothes, which contained no black at all. To my horror I saw that he was holding the tattered plastic bag with what was left of the bird stuffed back in it.

"What his the meaning of this?" the man said to Vietz.

"That's why we're here, Colonel."

"Colonel," Massachusetts said. "We're fucked."

Then, just because we were on a roll, just to seal our fate further, who should knock at the door but the Wartemanns, Anja and Wolf. The school must have called them. Anja saw the bag straight away and the green shape distinguishable through the plastic. She covered her mouth.

"Mein Gott." She took the bag from Michael's father's outstretched hand and opened it. "Gufi."

"Goofy?" Massachusetts said.

"When we saw he was missing, we didn't imagine this," Wolf said.

"So you have killed Gupi," said principal Vietz in English, sitting down behind his desk.

"Gufi," Wolf said. "Like the dog von Disney."

I glared at Julien who just looked at his feet.

"It was an accident," I said. "I can explain."

"Shut your mouth, commie!" Michael shouted, trying to stand up. So he'd figured out who the supposed commie was. He looked humiliated. Michael's father, standing behind him, put his hands on his son's shoulders and pushed him back down and leaned forward. "I don't know what you were hoping to accomplish here," he said to me, "but you will certainly fail."

"If you mean learning German," I said, nodding.

"Could someone back up a bit?" Julien said.

I looked at Chewy, who just shrugged his shoulders. He seemed really stressed out.

"Professor Uwingen," I said. "I think they think we're - "

"No one here speaks out of turn," Director Vietz said. "This town has suffered enough in this conflict."

"Conflict?"

"The Cold War conflict."

I looked over at Wolf and Anja, half expecting them to burst out laughing, to blow the lid on this latest gag, but they just sat huddled together, each with one hand on the plastic bag.

"In light of today's events, an uneasy coincidence has come to light, Mr. Prieto," Vietz said, peering at an open folder through his reading glasses. "I need to ask, how is it that a Cuban national, in search of an academic semester abroad, would happen to come here?"

"Here being."

"On the seam of the Iron Curtain."

"I'm American. My parents are Cuban exiles. My father's American now too."

"I don't have to tell you about our special role here," Vietz said.

"Actually – "

"We are the first line of defense along the Baltic. We all pitch in. We have patrols. We monitor press and radio transmissions. Keep an eye out for infiltrators. Unfortunately," he said, glancing at Michael's father, "they turn up just about everywhere."

"Have you looked into him?" Julien said, pointing at Michael.

"How dare you," said Michael's father.

"Don't stir the hornet's nest further," Vietz said.

I held up my hand.

"No one is above suspicion," Vietz said, glancing apologetically at Chewy. "No one can be."

"This Fall," said Colonel Baumann, "we learned that three neighbors were sleeper agents for the DDR. Herr Neusser. Blumenthal the Bavarian. Stefan Klein, who was like a brother to me. A baker, an architect, a minister. They were our friends - "

"We only learned about it after they'd fled," Vietz said. "And they only fled because the Americans were on to them."

"We would have found them eventually. They made off with very little. Only the blueprints for Hallersdorf's new SportClub."

"Three secret agents stole your plans for a gym?" I said.

"It was to double as a bunker. And we are now under an uncomfortable amount of scrutiny. Bonn has made its displeasure clear. If we cannot hold the line, then others will be brought in."

"I'd love to know what Herr Bonehead dug up on me," I said, gesturing at the folder in Vietz's hands. "Does it say there that my mother, Miriam Prieto, spent 18 months in a Cuban dungeon outside Santiago?"

"There is little here by way of background information," Vietz said.

"Do you people even know Cuban music? *No Me Busques Más*? Los Soneros de Matanzas? Does it say that she wrote songs critical of Fidel Castro's government and was accused of treason? Does it mention how she developed liver problems in prison and a skin thing? How being locked up gave her the gravelly voice? How to get out of that jail she had to publically renounce her work? Her ideals? And finally just ditch?"

Silence.

"Leaving her two kids behind? How they've suffered in school because of it? How my parents joined the anti-Castro movement in New York, where I was raised?"

Vietz was eyeing Michael with one eyebrow raised, tapping his report against his desk.

"If what you say is true, Prieto — "

"I haven't even started."

"Well. I'd say young Baumann's report lacks elaboration. And rigour."

"I will correct that."

"Unnecessary. We may have missed the Stasi Three but let's not get delirious either."

"Wait a minute," Michael said. "You're not going to just believe him. It could be a cover!"

"If it was," Vietz said wearily, "then you've blown ours. That is all."

Herr Baumann led his glowering son out of the room.

"Wolf, you'll have to leave me the bird," Vietz said.

"Of course."

"Then we are finished," Vietz said, "Take the boy home, *bitte*. And prep him, why don't you, for his first patrol. He is going to be of value. A true-blooded Cuban dissident might help us get back into Bonn's good graces."

"I'm American," I said.

"Yes," Vietz said. "You keep saying that."

"My first patrol?" I said from the back seat.

"Beach patrol." Wolf said.

"That's like, what, arresting penguins?"

"If only it were so exciting."

Anja was sitting on the bench seat next to Wolf, staring out her window.

"Listen," I said, "About Gufi Bird. It was an accident. I brought Julien and Massachusetts home with me during a break. We were gonna stay two minutes. Then Gufi, I don't know, he got all tangled in Julien's hair. It was like he was attacking him."

Anja looked at Wolf icily. "I knew this would happen. Letting such a strange character in. Damaged goods, I told you."

"Hold up," I said.

"We couldn't have known from his application alone," said Wolf, glancing at me. "He just arrived."

"It was obvious. The way he kept to himself all that first morning - "

"But today's only my second day," I broke in. "I'm not maladjusted. I'm just adjusting. I'll get you another parrot at the parrot shop - "

"God in Heaven," Wolf said. "We are not talking about you!"

"Gufi was a bad egg," Anja said. "We are very sorry for what happened."

"You guys are kidding, right?"

"Not this time," Wolf said.

"Yeah, well, Julien suffered the most. Gufi didn't even see it coming."

Anja closed her eyes. "I am always right about these things," she sighed. She turned to me. "I get a feeling. I call it my *Vogelgefühl.*"

"You know, you arrived just one day after Gufi did," Wolf said.

"Arrived from where?"

"From Lübeck," Anja said. "But they come from all over West Germany. People buy tropical birds as pets, then get bored with them."

"Parrots are not like dogs," Wolf said. "Not even the ones named after dogs. They don't give affection in the same way."

"So what are you, like a flying kennel?"

"A sanctuary," Anja said.

"How many birds do you have?"

"As of today," Wolf said, "one less."

When we got home it was dark. I still hadn't met their son Jan, sober at least. Today he'd gone straight from the Cheesebunker to

Astronomy Club. I peered out the living room window into the back yard. I could make out in the faint light of streetlamps a series of small cabin-like structures below high trees. Maybe they were more birdhouses. Behind me, in the long-hall, the chirping, cacawing and whistling carried on and on. I felt like whistling myself. I was getting treated by my new host-parents to a special dinner of rump steak and potatoes. Quark and red berries for dessert.

Anja called me into the dining room. Wolf was already seated at the small table. The meat smelled wonderful. And someone had cut my steak. How cozy and warm that house was, especially with all the snow outside. Glowing like a tiny ember in the night. The door opened. A tall kid with curly blonde hair in a ski jacket came quietly in, riding a wave of freezing air, hauling a black nylon sack with him. His eyes were large and round. I remembered him. He looked at me, then at my shoulder, and said "*Hallo.*"

"*Hallo.*"

Jan stomped his boots and huffed down the long-hall and ran upstairs. Five minutes later he was back, changed into a pair of stone-wash jeans and a red Hawaiian shirt. He looked at me and sat down and picked up his fork.

"Where is Gufi?"

How had he noticed?

"*Ich –* " I began.

"They killed him," Anja said gently.

Well, I thought. Just put it out there. Her son's eyebrows went up.

"The other birds," Anja said, pushing her hair behind her big ears. "They set upon him."

"Who is responsible?" Jan said. "John-Boy? Ralph Malph?"

"There were feathers everywhere," Anja said.

"Somebody should have been here," Jan said. "The first days are always hard for a new arrival."

"There's nothing anyone could have done," Wolf said. "You know that separating fighting birds is dangerous."

"I'll buy you another bird," I said.

"We don't buy them" Jan said disdainfully, displaying not one bit of the Humour he allegedly possessed. "Buying birds is the problem."

After dinner I helped Anja clear the table as much to solidify my good standing as to avoid going upstairs and running into Jan. He seemed very skeptical of his parents' version of Gufi's demise. Better to avoid contact with those big eyes for a couple of days, I thought. We finished the dishes and Anja turned out the kitchen lights.

"Good night, Milo" she said. "It's been a strange day, *oder?*"

"Pretty much as strange as I ever had."

"It is not always like this."

"It's cool."

"You seem 'cool.'"

"I am holding it together," I said, before realizing it. I saw how that made Anja look at me. "Could I have the address of the house?" I said quickly.

"Of course you can," she said, touching my shoulder.

"It's, you know, so that they know where I am."

"That's important." Her voice was so kind I couldn't look at her.

She wrote down the address on a paper towel in the kitchen. I muttered thanks as casually as I could and made my way towards my room. Two parrots dive-bombed me in the longhouse, banking away at the last second. A toucan penned behind chicken-wire in the far corner shreaked. It had a splint on one leg. Just behind me, the faint patter of droppings hitting the floor.

In my room again at last. I dug around in my still unpacked duffle, found the manila mailing envelopes and addressed one to Halsey, copying out my new address on the back. It had been more than two weeks since I'd watched her roll away. I was dying. To hear her voice, inhale on her pillow, sip her weird teas. And all the other stuff leading up to her balling my brains out. Remembering an article I'd read about how the olfactory sense is the strongest of our memory triggers, I kicked off my boots and stuffed my warm socks into the envelope and sealed it, no note. There was a knock at my door.

Anja popped her head in and handed me the airmail envelope. "Milo, with all the commotion today I nearly forgot this."

"Oh. Wow. Thanks."

Dear Milo,
Wie geht es dir?? Okay, back to English. I miss you every day more and more. I feel like there are bars on all the

windows here. I really am in a jail, even if you don't agree. I don't know if I can take it, to tell you the truth. I hope you are keepng my beginnings safe. My friend Janet is sitting next to me. She says hi. You haven't met her but you'd like her. She's a punk from upstate New York. Plays accordion. A senior. How is Germany? I'm sure ...

I turned the letter over.

...you're having the time of your life. My wrist is just about better. They took the brace off early. I know you didn't mean to twist so hard. Still, I was weak and should have dropped you on the spot. Against my better instincts, I call rematch. But until then I'm not sure what to say. It's going to be months. And then who knows if you'll even end up back here. Lots can happen. I know that you know how I feel so I won't even write the word. Surprise me on the first day of school next year. But in the meantime, keep heading wherever it is you're heading. If you don't you may never figure it out. The thing that's eating at you. And, worse, you might never come back.

Love (oops),
Halsey

I guess you could have called it patrolling. We were in formation, two-by-two, about thirty of us, all students, marching along the beach. A bald man in a red sweat-suit blew on a whistle. We picked up the pace, speed-walking parallel to the shoreline. The man shouted something and the pairs of students reached out and held hands. I was next to a girl named Heike. But in my head I was still at the Wartemanns trying to find the words to convince Halsey that I'd make it back to Wimple no matter what.

"I'm bored," the girl named Heike said.

"Huh? Then why'd you come?"

"It's obligatory."

"Would you switch sides with me?"

"*Ne*. It is forbidden."

"But if we're going to hold hands?" I pulled my empty sleeve from the left pocket and shook it like a snake skin.

"Where is the arm then?"

"You really wanna know?"

Heike tilted her head, studied me as we walked. Finally she said, "Under the circumstances." We crossed each other like square dancers. She placed her hand in mine, curling her fingers into a fist: a warm baby bird.

"Attention!" shouted the man in the red suit.

"Who is that?" I said.

"Herr Silberhorn. The village actuary. On Saturdays he's the head of the Strandschutzjugenddienst."

"You really think we could protect this beach from those marauding Reds?"

"I couldn't care less."

Up ahead the beach curved slightly. We neared a stand of several dozen beach cabañas, their colorfully painted wooden doors locked for the winter. We made our way past our school, jogging now, and out onto the cement promontory that jutted over the sea. If you knew how to hit a golf ball you could have hit one into East Germany from there.

We formed a single line, holding hands, facing the enemy. Watching for who knew what.

Silberhorn pulled out a megaphone and led us through West Germany's national anthem. Then he shouted some phrase, and we shouted in response: *"Für immer! Für immer!"* Forever, what? It seemed like forever since we'd been standing out there. It was past four and the light was fading. At the entrance to the Trave River the wind licked up tiny silver waves like minnows. Silberhorn came striding over.

"Would you come with me, Herr Prieto? *Bitte.*"

I followed him out to the iron guardrail at the end of the promontory. There was one of those pay-telescopes mounted there. Below us waves broke lazily against a bulwark of granite blocks.

"Begin please."

"What's with the horn?"

"For your message."

"I don't have a message."

"You must have. Each week there must be a message. Didn't they tell you?"

From the foremost white cement watchtower, looming right on the far shoreline, half a dozen East German soldiers in long green wool coats and hats that were not for combat came out on to a high catwalk. They leaned against the railing and appeared to be talking amongst each other and not at all interested in us. Some of them lit cigarettes.

"Ready, set," Silberhorn said, "and go. *Jetzt*. Now is the time! Say something!"

"You want me to pick a fight?"

"Don't forget to squeeze the button."

I thought about the protests I'd once gone to. The only ones I'd ever known, the ones I'd tried to make mine and Hipólito's together. I turned on the megaphone and held it to my mouth.

"Uno, do', tre'..." My amplified voice sounded so tinny and feeble against all that open water. I took a deep breath.

"Mejor Ford que un dictador! Mejor Ford que un dictador! - "

Another student, a tall, Turkish-looking teen, came over and took the megaphone from my hand. I shrugged at Silberhorn as the kid let rip an unfathomable diatribe. It was like the words were flaying into shrapnel in his throat before spraying past his lips. I was half surprised his mouth wasn't bleeding. What a language. So German was made for angry speeches. Our colleagues, the rest of the students, began clapping in unison. I saw for the first time that Michael Baumann was among us, but he was so bundled up against the cold I could barely see his face. Or maybe he was concealing himself from me. The guards on the East German catwalk flicked their cigarette butts to the beach below and went back inside. I assumed they hadn't heard us. But before shutting the door the last one turned and flipped us the bird. Holy hell broke loose among our ranks. Everyone started screaming and laughing and giving the finger back. The Turkish boy put down the megaphone, grabbed his crotch and began thrusting over and over, his other hand behind his head. Then the East was back to looking like before: a dull land scoured lifeless by plague.

On Monday I swung by Vietz's office.

"I'm not doing the patrols."

"We need to get your German up to speed. I've ordered a special tutor for you."

"I'm not interested in politics."

"I know you're not. And I know you're not a spy. Far from it. But I need you. I'm giving you a column in the student newspaper as well. Every week you're to write something. It could be political, social, or economic. But I'd suggest always some sort of comparative criticism."

"Of…" I said, jerking my head eastward.

"Yes, of them."

"I thank you for your interest. But I'm not going to become a cheerleader in a conflict that's not mine."

Vietz leaned forward. "If you don't like it I can have you expelled tomorrow, for fighting. You'll be out of this program and on a plane. And you know where that plane will land."

"No I don't."

"I know more about you now than I did a week ago. I know about your wonderful second chance."

"That's the American way."

"And this is ours. Please say yes. I wouldn't want any of this to reflect badly on Professor Uwingen."

"And they're the bad guys?"

"You decide."

"You got me. I'll write the column."

"And Saturday Strandschutzjugenddienst."

"And Saturday Somethingdienst."

The week passed without any more news from Halsey. I'd sent her my socks anyway. "Lots can happen," she'd written. "Keep heading wherever you're heading." In my follow-up letter I'd asked her what she meant. And if she was putting us on hold then how much that idea stunk. More than the socks, in a side-by-side comparison. Yet still the silence. I didn't want to but I was starting to take it as an affront. Was she setting me up for the big blow-off? *Ninguneándome?* Could she? The fear began seeping in. The churning in my gut.

On Saturday, when I was feeling really down, Heike sought me out in the line-up. We marched out to the promontory, shouted for a while into the icy wind, then about-faced. For the return she maneuvered us into tail position. A light snow began to fall. We passed the summer cabañas. Suddenly she leaned close and whispered, *"Pass auf!"* and pushed me sideways, knocking me to the ground behind the nearest cabin. That's how I learned that *pass auf* meant heads up. She helped me up and held a finger to her mouth as she reached with her other hand inside the neck of her coat. There was a shoelace tied around her neck and she grabbed it and pulled out a small metal key that actually steamed for a second.

"I'm a latch-key kid, too."

She led me behind the row of cabanas, tiptoeing even though it was sand, and stopped before number 143. She opened the padlock and pushed open the door and I followed her inside.

"This is less boring," she said.

"Yeah?" I said nervously, stamping my feet. "You got Atari in here?"

Heike shut the door again and it went as dark as night. She rummaged around without speaking until she announced that she had found a beach mattress. Then the little bird-hands came and found me. She took my hand and guided it to the place where the key had been. She was like a wood furnace under all of those layers. I did not think overly much about stopping myself. My heart was frozen on a pond in Maine but this was me, right now, not being ignored. I was exactly one girl north of being a virgin and being touched physically was the high to beat all highs. Halsey had gotten me hooked on it, then left me spasming in withdrawal. She'd have surely disagreed, pointing out the obvious: that I'd left her. I'd had no choice but she didn't know that. She didn't know about Swope or the mayor's car or any of the baggage that came before. So there I was. In that moment, in that darkness, with no words of reassurance whatsoever to buttress me. How was I supposed to be strong or faithful or whatever? I wasn't. I unzipped Heike's jacket, helped her pull down her jeans, pretending they were someone else's. That day and on several Saturdays to come.

The next day, Sunday, I got up early and walked down to the boardwalk. I was hoping to see the rescue helicopter. Always good for a laugh. When I came back there were more letters for me, propped on the fourth stair. I scooped them up without a glance and took the stairs two at a time, my heart beating wildly.

"*Hallo.*"

"*Aiiiiiiii coño!!!!*" I screamed, falling forward.

Jan was standing on the top landing.

"Sorry, Jan, I didn't see you. Jesus. When did these arrive?"

"Yesterday. My mother forgot to give them to you. Do you have a girlfriend?"

"Uh, yeah, I do."

"Sometimes your post smells like perfume. I'd like one."

"Well," I said, moving past him, "I could introduce you to a girl with a cabana right on the beach."

"We have a cabana. It's green and yellow. Number 37."

He was just standing there. Not smiling, not frowning. I was pretty sure the bird incident was behind him now, though since that night we'd barely spoken at all. Just, good morning. Bye. Hello. It would be good to have a little more communication. But not right now.

"Sorry, Jan. I just got these to read. Maybe later you can show me that cabana."

"*Ja, natürlich -*"

I shut the door and dropped my books onto my bed. The postcard first. On the front was a photo of Wimple's church steeple. I turned it over. You had to be kidding.

Dear AIM representative Prieto, I hope you are settling in to your new surroundings, and learning a lot. I trust also that you are serving as a fine example of what constitutes a law-abiding American citizen overseas. Make the most of your time. Steer clear of the troubled waters. Surprise me. Powders

AIM representative Prieto? I was five thousand miles away from Wimple and I still couldn't get away from this guy. I wondered if his note wasn't another veiled warning about Massachusetts. What did he mean by "the troubled waters"? Like there was some shoal I could find on a chart. I tossed the card on my bed, picked up the other letter and bit into one side of the envelope, making a hole. Then I knelt on the envelope and slipped my forefinger into the hole and ripped the side open. This one did not smell like perfume. It was in Spanish.

Milo,

Gunnar called the other day asking how to reach you in prison. What a surprise. I suppose he found out through someone on the scene. Also a surprise to learn that you got yourself out of jail. And out of the country. Gunnar called back to tell me, and to give me the address. Germany's pretty far away. I'm not sure what you thought you could do there. But I am leaving VertiVille so your old key won't work.

Hipólito

It was enough to get your gut in knots. But fuck him for the moment: his news had me floored. Three Bags had actually gotten in touch? My uncle, the magnificent one-foot-in-both-worlds weirdo? I hadn't heard from him in years, not since he and Hipólito had had their falling out. Now he was apparently sniffing around. Why? The very idea of it set off a burst of hope and excitement and longing. Would he write as well? Or call? Or would he just come loping down the sidewalk, the way he'd loped away that night? I reread the letter for any clues, found none, hid it away in a book.

When I came downstairs Jan was in the long-hall.

"Was machtst du?" I said.

"Changing the water and feeding. You must do so everyday."

"Listen, if you want, we can have a little belated funeral for Gufi in the garden or something. Did he have a favorite toy or something? We could bury that."

Jan shook his head. "Thank you."

"You got plans right now?"

"Nee."

"I was gonna go for a walk."

"I can show you our cabana."

"All right."

It was a freezing, cloudless morning and the low sun lit up everything pretty. Even the East looked like a place you could visit. Jan was acting less distant. As we walked along the icy boardwalk he asked question after question, bouncing along on his toes. Where was

I from? What was it like? Who was my American girlfriend?

We reached the open beach and the cabanas. The wind was howling in off the sea. "Here is ours!" Jan yelled, tapping the green and yellow door of cabana 37.

"Go ahead!" I said. "Open her up!"

"I don't have the key. Which belongs to your German girlfriend?!"

"German girlfriend?!"

"You said there was a girl with a cabana!"

"Ah, Heike! Follow me!" I skirted along behind the cabanas, retracing our steps from the other day. "Here!" I shouted. "I'm pretty sure it's this one! You treat Heike right and she might just invite you in!"

"When?!"

"After Beach Patrol, on Saturdays!"

Jan smiled, then laughed. He seemed genuinely happy, and that changed his whole face, lit it up. He went bounding home, but I stayed because you could hear the rescue chopper pass overhead. This was happening like crazy-often. 1986 was one of the coldest winters on record in northern West Germany. The Baltic had seized up like a giant lake. The ice now extended nearly a mile out to sea. To keep the ferries and commercial ships running, each dawn a pair of icebreakers from the Lübeck shipyard came out to chop their way through the white sheets clogging the shipping lanes on the river. From as far away as the Wartemann's you could hear the vessels out there groaning like metallic walruses.

Because the ice got so thick lots of people would walk out on it, especially tourists. Sometimes the dumb-asses wandered too far out. Before they knew it they'd find themselves drifting towards Leningrad. You'd see their little arms waving. And waving. At which point a guard posted in a white hut on shore would get on his radio, and a couple of minutes later Hallersdorf's small, red rescue helicopter would swoop in. It was something to see.

When I heard the whirring I hurried for the boardwalk to watch the latest. The chopper was hovering over the stranded victims –a couple with a small child – like some curious insect. A guy inside was lowering what amounted to a giant picnic basket for them to climb into. The parents got their kid inside and up he went. Next was the guy's wife, but you could see her just shaking her head. After a minute the basket zipped up again, then came down with an officer inside. He and the husband tossed the woman into the basket. When the husband was safely up the chopper veered toward shore. In the white hut the folks got their cursory lecture about how ice works, not being stupid, how to pay their fine and please enjoy the rest of your stay in Hallersdorf.

Inside I could hear the parents yelling. At each other, the Coastguard guys or their kid, I couldn't tell. They came out and hurried away quickly. I was going leave myself when I thought I saw Chewy, all alone, way out on the ice shelf. I ran down the ramp to the beach, slid across the ice.

"Professor Uwingen!"

Chewy glanced over his shoulder.

"Watching the excitement?" I said, breathless. We were probably 400 yards from the shoreline. I remembered the last time I'd stood on ice like this, with Halsey. The sadness and the cold.

"What do you think it costs them each time they have to come rescue someone?" Chewy said quietly. He was staring toward the East.

"No idea. Can't have tourists drifting into the DDR though."

"I can't get over how odd it is to be so close. So close to that, that mouse-trap."

"Me neither."

"When I escaped it was like crossing some imaginary line in a kid's game. The ground didn't look any different on one side or the other. The construction had barely begun. I could have shouted 'Base!' Is that what kids say? Base? When they reach safety?"

"Yeah."

"There was no base for my family."

"I remember the story."

"Not one word after that day," he said. "You might have thought."

"No letters?"

"No letters."

"Is there any way you can investigate?"

"Just one way," he said. He put his hands over his head and leaned like he was going to dive into the water. He laughed, and straightened up. "It'd be a long cold swim."

"Even if you made it," I said. "You'd never get back out."

"I would not care. When you lose the people close to you everything else can lose its meaning."

"Yeah," I said. "For real."

So maybe this was why Chewy had organized this semester abroad here, right on the border. To get as close as he could to what he'd lost as a kid. Even if he could never quite cross over to the other side. There was something about the idea that I liked. That I loved. I wanted to talk about it but Anja and Wolf were waiting to take me on a bird rescue in Timmersdorf. "You wanna walk back with me?" I said. Chewy waved me off, his eyes still on the East. "See you in class," he said.

A couple of weeks later I came home from school just as the postman was walking up the driveway. "*Hier,*" the guy said. Among the mail were two envelopes for me. The first I stuffed in my coat pocket. The second was from one Gunnar Gunderson, with a Norwegian stamp on it. Hipólito had tipped me off but I was still surprised. I tore it open.

Dear Milo,

I called Hipólitos to find at what detention centre you were being held in. That's how I eventualy got your address in Germany. It's been a long time since our problems but I don't think he was any less angry. I don't blame him. I do wish he had let us keep seeing each other. I'm writing because I have some things I want to share with you. Now is the time. Could I come by to your house there? I don't want to write it down. As for me, I'm still playing the trombone but travelling less. And, I have met a wonderful Norwegian girl. Who would imagine. I returned to my roots. Maybe that's why I started to think a lot about you. I am in Norway now. Please, let me know when I could visit.

Love,

3B's

At the bottom of the letter there was a telephone number. I ran inside to my room and looked at the calendar on my desk. Then downstairs to the kitchen. "Anja, may I make a call? To Norway? It's a family thing."

"I didn't know you had family there."

"Remember I told you about Three Bags?"

"Do you have the number?" Anja said. "Well, then give me the number."

"Ja, alo?"

"Uncle Three Bags?"

"Milo?" he said, his voice faint down the line. "Wow. That is something amazing. You got my letter already."

"Yes. I – Hello? Threebs?" There was a continuous pinging on the phone line.

"Ja, I am here!"

"I wanted to call because. Well, I'm leaving Germany soon for Spring holidays, for three weeks. Your letter sounded urgent. How are you? What're these things you need to tell me?"

"I need to take you somewhere."

"Where?"

"I'm sorry but not on the phone."

"Come on."

"Don't worry. There is no reason."

"I'm not worried," I said, steadying my breathing. "What is this about? After all these years out of nowhere you're back. With something you gotta say but that you can't say. Some place we gotta go? It's wack. And you called Hipólito?" I tried to keep my voice

198

even. I missed him, that simple. Just as badly as in the days, weeks and months after Miriam's death. Hearing his voice, I felt like a four-year-old. Soldered back to the old awe, and longing, and anguish.

"I wish I had seen you sooner," Three Bags said.

"Can you come right away?"

"I have some shows here. When are you leaving?"

"Tomorrow," I said. "But wait, we could meet up in a French town called Cerbere, on the Spanish border, on March 14th if you want. I was just checking the schedule. We're going by train. We could meet at the station entrance. Nine-thirty arrival. You could come with us to Andalucia. Then we could go wherever it is you want to take me."

"You are going to Andalucia? That's perfect!"

"Yeah? My friend Julien's girlfriend is from there."

"But I'm not sure if I can make it by th - "

"Threebs? You remember when I saw you last?" I said.

"In the window."

"Did you really love her and all?"

The line was pinging and pinging, like a submarine sounding the darkness. Like some fish pecking algae off the subsea trunk line. Like maybe Colonel Baumann listening in on our call.

"Three Bags?"

Either he'd hung up, or someone had hung up for us. It felt like the air had been sucked out of my lungs. Would he show? I'd call him back. But first I had the other letter. I grabbed my backpack, already jam-filled for spring break, and left it by the front door. Then I walked down to the beach, sat down in the fading light under a street lamp.

So she'd broken her silence after all. I knew she would. How glad I was to see she was as hooked as me. As in love.

March 2nd, 1986

Dear Milo,

I just received the photos of you going into some beach hut. With some girl. Obviously you didn't take them and didn't know they were being taken. But you must have been in there a while because when you come out the moon's a lot higher in the sky. Don't want to know her name, don't want to know where this is, don't want to know anything more about this or you. When I said keep going I didn't mean into someone else's arms. But this is your choice. You didn't trust me, not even with my parting gift. I can already imagine the letter you'll write in response to this, talking about your weird childhood and how it's left you damaged and afraid of loving and blah dee blah. Obviously you're not too damaged to hook up with whoever this girl is. I was going to write that I hope you find happiness with her but I'm not feeling that generous. Then I was going to write that I will track your ass down. But it's time for me to get away from weak people altogether. Goodbye in all the languages you now speak.

No signature. Oh boy. If I couldn't breathe after Three Bags' call Halsey had just ripped my lungs out. Who the fuck would have taken those photos? And why? Who even knew about Heike? I hadn't told anyone.

Except I had.

"Milo!" Anja said, when I walked through the front door. "Don't forget I have some things for your trip." A parrot landed on my shoulder. The house smelled of Käsespätzle. I was sorry for what I was going to do next.

"Is Jan still home?"

"He's upstairs. Wolf will be home later."

"Be right down."

I bounded up the stairs and walked into his room without knocking. He looked up at me from his books, startled. "*Ja, hallo Milo!*" he said, half standing. He was acting all happy to see me.

"Where's your camera?" I shut the door.

"*Was?* What's gotten into you?"

"Don't play games with me, asshole. I want your camera."

"But – "

"You wanna fuck with me? Get your camera out. I want you to be ready."

"What for?" Jan stammered, his eyes wider than ever.

"For when I start breaking parrot necks. One by one. Let's go asshole."

He looked positively horrified now, red in the face like he was going to cry. Like he'd been made to eat bird droppings. He stood up. "Milo," he stuttered. "You are...! What has happened to you?!"

"What's happened is she got the photos, fuck-face. What's happened is you wrecked my life."

"What photos?" Jan said, trembling. "What camera?" He splayed his hands out like that was proof. "I don't have a camera!" I never saw a guy so desperate.

"Don't bullshit me."

I reached out and grabbed his throat and tried to push him down on his bed. But it turns out that Jan was as strong as an elk. He walked me backwards like I was cardboard, slamming me into a black plastic shelf stacked with homemade cassette tapes. They came crashing down on top of me.

"I don't have a camera! Ask my *Mutter*! And get out of my room!"

"Ask my *Mutter*! Ask my *Mutter*!" I said, getting up. I stomped on a tape or two on my way out

"Anja?" I called, hustling down the stairs.

"*Ja?*" she said from the kitchen. Luckily she had the little TV on loud. On the screen was an image of a building on fire. People were burning American flags. The caption said something about Libya.

"Have you seen Jan's camera?"

"I haven't."

"So he does – "

"He doesn't have one."

"Be right back."

I ran back upstairs.

"Jan?"

"Get out!"

"I'm really sorry man. I thought you'd done something majorly dickish."

"You are crazy. I knew it!"

"Somebody was following me. Taking unflattering pictures."

"I don't have a camera," he said. He didn't look scared anymore. He took a step toward me.

"I thought it was you because, because I'd shown you where Heike's cabana was...just forget it okay?"

"Get out," he said.

I did. I grabbed my passport and ran down the stairs and slung on my pack. What the fuck had I just done? I'd shaken Jan to the point where now he probably would spend all night plotting how to cut me into pieces. I hoped more than anything that he wouldn't go to his parents. I'd just sunk myself deep into doo-doo without resolving the mystery: who would want to fuck me over? I reached the beach and was going to walk down to the ice's edge. Maybe keep walking. Maybe now was the right time. Or did I need more proof that I could only screw up everything good that came along? I took out Halsey's letter for one last read. A car pulled up alongside me. It was a red Volkswagon Golf convertible with a white leather roof. The driver's side window came down.

"Going on holidays, Prieto?" Michael Baumann was smiling all smug-like, like some just-made mafia goon.

"What do you want?"

"Just checking in," he said. He looked tanned and refreshed. I wasn't in any mood to deal with that douche. Seeing him reminded me of all the concocted conspiracies and border bullshit I was so happy to be leaving behind for a while.

"Go check on your jockstrap," I said.

"I see that you have received post," he said, winking at me.

"Mail, you mean?" My hand gripped the letter instinctively. "What's it to you?"

"That depends." He winked again. That douchebag smile. I stuffed the envelope in my pocket. I started across the street.

"You're dead."

"Wait!" Baumann said. He was laughing and fiddling with the clutch. I lunged at him and caught him, unprepared, by the collar. He shrieked and popped his car out of neutral, jolting forward and sending me spinning to the slushy street. I got up and ran at his car again.

"You're dead!" I shouted. I nearly caught the driver's side door but Baumann sped ahead again, then braked. My left knee was starting to hurt. People were watching me. A zombie hobbling down the middle of the road like that, my loose jacket sleeve flapping around, dirty slush in my hair and on my face.

"Why did you do it?" I shouted.

"You hit me," he said. "In the face. With a toucan."

"Get out of that car."

"Get out of my country."

He sped off.

I sat down at the far edge of the boardwalk and watched the black sky. Halsey's letter was – holy shit, where was it? I reached into the front inside pocket of my coat. It wasn't there. I checked the other. Nothing. But I did find something thin and long. It was Michael's pen, that fancy-pants monikered number I'd picked up the day of our parakeet rumble. I should have stabbed him with it. I got up to search for Halsey's letter. I must have dropped it chasing Michael. I searched for what felt like forever. I needed that letter, to search for clues in it as to how to undo her words. The pain and intention behind her words. But no luck. Dejected, I popped into the only eatery open along the boardwalk in winter. A rotisserie chicken chain that had beer on tap. Four or five glasses later I stumbled back out to the beach.

And that's when I saw the man coming across the ice.

It was more like a swagger, the slow swagger of an exhausted surfer. There was so much wrong with this picture, I thought. For starters it was past 11 o'clock at night and probably 20 degrees out.

"*Hallo!*" the man called.

I ran across the sand. In the moonlight I could see the water glistening off his dark wetsuit. It was one of those short-sleeve summer suits, inadequate for these waters in winter. The guy must have been freezing. But that wasn't the only thing. I noticed that his surfboard wasn't really a surfboard. It was shaped like a surfboard but you could see how the edges were all jagged, like he'd cut it by hand. In his other hand he carried something heavy by a couple of straps: a metal box of some sort with a shaft attached to it and a small propeller at the end. This dude had to be East German. He must have just escaped. Several attempted to every year, they'd told us. But I couldn't believe it.

"*Können Sie mir helfen?*" the man called, dropping the heavy contraption when he reached the sand. I ran towards him. "*Ja*, okay!" I yelled. "You're okay. You're okay now!" The guy was tottering forward. I grabbed his upper arm. It was caked with a clear slick substance, like Vaseline. So was the guy's neck and bald head and face and pudgy legs. "Jesus man!" I cried. "How the hell? Nice work!" I pointed at myself. "*Amerikaner*," I said. The guy had a really dazed look on his face. "Uh, *Willkommen in der Freiheit!*" I said. Welcome to freedom, motherfucker! This was amazing. What were the chances? I remembered I had my Beach Patrol Whistle in my coat pocket. "*Komm*," I said, fishing it out. "Come with me." I started tooting and walking toward the boardwalk.

"*Hilfe*," the man said. He said it really softly. I could barely hear him.

"I am your *Hilfe*, *Kamarad!* We gotta get you warmed up inside somewhere. Come on!"

I took two steps forward but could sense that my new friend was not following. I turned around. "You can't just stand there," I said, waving my arm. "Come on, take my coat." I hung the whistle around my neck and was fiddling with the Peacoat buttons when the man dropped the surfboard. "You won't be needing that anymore," I said. "Here." I whipped off my coat and held it out. "What's your name?" I said. "*Wie heißen Sie?* Eh? You gotta name?"

At first I thought I was falling, it happened so slowly. The guy who'd apparently just jet-propelled himself across the night sea on a slice of Styrofoam, dodging East German gunships and spotlights and razor-edged chunks of ice, enduring the freezing water, lathered in lard, fucking barefoot for god's sake, went over face-first like a pillar of cold clay into the sand.

"Hey!" I screamed. This was not good. "*Hilfe! Hilfe!*" I tooted on the whistle some more. The man wasn't moving. I knelt next to him and touched his neck, like I'd seen on TV. Like I'd once done with Ronny Linky. It was cold and slimy like his arm. Then I saw something, a small hole. It was in the side of his left thigh. I went behind him and kicked his legs apart. There, on the inside of the same thigh, the exit wound. Big, messy, with the neoprene and the skin blown outward.

Worse though was his right thigh, because the bullet in its trajectory had pierced it too, and as far as I could see the projectile hadn't come out again. There was no blood to speak of outside the man's body but maybe he'd bled plenty on the inside. An East German bullet must have hit him. But I hadn't heard any gunfire. Maybe they'd gotten him right at the beach just as he was pushing off – they said that was the moment of greatest vulnerability. Between the dogs and the trip wires and the patrols and the towers. If that were the case, this poor guy had motored that entire distance – two, three, five miles from shore to shore? – already bleeding to death.

While I was playing the conjecture game, standing over the dead-still man, quite drunk, something dire occurred to me: what would people say if they saw me out here with the body? I'd already begun imagining myself a hero. But who was I kidding? I was going to be in even deeper shit. Prieto, the kid some folks not so secretly suspected of being a lefty collaborator, or sympathizer, if not outright cloak and dagger spook. This would not look good. In Hallersdorf the rules of war applied. Maybe this guy was actually a spy. That didn't seem right, but you never knew. Maybe he was one of the Stasi Three who'd escaped from Hallersdorf some months ago – the baker? - sneaking back in on some sinister mission.

If he was a spy, what would that make me? I had to get the hell out of there and fast. But first I knelt again and felt for a pulse for real, on the man's thick, gooey wrist. He was colder than the sand he lay in and I could not find a beat. I waited another minute, then tried again. The guy was toast. Still crouching, I ran toward the water then west along the shoreline. I was like a quarter mile away when I decided to circle back one last time. This whole thing had me scared shitless, but not so scared that I wasn't still mulling the other complications in my life. I reached back into my pocket and pulled out Baumann's monikered pen. I wiped it down with the edge of my shirt, set it gently in the sand next to the body.

"What's her name again?"

"Lola."

"How'd you guys meet?" I said.

"We ran around together every summer as kids. Until the day she realized what a catch I was."

"Billets, s'il vous plaît."

We were a week out of Hallersdorf, riding the overnight trains too crowded to lie down on. We'd skipped town several hours earlier than planned on account of my having assaulted Jan, and the less than understanding reaction of his parents. When I'd come in the front door after ditching the dead guy, Wolf and Anja dove down the stairs like a pair of falcons.

"What's wrong with you?" Wolf said crossly.

"Nothing," I said, out of breath. "Just back from a walk. Hey Wolf. Nice to see you too."

"I have a mind to call the police on you."

"What? Oh jeez. That. It was a misunderstanding. I feel terrible."
Wolf didn't look at all convinced. Nor did Anja.

"You will have to find another place to live," he said.

"Like, now? Can't you give me extra chores or something? Isn't that how normal families punish their kids?"

"You are not - "

"Wolf," said Anja. She turned to me. "Jan is very upset. As are we. You had no right to accuse him like that."

"I acted on bad intel," I said, hanging my head.

"We're going to call Professor Uwingen and ask him to find you other lodgings for the last six weeks."

"Wait. Wait. Let me tell him at least. First thing in the morning. I promise. Please."

"No."

"Only on one condition," said Anja. "You come back directly after school to get your things."

"Okay," I whispered. "I'm sorry." And I really was. Anja had been so nice to me. Nearly too nice, I'd thought more than a few times. It killed me to see she'd reached the same conclusion.

Anja and Wolf must have completely spaced that I was leaving for Spain in the morning. I had nearly all of my stuff in my pack already so I left straight away, taking the bus to Massachusett's place. I slept on his floor like I'd slept on his floor when Bigelow was after me. At dawn we were in the Lübeck station, scanning departures. Now in a few minutes we'd be inching into Cerbère. The air was warm, my nerves were frayed. The conductor stood impatiently in the doorway of our compartment. My hand was shaking as I fished for my documents.

I hadn't told Julien or Massachusetts about Three Bags yet. I hadn't been able to. Where would I start? With who Three Bags was? How we knew each other? That part was easy. But then? When we'd last seen each other? The fucked-up circumstances that had driven him away? This was all the dumb shit I'd preferred to gloss over with Halsey and the rest of planet earth. AIM was about getting a new start, not about centrifuging out our heavy material for analysis. But I was out of time.

I took a deep breath.

"A friend of mine is meeting us here," I said. The Cerbere platform came into view. I saw how small it was, and that there was no one on it. Three Bags was not there. My heart sank. Why hadn't I kept my mouth shut three seconds longer?

"What do you mean?" Julien said, putting his guitar away. "You know someone here?"

"Not from here. From Norway. Well, from The Bronx. A family friend. Three Bags."

"Three *Bags*," Julien said.

"He used to play music with my parents."

"This requires a group meeting," Julien said.

"What do you call the three of us sitting together on a train?"

"So he's old," Massachusetts said.

"Yeah," I said, although I'd never thought of Three Bags as old, nor, come to think of it, even considered that he'd have aged since I'd last seen him. Would I even recognize him?

"But he's not old in his head. Anyway I don't see anyone out there."

"Why was he coming here?" Julien said.

"I don't know. He wrote to me just before we left Hallersdorf. We agreed to meet here."

"Why didn't you say anything?" Massachusetts said.

"I just did."

Massachusetts looked out at the sea, squinting into that brooding, grey light. "I guess Three Balls is in then." The train stopped. He picked up his pack. "Let's see what this Nordic wack-job wants with our boy." He jumped down from to the platform. Julien followed. I came behind, craning my neck.

But I guess I wasn't meant to find out what Three Bags wanted. There was no sign of him as we wound our way through customs and passport control. I was crestfallen.

"*Pasaporte*," the Spanish customs officer said.

"Have you had a Norwegian pass through here?"

"*Sí señor.*"

"Today?"

"No. Not since last summer."

We walked outside to the other train platform where the Southbound wagons waited. The first thing you noticed was that it was cover-your-eyes sunny. We boarded along with the rest of the passengers from Cerbère. Second-class on this narrow-gauge jalopy consisted of two rows of rigid bench-seats upholstered a very long time ago. We sat with our packs between our legs.

What had happened? Either he'd been delayed or this was playing out just like it had fourteen years before, when on the street he'd made the phone-call gesture then never called.

Strange, I thought, how his voice over the phone the week before had been like someone opening an old kid's book on my lap. All week I'd been imagining what it was going to be like seeing him again. What I imagined had two endings: me hugging him or me punching him in the adams apple for having ditched out on me. As the minutes ticked by and the Spanish countryside slid past, the adams apple version was gaining the upper hand. Then I saw him. His hair was totally grey, including his walrus mustache, but he was just as tall and funny looking and unmistakable.

He was pushing his way through the doors into our car, his soft trombone case held out in front of him like the prow of a Viking ship, his green frame pack over both shoulders, a little burgundy prayer satchel visble beneath his open coat. I stood up in the aisle.

"Hey."

"Hey," Three Bags said, stopping.

"Do you recognize me?"

"Barely," he said quietly, standing his trombone case on the ground. "Barely at all. Oh, brother. You have grown. That's for sure." He pushed a lock of white hair out of his face. "You are so big." He opened his long arms and surprised me by taking me into them. His embrace was strong. He rubbed my head with one big hand.

"Three Bags fuckin Gunderson," I said, trying to sound self-assured.

"However, the blond has not changed," he whispered against my head. "The duck has not lost its feathers."

"*Comemierdas*," I said, going deeper into his embrace, resting the side of my face against his chest. I didn't know what to say next. All of my imaginings were gone. There were no punches to throw, there were no smiles. Just a feeling like a wave slamming into you. He smelled like a soapy horse. Like music, like mischief. Like the Bronx itself, or at least that small, wonderful part of it, from the finite early days.

VertiVille, The Bronx, November 1971

He appeared in the doorway, his foot tapping clave. I was sitting on my crate on the far side of the laundry room, before my faithful audience of rattling dryers, my little radio at full blast, practicing over and over the switch from the bongos – my first ones were makeshift, fashioned from old paint cans - to the cowbell at the *montuno*. If you were fast, not missing a beat from the final cha-cha stroke to the low downbeat on the bell's open edge, it was nearly like sleight of hand. If you were slow you train wrecked.

"Keep the clave tucked under your right leg," Three Bags called over the music. "That way you only have to bend over for the bell."

I tried it. It was much easier that way. "You. Are. Right," I said as I played. "Yeah."

"Where is your mama?"

"Out!" I said.

"*Y papa?*"

"Sleep! Ping!"

"Would you tell them I came by, Patico?"

"Si!" I still had not yet mastered the art of playing and talking simultaneously. The best I could do was shout single syllables, in time to the music.

"Okay then!"

"O! Kay!"

But a minute later he was back.

"How long have you been practicing today?"

"I don't know," I said, putting the bell down. I turned down the music.

"Just getting warm," he nodded knowingly. Like we were both seasoned pros.

I fanned myself and stuck out my tongue.

"You want to come jam in the playground?"

"The playground is for kickball, stickball and basketball."

"Not this playground! A bigger one! Come on. We'll leave a note!"

Unlike my parents Three Bags did not have a car. So we left a quick note in my kitchen then crossed the overpass from VertiVille, me holding his huge hand, catching the bus south and then across the Pelham Parkway north of the zoo.

"Are we going to the zoo?" I asked. I was sitting on his lap, with my head against his chest.

"No."

"Cuz if we are, the zoo's not a playground."

"You are barking at the wrong tree, boy."

A woman sitting across from us smiled. "Handsome child," she said.

"He is lucky," Three Bags said, "That I am not his father! I am only his uncle."

"You're not my uncle!" I said, pretending to slap him. But I loved that he'd said it. We jumped off the bus on a busy road I didn't know and walked a couple of blocks and stopped in front of a restaurant. Haitian Soul, read the awning.

"Well?"

"What?"

"What do you think?"

"Three Bags!" I whined. I was getting tired, and hungry. I sat down on the little ledge in front of the restaurant and put my chin in my hands. Three Bags did the same.

"Well?" he said, waving a hand before him.

And then I saw what he wanted me to see. Right across the street. A brick building, two stories tall, with a vacant lot on either side. A big white sign near the roofline: Botnitz's Music. In the windows I could see violins, horns of all kinds, and drums.

"Let's play," Three Bags said, rubbing my head.

"They let you play?"

"They will when they hear you."

The drum section was upstairs. There was a young guy working there who Three Bags introduced as Felix. He told Felix I was the future of Latin jazz.

"The great hope of VertiVille."

"No shit, you live out there? What's that like?"

"I dunno," I said, looking at Three Bags. "Fine. Tall."

"The boy is interested in the Valje bongos."

"We've got some starter bongos," Felix said helpfully.

"He would destroy those."

"Ooh," said Felix, doing a quarter turn like a soldier, then skipping off into a storeroom.

"I don't like these plastic *guiros*," Three Bags said, picking up a fake gourd from a whole shelf of them and raking the plastic stick along its edge. "They are too loud!" he shouted.

"Let me see," I said, sitting on a black swivel stool.

I was scratching along when a song came on over the store stereo at a slightly slower tempo. Watermelon Man, featuring one of the fat-cat *congueros*, Mongo Santamaria. When Felix came out with the bongos in their carrying case he was grinning. *"stá bien, muchacho."*

"Gra. Ci. As." I said.

Felix signaled for me to switch with him. I loved playing to Mongo because of his precision on the skins and his down tempos. Going slow was how you were supposed to learn any instrument, mastering technique, establishing good habits that would keep you from tiring or hurting yourself or holding you back when you played faster. When you improvised. Mongo Santamaria was my flight school. I began smacking and cracking around his improvs like we'd grown up together. For me it was true, musically speaking. Except for the Valjes being too big for my legs and slipping every so often, I was on fire. I didn't even mind having an audience. Felix was playing the guiro and watching my hands.

"This boy is the real deal!"

"I can see that, *hermano*."

"*A. Zu. Car!*" I yelled, making myself laugh.

"*Azucar!* Where'd you find this kid?" Felix jumped up and ran back into the storeroom.

"Spain!"

"You guys know this?" Felix called out, not saying what it was. "You're gonna love it." He came running back over and picked up a little shaker-egg. "Tjader. This is gonna sell millions."

After a quick horn section lick, an up-tempo rhythm kicked in with a flange electric guitar floating over the top. Then the strange lyrics. "Sombre Guitar/Harmony's down/day into day/just hanging around..."

I grabbed a conga and played straight, feeling my arms tire quickly at that pace, trying to focus instead on Three Bags who was now tearing a hole in the universe with his bone. I'm not exaggerating. One moment he was like some flatulent sea lion trying to roll over on us, then he was soldering something way up high near the water pipes along the ceiling, then he was a runaway jalopy bouncing down subway stairs, honking his hooga horn in warning. Can you imagine what any of that really sounds like? Can you imagine a guy with a shock of crazy sandy hair and a walrus mustache, standing six feet five inches tall, skinny as a pole, bent at the knees and rocking back and forth and side to side at the waist, in sky blue denim bell bottoms and red Keds sneakers, just blowing the living hell out of a long brass noisemaker as weird-looking, if you stopped to think about it, as anything Dr. Seuss might have drawn? And all of it sounding so beautiful like it was prewritten or preordained and you have the absolute out-of-body pleasure, as a four-year-old, of playing alongside it? Or, better put, of hanging on for dear life alongside it?

When the song was over Felix zipped the Valjes up and took them to the register.

"You want I put them in the original box?" he said to Three Bags. My heart started pounding with the sudden possibility that I might go home carrying that black bag over my shoulder.

"I am not going to buy them just yet."

"Kid deserves 'em."

"Ya, that's what I brought him here to show!"

Man, I thought, so I'm not getting them?

"Your call, Mr. Gunderson."

"How do you know his name?"

"If I didn't I'd be working somewhere else."

"I think we are going to wait," Three Bags said, rubbing my head.

"Oh," I said. "Okay."

"We must ask you father first. And Christmas isn't far off."

We jumped the bus back. At home Hipólito smiled thinly as Three Bags and I recounted our adventure. When I got to the part about nearly buying the drums his face went flat. He looked at Three Bags and shook his head.

"Valjes are not kids drums."

My father had strict ideas about drums. Traditional ideas. I wasn't allowed to even touch his three consecrated batá drums. They were sacred, for religious purposes mostly. And even with 'recreational' drums – bongos, congas – you had to earn the right to play. You started with clave, or *palitos*, until those were second nature. Only then, and with the nod of an elder player, would you find yourself seated before the skins.

When Three Bags left later that evening, I went into the kitchen and asked Miriam if he was really my uncle.

"You can call him that," she said, pouring me a glass of Hi-C. "He's like family." Hipólito came into the kitchen.

"Your uncles are all in Cuba."

Miriam looked at him. He grabbed a beer and went out to the living room. I followed him out and climbed up on his lap on the couch. There was a college football game on the TV and he was watching it, still trying to figure out how you played. I snuggled against him but he acted like I wasn't there so I went to my room. I turned on my little radio, spinning the dial, hoping to find that Tjader tune again. What was the line from it? Harmony's Down? My door opened.

"Turn that off," Hipólito said. "Come help me watch the TV."

"What else about you hasn't changed?" Three Bags said.

"Everything's the same. Just bigger. I thought you weren't coming."

"It was easier to fly into Barcelona and meet you on this side."

"So much effort out of the blue," I said. "I can't wait to stop not getting it."

"There are two boys staring at us."

"Eh-how-you-doin'? So you're the Norwegian trumpet player. Julien plays guitar. I carry it for him."

"The trombone," Three Bags said.

"And you're carrying, surprise, three bags," Julien said.

"You never know when the phone is going to ring."

"What's in the little one?"

"The Buddha Shakyamuni."

"Yeah? Well take a seat, Three Buddhas."

"So then," Three Bags said, sitting down, "you are all students in

Germany. Wonderful." He had a week's worth of white stubble on his cheeks and chin and his hair was just as wild as before. He looked even more like a tall, skinny version of Albert Einstein. I was still having trouble believing he was actually here. He reached up and took my hand.

"But you have been in trouble too."

"We," Massachusetts said, "are America's troubled youth."

"Sprung on the promise that we won't screw up again," said Julien.

"That's good. That's extremely good! You can still learn something. Of course you can. Brother. You are showing the world that that one is possible."

"Have you been in jail?" Julien said.

"No. But it's not too late!" Three Bags said, sitting forward then back. On his face, this look like we should all be laughing.

The ticket conductor passed through the car. When he was gone, Three Bags lowered his gaze slightly and shot his eyes among us. Like peering over reading glasses, except he didn't wear glasses.

"I would like to know what you all did," he said. "Before we go one inch further."

"Don't be scared," Massachusetts said.

"I got caught smuggling hashish from Tunisia to the U.S.," Julien said.

"You were in jail there?"

"Briefly. My family got me out. It was a very small amount. I was doing my time in Connecticut."

"Connecticut?" Massachusetts said. "Sounds tough."

"And you?"

"I, uh, hit a guy. Too hard."

"Was it self defense?"

"If defendin' your interests is self defense."

"Those are two different things."

"That's what the judge said."

"That's a dangerous one. Too much aggression. You have to work on that one."

I thought Massachusetts might get a little defensive but he was just nodding his head, like a kid.

"Patico. I heard about the cars."

"From who?"

"The music world."

"Yeah, well," I said. Unlike Massachusetts, I was uncomfortable with the subject matter. "Gotta work on that one myself."

"Do not treat only the symptom," Three Bags said. "You must treat the cause. The mental afflictions."

"Milo is quite mentally afflicted," Massachusetts said.

Thankfully, Three Bags changed the subject. "Now, just as important. Have you brought any sun cream?" He leaned forward again. "I forgot my sun cream. In the sun I'm like a walrus without his fur!"

"We'll get some." I put my hand on his shoulder. He looked up at me briefly.

"We need to make time."

"We just need to find a supermarket."

"No," he said, switching to Spanish. "For what I came for. For what I came to show you."

By late afternoon we'd trundled past Barcelona, skimming across the flat beaches south. Skirting Tarragona's Roman ruins. We were making good time through what appeared to be one giant, never ending coastal orange grove. The late afternoon sun was a deep orange color itself.

"Why don't we sleep outside tonight?" Massachusetts said, breaking a long, sleepy silence.

"Because there are hotels," Julien said.

"Look at it out there. It's a gorgeous evening."

"Go for it."

"Wussy."

The train slowed quickly. Julien's guitar, propped on a seat like a passenger, tumbled to the ground. The train stopped. Outside you could hear a whistle blowing, and lots of yelling.

"What are they saying?" Julien said.

Our ticket puncher came into the car. His tie was loose and he was holding his cap in his hand.

"*Huelga!*" he shouted. He motioned with both hands toward the door. "*Huelga, colegas! Vayanse del tren.*"

"What's welga?" Massachusetts said.

"A strike," said Three Bags.

"You can get off the train or stay on," the ticket guy said.

"When will it begin to move again?" I asked.

"When we feel the railroad has responded favorably to our demands."

"And when is that?"

The man laughed. "It has been many years already."

People were wandering off across the inland orange grove, suitcases in hand, following a swift old nun dressed in grey who apparently knew where we were.

"Hey," Massachusetts said, snapping a finger. "This way." He walked to the end of our car and stepped over the couplings. We followed him down a grassy slope and across a dirt maintenance road. Soon we were beneath the pines we'd seen through the windows, their canopies bathed in the last red light of the sun. We were standing at the edge of a sandy drop-off. And there it was, the cobalt blue Mediterranean, licking at the rocks below us. The cool air coming off it.

"So, Grizzly Jones," Julien said. "This is the spot?"

"Adams," Massachusetts said. "And no. You guys wanted to get further south. Come on." He marched off at a solid clip south through the trees. After fifty feet he stopped.

"Here," he said, slinging off his pack. "Further south."

"Just to be a dick," I said.

"Just want everyone to be happy."

"I am ecstatic," Julien said. We all sat down on our packs. Less than a minute later the guitar was out. Three Bags quietly unzipped his trombone case and worked the mouthpiece into the neck. He blew a round, reedy low E. Julien strummed an open E chord, frowned, went back to his tuning knobs.

"Play whatever you want," Three Bags said. "I just want to listen."

Julien started to finger pick one of his go-to numbers, The House of the Rising Sun. His hands were steady, but as usual his memory was not.

"Now brother, don't you listen, to the words that I have sung/Or you'll spend your days in loving misery, in the house of the rising sun..."

Three Bags sat facing forward, his lips half stuck to his mouthpiece, like he was pulling out of a kiss, his eyes sideways on

Julien, tapping one Birkenstocked foot on the pine-needle floor. He was running alongside the train. After a little while he jumped. But jumping's the wrong word because it was like he never came down. He just went sailing on up and up on the currents of that simple scale. Sliding along the notes, quiet, controlled staccato grunts dissolving into long, pliable plaints. Just right, I thought, always just right. A couple of times Julien lost his way, but soon even he was playing at a level I'd never heard out of him. His fingers worked on the forward edge of the tempo, and as he reached his own version of musical rhapsody his mind-mouth nexus directed him to sing:

"There is a train in southern Spain, they call the Strike Brigade/And if you're southward bound and thrown to the ground head west, boy, into the shade/Now sooner, or then later, all together we'll see the moon/It'll be 70 degrees on a sandy beach, the spring can't come too soon."

Massachusetts pulled from his pack two bottles that said "cava" on them. He twisted one of the corks until it blew out over the cliff. The bottle went around. From Three Bags to Julien, Julien to me. And around again. Julien broke out two baguettes, some cheese and a tomato.

"This is goo breh," Three Bags said.

"Julien pretty much bought out a French bakery before we crossed over," I said.

"I cannot eat Franco bread."

"He died like a decade ago."

Massachusetts threw a little stone at Julien. It hit his guitar.

"Hey, what the fuck!"

"Chill, dude."

"What an incredible penis you can be."

"Easy there Frenchie," Massachusetts said. "It wasn't on purpose."

"Gents," I said.

"How long have you three been travelling together?" Three Bags said.

"About a week."

"A year," Massachusetts said, yanking his sleeping bag from its sack and laying it out a good 30 feet away.

"Ten years," said Julien. He picked up his pack and guitar and moved off in the opposite direction, made his own little camp.

"Great idea, camping on rocks!" he shouted.

Our first full-on travel spat, I thought. But I was glad for it, because it left Three Bags and me alone for the first time that day.

"Should we make a little fire?" I said.

He switched on his flashlight and balanced it facedown on a small rock. "There. A flashlight fire."

I fished for my sweater in my pack, pulled it out, put it on.

"You do that pretty well," Three Bags said, hunching his knees up to his chest. "The sweater. The pack. Everything so organized."

"Growing up it was either that or starve to death in bed. My choice."

"Hipólito was not that way."

"We talking about the same guy? Cuz that's a quote."

Three Bags looked out over the water. "How death can change a man. I sort of didn't want to believe that one. Even after I found out you were in jail."

"Yeah, well, and you?"

"I went downhill. But I need to tell you some things Milo. Firstly, about your mother. She and I -"

"I know," I said, getting into my sleeping bag. "I always knew. Hipólito put it pretty bluntly. The night you were in our garbage. When he threw a toaster at you."

"A clock. You remember that. I barely remember anything from when I was five. I remember my father knocking me over with his bike because I wasn't walking fast enough to church. In front of the whole village, that one. I remember the caribou standing on our street one evening in Autumn, right in front of our house. Blowing steam from their noses. Like they were waiting for me."

Three Bags got into his bag, then lay back looking at the moon and the faded yellow halo around it. "Over these years," he said, "when I thought about you, I always thought that all this would have faded away. I hoped for that."

"Yeah, well. I guess I took all that uncle shit literally."

"What uncle shit?"

"When you said you were my uncle. When we went to Botnitz's."

"That was a wonderful day! But I hoped that you would forget me as soon as possible. There was no other way. Things went terribly. The drinking was bad. The guilt. Maybe I could have called, or visited you at school, but that would have been worse. At least, I said to myself, with time the boy will forget me and this whole mess. The best was to forget each other. And your mother. So I left New York."

"What did you feel guilty about?" I said.

"The accident, of course."

"Why?"

"Well. Listen. Miriam was going to leave your father. Probably, we would have all ended up living together. That was what we imagined."

"I didn't know that," I said, stunned.

"In the grave hole," Gunnar said, "at Miriam's funeral, for a split second, it was like we had made it." His voice dropped to a whisper. "I remember thinking, we were together."

"Kinda late, there."

"I was not thinking straight. Not then, not before. So selfish. I wrecked one family dreaming about another."

"It wasn't your fault. You weren't even there."

"Is that what you think?"

"I know," I said. "I've watched the replay a thousand times. It was just me and Miriam. And Imaginary Mom."

"Who's that one?"

"No one you'd ever want to meet."

I wanted to tell Three Bags about how Hipólito had dared me to go with him, the night of the garbage incident. And how I'd wanted to. But I figured it'd just make him feel even worse. "You know," I said, "not having a family isn't necessarily a bad thing. And you could start one anytime. Maybe with your new Norwegian honey."

"Stranger things have happened," Three Bags said. "Like you ending up in jail."

"Juvi."

"But things are looking up for you now."

"Anytime you can make it to lunch without someone swinging you in circles by your legs, things are getting better."

"Where will you go when this is over?"

"I haven't worked that out."

"Maybe where I am taking you will help."

"Where?"

"Did I hear you right? Did you call her Imaginary One?"

"Imaginary Mom," I said. "Eleanor. Miriam slipped up once. I never forgot. She's actually caused me lots of trouble for someone who only exists in my head."

"In many heads,' Three Bags said, shaking his. The battery in his flashlight was going dead. He turned it off, lay back down.

"You knew Eleanor?" I said. "Or am I not getting you again."

"I knew her well. I had my base in Spain in the 1960's. Tried to anyway. The Franco government was not so open to jazz and its unconstrained creativity. That's where I met her."

"Was she a hero?" I asked.

"I don't know. Strange question. Maybe. She came to Spain a dancer. She got involved with a crazy, very well-known flamenco guitarist. Married. She was his lover for years. The relationship nearly destroyed her. She came to live with me for a while. That's how I met Miriam and Hipólito. Anyway, I always thought one day you should know this. That it might help. When I heard you were in jail I thought now is the time."

"Help how?"

"To understand how you got here."

"That's it?"

Three Bags leaned toward me in the dark. "You did not fall from a star."

"I never – "

"You were born into a towel of blood and placenta, attached to your mother by a tube. Like everyone. Like every single person."

"You've gotten even weirder than I remember."

"You have the same right as all of us."

"What right?"

"To exist," he whispered. "Even if in two worlds at once. One foot in each, and everything constantly shifting."

What was this? Had he found out about my plans for the final scalping raid, the night of my last arrest? Was he just being poetic? Or was he now officially nuts. Blood and placenta. Fallen from a star. Jesus. He'd stuck his finger right in the wound. How had he done that? I was grateful the light was out, that he couldn't see my face.

"She was poor, right?" I said. "That's why she gave me away."

"No," Three Bags said quietly. "She just didn't want a child. Though my guess is she's changed her mind. We'll find out soon enough."

The next morning we hiked to a town and found a train to Torremolinos. Julien was as amped as I'd ever seen him. He kept using the bathroom at the end of the car. Each time he came back you could see he'd redone his ponytail.

"We'll drop off our stuff at my parents', take a dip in the pool, then find Lola."

"She know we're coming?" Massachusetts said.

"I promised her I'd come."

I got up and pulled Three Bags into the hallway.

"Same question for you," I said, on edge. "Does she even know?" These were actually the first words I'd said to him since the night before. When our holiday had taken a decidedly different turn. You could say I was in a bit of shock.

"She doesn't know," he said. "No. Not yet."

"Then I'm out. I don't need to see her. I prefer her exactly where she is, wherever she is."

"Haunting your dreams?"

"Better than haunting my reality."

"This is your one chance," Three Bags said. "She's not going to be here much longer."

Julien's parents' villa was in the hills above the beach town. It was so white you couldn't look at it. My eyes took cover among the bougainvillea along the southern façade. In the cork oaks darkening the hills.

"The key is, yes!" Julien had a terra cotta planter tipped up with one foot. Massachusetts picked up the long iron key and had the front door open in three seconds. We dropped our bags in the foyer.

"Holy shit," I said. I hadn't ever been in a big old farmhouse. The scale of everything. Where the sofa was in the living room you could have had five. In the kitchen there was space for a band rehearsal. The walls the same white as outside, the windows cut small, I guessed, to keep that glare at bay.

"Your life sucks," I said.

"Not so bad, eh?"

"Who else is here?" Massachusetts said.

"Just us, boys." Julien put an arm over each of our shoulders. "Just us. Come on."

"Julien? Is that you?"

Julien practically fell down trying to get out the front door. But he made it. So when the lady appeared at the stairs she only saw me, Three Bags and Massachusetts.

"I'll call the police," she said in broken English. What are you doing here?"

"Juuulien," I said.

He reappeared in the doorway, squinting.

"Hello Darianne. These are friends from school, that's all. Plus, a famous musician. Gunnar something. I didn't think anyone would mind if I showed them the place."

"I think your grandfather is going to mind very much."

"It was a mistake, then. We were never here." Julien was already picking up his pack and guitar.

"Except here you are," said the woman. "And Mr. Bowles has asked that I alert him to any such occurrence."

"I'm only here because you see me here."

"Yes. I see you. Quite clearly."

"Well then fuck it then," Julien yelled, stepping back outside. "I thought maybe you'd grown nicer with time."

"And we'd thought you'd have grown up."

We ambled back down the entry drive. It killed my shoulders to have the pack back on. "What the hell was that?" I said. "Who the hell was that?"

"The gatekeeper," Julien said. "Normally she's at the flat in Paris. I don't understand."

"The flat in Paris? We were in Paris a week ago."

"Why won't your grandfather let you come here?" Three Bags said.

"Long story."

"So now where do we go ?" I said.

"To the beach!" Julien said. "To the bar where Lola works."

"Any beach that's not frozen sounds good to me." said Massachusetts.

At the beach we followed Julien along a tiled promenade past a dozen tourist hangouts. The town was jumping and it was only noon. Brits and Danes and shirtless Belgians strolled around, showing off their their pink skin, drinking sangria from plastic cups.

"Which bar does she work in?" I said.

"I think...I'm pretty sure it was this one."

"You don't remember?" Massachusetts said.

"It was this one, I said."

"When was the last time you were here?"

"Excuse me, is Lola here?" Julien said to a bartender.

"Who?"

We sat down at a table.

"I don't get it," Julien said. "I'm sure it was this one."

"You said you told her we were coming,"

"I said, I'm coming back. I promised. I told her to wait for me."

"When did you say that?"

"Three summers ago."

"When you were fifteen? How old was she?"

"Eighteen."

"You shitting me?" Massachusetts said. "And she was your girlfriend?"

"She said I was cute. That I could be. There was always a spark there."

"Okay," I said. "Let's recap. We come all the way to the south of Spain to a house we are not allowed in, to meet your girlfriend who never actually was."

"And her pretty friends?" said Massachusetts.

We ordered a round of beers. "Once upon a time there was a rich kid named Julien," said Massachusetts, "who pooped lies from his mouth."

"Yeah, out with it," I said. "Why doesn't your family want you around?"

"Okay, my bonafide criminal friends," Julien said. "If you must know, I once stole some money. From my grandparents. Three thousand measly dollars. But they've, well, struggled to forgive me."

"That's quite bad," said Three Bags.

"They were rich. They are rich. They weren't going to miss it. I was visiting them over the summer, in Connecticut. My father had sent me so I could get a job in the U.S., like other American boys, but where? Where was I to get a job? And how?"

"By walking into any of a thousand stores and asking?" Massachusetts said.

"I had never worked in America."

"And in France?" I said.

"Living with my grandparents I didn't have any expenses," Julien said. "I just needed spending money until I went home. I was going to tell my grandparents I was working and show my father the money as proof of my American summer-job. Then I'd buy something for Lola. They kept cash all over the place, so I didn't think they'd miss it."

"How'd you get caught?" Massachusetts said.

"My grandfather was watching me."

"What'd he have, one of those paintings with spy holes for eyes?"

"No, he was in the room. His office. Asleep in a corner chair. I didn't notice him."

"What the," I said.

"It was dark. He didn't see me either. Until I woke him opening the desk drawers. He started screaming, 'Betty! Betty! Intruder!' He didn't have his glasses. It was pretty late at night. He shot me."

"What?"

"He had a shotgun there on a shelf. Just lifted the barrel and sprayed the room. Nearly blew off my left foot. Some of the nuggets are still in it."

"Buckshot."

"And he called the cops?" Massachusetts said.

"No, he didn't," Julien said. "My father did."

"Damn."

"Before or after they realized it was you?"

"After."

"Sounds familiar," I said.

"And the drugs?" said Three Bags. "The Tunisian jail?"

"I have been to Tunisia. Twice. My mother is from Tunis."

"Your own father ratted you out," said Massachusetts.

"He wanted to teach me a lesson. As you know he's a lawyer. And a stickler for the law. The family court judge was an old friend of his. He thought my dad was serious so he made sure I got the 8 months in juvi camp. My dad was surprised, he told me later. But then, you know, he started coming around to the idea."

"Camp?" Massachusetts said.

"In Connecticut they send you to a camp. You live in wooden barracks."

"And what did you do all day?" Massachusetts said. "Chase girl scouts?"

"Planted trees," Julien said. "Cleaned up litter along roads."

"The summer job you couldn't find," I said.

"And then AIM came along."

"I knew there was something too wussy about you to be a narco," I said. And then boom, it hit me. Julien's life of crime might have been underwhelming, exaggerated, but maybe Massachusetts' had been just the opposite. And that's why Powders had warned me twice to steer clear of the 'troubles.' What if the trouble he'd hinted at really was larger than we knew?

"And you," I said to Massachussets. "Your turn. Full disclosure."

"Yeah? Okay, you got me. I was really in jail for – I can't say it – okay! For not helping an old lady across the street." He turned to Three Bags. "Fucking pansies. You believe it? Two outta three of us is livin' the lie."

"Two out of three," Three Bags said, chuckling. "That's not bad."

"*Ain't* bad," Julien said. He opened his guitar case. "Meatloaf."

Meatloaf! That got me to smile. Julien coming clean was making me feel like I'd put a weight down. Finally, I wasnt the only liar. Even if I still hadn't told them my real deal. Even if what we were really doing was rolling towards Eleanor, no matter how many pitstops we made along the way. No matter how many distractions. I still wasn't sure I'd go through with whatever Three Bags had in mind. To distract myself I watched Julien trying to sound out Two Out of Three Ain't Bad. "I remember how she left me on a stormy night…" I sang. Julien tried to follow along but, who'da thunk it, he didn't know the lyrics. So he did what we were all good at. The thing we had in common. He made his lines up.

But Three Bags wasn't having any more of it.

"Time to get real," he said.

He led us to the bus station.

We wound our way up into the bare mountains above the coast. The bus stopped once at some brightly lit roadside bar then slid into forests, still climbing. A window was open and the air blowing in was cool and smelled like pinecones. I was going along with all of this because I couldn't see what other choice I had. Because I was weak. Three Bags had reappeared in my life just as everything else had fallen apart. He was back and had become, just like that, all that I had left.

The bus stopped and we clambered off. We were on a paved road but the roads running off of it all looked to be dirt. There was a stone chapel, lit by a lone streetlight, and a series of white houses disappearing up a road behind it. Otherwise just forest all around. Three Bags walked to the chapel. There, in the shadows, he reached for something square hanging on a wood post. It was a payphone. He fiddled around in his pocket and pulled out some coins.

"*Hola Antonio, qué tal? Soy Gunnar. Sí! Sí! Cuánto tiempo…Mira, una cosa...*

"How did he know there was a phone here?" Massachusetts said.

"He's talking to someone he knows," I said. "He must know the area."

Three Bags hung up the phone. "He will be here in fifteen minutes."

"Who?"

"Antonio. An old friend. He will take us the rest of the way."

"To where?"

"To take the Imaginary out of Mom."

"What's he smoking?" Julien said.

"Gents," I said. "Three Bags' got a little surprise for us. And I apologize in advance."

Three Bags' pal Antonio was an old swarthy, thick-necked guy with bowed legs and a gruff, suspicious attitude.

"You know she's not well," he said.

"I know."

"*Coño,*" he said, scratching at his nose. Then he looked at us and switched to English. "She is going to cut me off the balls."

"What?" Massachusetts laughed.

"*Vámanos!*" Antonio said. "We go."

Massachusetts and Julien jumped into the crowded cab, elbowing each other. Clearly they were excited. I was beginning to spiral.

Three Bags and I climbed into the open bed.

"When did you find out about her being sick and what not?"

"Just before I wrote to you."

"I don't wanna do this, man."

"On another day I would say okay, let's just go to the beach. But not today."

"What's different about today?"

"There has never been another day like it."

Antonio turned off the paved road onto a bumpy forest track. Ten minutes later he stopped. I climbed down and puked behind a tree. In the yellow light from the nearby cottage you could see the puddle at my feet. I wiped my mouth. Everyone was watching me. Three Bags and Antonio began taking all our stuff out of the truck and laying it on the roadside. Then Antonio just sped off.

"*Espera!*" I yelled as he throttled up the mountain. "Wait!" I panicked, went tearing after him, waving my arm. But it was dark and the road was steep and I stopped running after a few seonds. "You stupid jerk-off," I said. My legs trembling.

"Dude," Massachusetts said. "Why are you spazzing out?"

"Jesus. I should have had a say in this. This can't be happening."

"We have gotten very lucky."

"Whenever someone tells me I'm lucky – "

"She has not yet achieved samadhi."

"That yoga?" Julien said

"It is leaving the body," said Three Bags.

I sat down on the dirt. Three Bags came and bent his knees and put his hand on the back of my head. "We are going with the flow. There is only moving forward."

"But what's the plan?" I said. "I am out of gas."

"She is terminal. There is no hope for her whatsoever."

"I guess we have that much in common."

"You asked me why we're here. Maybe that's why. To change that idea. At least for one of you."

A smallish woman with black hair trussed up in a ponytail came out of the nearby house and tried to take our bags without making eye contact.

"Buenas, Maribel," Three Bags.

"Hola, señor Gunderson," she said coldly. "Tell them to follow me. And to not make any noise at all."

"Follow Maribel," Three Bags said. "And no talking." Massachusetts and Julien picked up their packs and stood like kids lining up for recess. They were looking at me. Maribel and Three Bags too. I was still sitting in the road, cross-legged, my head low.

"I'm coming already," I said.

Maribel glanced at Three Bags.

"Está bien," he said.

The four of them walked up the gravel entryway toward the old, stuccoed cortijo. There was some moonlight and you could see that the house was whitewashed and that it was big and sat on a slope, and that there was a fire burning in a fireplace somewhere inside. I tried to tease out something more definitive from this, some telling detail about the woman apparently 'achieving' death inside. Achieving in Spain, I thought. What was she dying of? Was this even her house?

Had she lived here forever? And the oddest, most tantalizing, question: Was I born here? A cold current of air was tumbling down the slope, down the track I was sitting on, and it caused me to shiver more. I realized I could sit there and hide behind a thousand questions until my nose ran, or I could get up and make myself go inside. The truth was I had no choice. Three Bags was right.

I stood and shook my legs. They felt so heavy. Each step along the gravel path was like those of a boy pushing a metal hospital gurney towards a set of elevators. Except that this search was not my idea or doing. It had been my shameful desire since I'd first heard her name, but I'd never imagined the imaginary turning so suddenly real. I moved my legs, and the steps took me further back, to the maps. From VertiVille down to Carnegie Hall, then flipping the pages to cross the ocean, to Madrid, over land to Milan and back across, licking my fingers, thumbing my way to Mantanzas, that former slave port on Cuba's north coast, to Miriam and Hipólito's origins. In this exercise I never found my own beginning, but it always made me feel somehow like I was on the heels of it. The problem with maps was that they gave a birds-eye view, which meant you couldn't ever get up close for a real peek at anything. But now this bird was tethered to the ground. Maybe Three Bags was right. Maybe this was my chance for something somehow less rotten. That's how I managed to reach the door. It was open.

Inside, a cozy living room with a cathedral ceiling. My friends were nowhere to be seen. But I could hear some clumping around upstairs. I looked around. The room was filled with the stuff of a lifetime, with objects I can't describe because my eyes went straight to one: a black-and-white photograph in a wood frame on a cracked wooden table by a set of French doors. I picked it up. There was moonlight coming through the doors and I tilted the frame to get the reflection from the glass out of my eyes - only to find my own face reflected in the photo behind.

In it, she was alone in a wooden boat - some kind of canoe, the ribbing visible - paddling away but looking over her shoulder, strands of blondish hair blown in a semi-veil across her face, smiling mischievously like she'd just splashed her portrait taker and was making a run for it. I knew that smile. I knew the way her eyes crinkled. The nose. It was the oddest feeling, seeing someone you looked like for the first time in your life. The invented version, good ole Imaginary Mom, vanished instantly, exposed now as the powerless piece of fiction she was. It made my feet feel even heavier, like they were fusing to the floor itself. I couldn't have described the feeling beyond that because I didn't have the chance. Something caught my eye outside the French doors and I looked out and saw her, seated on the stone terrace overlooking a fog-shrouded valley, with a blanket wrapped around her, covering her head even. From behind, with the moonlight spilling over her, she looked like an apparition of the Virgin Mary. But I knew it was her because there was no halo and her seat was a wheelchair. I was frozen with dread. Utterly unprepared. But I couldn't not approach her. If I stayed still she'd eventually turn around, see me just standing there, which would be worse. I had to move. I opened the door. When the latch clicked the blanketed head moved slightly. I stepped through.

I walked up and stood a long pace from her, facing the valley like she was. The night air. The smell of pines. There was so much fog on the trees below us. "Hello?" I said. My voice sounded froggy. I cleared my throat. "Eleanor?" I said.

"They named you Milano," came her voice, dry and soft. I felt a shiver run through me like a lance from the stars skewering me to the earth. It sounds unpleasant, but it wasn't. It was energizing.

"*Sí,*" I said. "*Me llamo Milano.*"

"Well," she said, sticking with English. "Well fuck me, then."

She swiveled slowly in her chair and looked up at me. I leaned back. This was indeed the same woman from the photo I'd just seen. A sick version of her. Her cheeks where drawn, her hair gone. Her eyes wide and glassy.

"So," she said in a loud whisper. "Gunnar wasn't lying. Then again, he never does, does he?"

"I can think of a couple of doozies. He lied to get me here."

Her hands were outside her blanket, on her lap, and she was flexing her bony thumbs. "What timing. I was nearly out the door. I was nearly there. I am cursed."

"What, you wanna die?"

"I want to die alone," she said, looking at the moon. "What is your accent? It's American."

"I'm from New York."

"So they went and stayed. That was all so long ago. What do you want here? Did they send you? I have nothing to offer you. I hope they told you that much."

"I didn't even know where here was until a couple of hours ago."

"There isn't even coffee left. I've used everything up, stripped things down to the bare minimum. I won't apologize, if that's what you're after."

"I am not after anything."

"Or money. I have very little. You can ask Gunnar."

"Three Bags – uh, Gunnar - brought me here by surprise. Just now. I hadn't seen him since the accident. Then he just shows up out of the blue."

"Accident, you say."

"Car accident."

"One of those bad ones."

"Yeah, bad."

"But you're all right now."

"Depends on how you define all right. My, uh, mom, didn't make it. That sorta changed the course of things."

"I see. Well. I am sorry for your loss."

I was about to say, it's not your fault. But it always had been, hadn't it? That, at least, is what I'd always told myself. Here was the woman whose name alone had had the power to wreck a family. I held to this reasoning now. I had nothing else to hold on to.

"I'm willing to do something for you," Eleanor said. "As a favor to Gunnar. If you're inclined to know what happened, I will tell you. I suppose that's it. That that's what you're after. In return you're to leave. It is late. Tell me now if you accept. Otherwise I am going to bed."

"What are you sick with?" I said, stalling for time. Did I want to know this story? Didn't I know enough already?

"My lungs are a broccoli patch of cancer," she said, touching her chest. "That's what my doctors said. One of them. The poet. Do you smoke? Don't. I quit after you were born, you may want to know. That was 20 years ago. But apparently the damage was done."

"Nineteen years."

"Nineteen or twenty, there's no time left. Do you want to know?"

"Well," I said.

"You look like your father," she said, studying my face. "I hope you don't act like him." She coughed. "I never imagined telling you this story. Not once. Forgive me if I omit anything. I was against kids my whole life. Against the idea of them coming out of me. Against them crying to me. Or over me. Even when I was one of them. Imagine that. You can take this all personally but I wouldn't recommend it. I didn't know you before, during or after your birth for that matter. Don't think I'm cruel. This is what happened."

I nodded.

"I was 35 when I got pregnant. It was hands down the worst scenario possible. If you're from New York then you didn't grow up like I did. I was raised by my mother on a ranch in Arizona, where all the girls in my family wore white gloves to church and acted like there were no farmhands who made our life possible or, for me, a torment. Those same farmhands who taught me Spanish. Mexican Spanish. Out in the fields when we were very small and on the loose. Then they started to teach me more, things I didn't want to learn at such an age, or probably ever. Threatening men who would bow their heads and remove their hats when my mother came around. She was a powerful, intimidating woman."

"Threatening you with what?" I said.

"I finally got away, went to school. Moved here. I'd grown up reading about princes, you know. That's what they fed little girls. Corn to the pigs, fairy tales to us. On my second day in Madrid I met Diego del Arenal – "

"*El Rubio?*"

"Yes. He dyed his hair, but yes. I don't give out advice but I'll say this. Don't become anyone's lover. Especially if they promise you something. If I knew now what I knew then."

"What."

"That the clock's ticking the whole time, not just at the end when it's loudest. There's a long period in the middle of life when you think you're off the clock altogether. But you are not. Diego was like me, against kids, but he ended up doing what all lazy men do. He gave in when he should have pulled out. I hope that doesn't sound too crass. When the doctor told me I was pregnant I nearly drank gasoline."

"Wait," I said. My head was spinning.

"Would you like a chair?"

"No," I said. "No. I - "

"Shall I go on?"

"Yeah, go on. But, so then Diego del Arenal is my father?"

"Yes. Was. He's dead."

I sat down.

"When I told him I was pregnant he was in total agreement that we had to remedy the situation. I had no money to speak of. Diego was rich as a bullfighter, but his wife - we looked alike back then – she was a *Gallega*, and she controlled every cent that came in to their unhappy house. At any rate abortion was illegal back then under *El Generalísimo* so we had only homemade remedies at our disposal. A local gypsy woman whose two daughters still live near here, she made me several types of tea that flushed everything else out of my system but you. She spoke unintelligible things with her mouth against my belly. I lost twenty pounds. But not the fetus. I used to picture you in my belly, like a little pink Tarzan with your umbilical cord wrapped fast around your wrists and ankles. But we were determined. We borrowed a friend's jeep..."

"Not Antonio's?"

"The very same. The beast that won't die. We took his jeep further up into the mountains, on the bumpiest roads we could find, slamming over roots and rocks, hoping to loosen your grip. But it didn't work. Nothing did. Not going to the beach and jumping off the cliffs onto the hard sand. I burst a blood vessel in my eye from trying. It has never really healed.

"As the days went by Diego grew more and more irritable. Well, what great ideas do you have, then, I asked him. He told me he'd found a doctor in Madrid. That surprised me. We literally passed a hat around to all of our friends – our artist and foreign friends. Most of our Spanish friends were reluctant. Some believed in women's rights but only in theory. Others were aghast. We got the money finally – it was 500 dollars – a fortune back then. And we drove my old Peugot to Madrid. Eight hours. That day wasn't supposed to be your lucky day.

"The doctor received us at his weekend home in the sierra, la Cercedilla. He had a little operating room in his basement. A metal table, a sink, an electric stovetop, a nervous wife. I don't know what his politics were, but I know he wasn't just after our money because he refused it in the end. He examined me, alone, then asked me to wait upstairs with Diego. To our surprise he came up and announced that he wouldn't do the procedure. Why not? I said. We have the money. We've driven all the way from Granada, Diego said. He sat there with hands folded like a kid at church. Because your lady friend is beyond the first trimester, the doctor said. He wouldn't look at me. That's impossible! I said. The father has only been back in Spain for two months. Diego looked at me with a look I didn't like at all. I don't know what to say, the doctor said. He was very smug and you knew he wasn't going to budge. Still, I tried to go back downstairs. Where are you going? He looked alarmed. I told him he was going to do the exam again. I know what I know, he said. That baby is at least 12 or 13 weeks. That's when Diego, my lover of four years, the man who was always, always, about to leave Julia for me, came straight out and declared that he couldn't be the father. He said it to the doctor. The doctor shrugged. I haven't been with anyone else, I said. All I know, Diego said, is that I've been on tour. And I get home and come to see you, and that was a lot less than 12 weeks ago. What does that make me? he said, riling himself up under false pretenses. Not only not the father, he said. It makes me a *cornudo*. You? I screamed. A cuckold? Can you be a victim when you've been victimizing two women simultaneously for years with your indecision?

"That's when the doctor asked us to leave. His wife gave me the envelope back and he practically pushed me out the door. You're making a mistake, was the last thing I said to him. Maybe so, he said, just to keep me moving. Then the door shut. Diego and I were just standing in front of his house there in the hills. It was cold. I wanted to reach out and cut his ponytail off.

"You are not worming your way out of this," I said.

"You're not worming your way in," he said. "You are not going to entrap me. Go find the real father and have your cursed baby."

"He said cursed?"

"I was so furious I got in my car and drove away. I left him standing on the curb in the middle of nowhere, and I never saw him again. I wrote him a letter once asking for money, because I had none, literally, but he didn't respond. Can you get me a glass of water? Just inside the kitchen door there's the pitcher."

My legs carried me to the kitchen. The numbing buzz in my head. Like a lead pipe to the nape of the neck. Had I finally found the killer I'd been seeking? She had, I was learning, tried several times already. On the way back from the kitchen I could see Eleanor's blank, sallow face. She was clearing her throat over and over. I handed her the glass.

"As I was saying," she said, "that day in Madrid was not meant to be your lucky day. But it was. One of many, I would guess."

"I could count them on one hand."

"I don't know your life."

"It makes yours - "

Eleanor interrupted me with another round of coughing. She lifted a pale hand to her mouth. Then she pointed at the empty, dangling sleeve of my Peacoat. "Is that from the accident? You weren't born that way."

"Yeah. We were - "

"That's enough. You're not here to tell me your stories. But to hear mine. That's the deal. Isn't that right?"

"Damn."

"Tell me to stop anytime and I will." We stared at each other for a long moment, then she continued. "The pregnancy. It was misery. Getting out of it should have been the simplest thing. But 'Spain is Different,' right? Soon it was too late and I was trapped. I returned to Madrid and tried to focus on my business. I had become a concert booker. That's how I met your parents. I worked some with Anagram. Anagram is a Cuban – "

"I know the label."

"I got Miriam and, what was her husband's name?

"Hipólito."

"I got them from Italy to Spain. It's true I had an ulterior motive."

"One thing before you go on," I said. "Why were you so against kids?"

"You reach an age," Eleanor said, slowing down, selecting her words, "where certain things become unbecoming to speak about. Even when I was young, I was discreet. I reserved its telling for men trying to understand me, for men I idolized too much, and for friends who were once close. No such people are in my life anymore. Don't think you're going to get special treatment. Do I sound cold to you? I'll say this. That whenever I thought of having kids I could only imagine my own childhood, which would make thinking of kids impossible, for anyone.

"When I met your parents, especially your mother, I saw a way out. The deal was simple, and easy to do in Spain. Giving up a baby for adoption wasn't a legal hassle. A doctor or nun would sign the papers without blinking an eye. Sign and take the money. They did it all the time. When they learned I was unmarried and uninterested in motherhood they started circling like vultures.

"But I'd already lined up your parents. They were famous, they'd just defected, so to speak, which made it even easier. After a show in Milan they skipped out on their handlers. I helped them, driving the getaway car. What fun that was! I also gave them some money I couldn't afford to give, and I promised to bring them to Spain, then to America, if they would consider helping me. If they would take the baby I was being forced to have. Miriam knew better than her husband that going home was going to be impossible. The idea of a child - another child, a replacement child, whatever you want to call it – seemed to strike a nerve. He was against the idea. He thought I was calculating. He was right. But what was he going to say? In Madrid, while I was waddling around like a water buffalo that summer, they were already making decent money. Miriam was over constantly. Everything was planned. And then, when it was time to, you wouldn't come out."

"Can you blame me?" I muttered.

Eleanor made like she was going to stand, and for a second I thought I'd offended her. But she wasn't standing. She leaned her head back and extended her legs off the wheelchair supports and made a slight whistling sound on the exhale. Her hands gripped the wheels like a couple of disc brakes. "The bones," she said quietly. "It's in the bones. Something I don't wish on anyone."

"I'm sorry," I said. "Can I get you some kinda medicine?"

"No. Mirabel administers the morphine. I get it from France. Spain doesn't even know I'm sick. Otherwise I'd be in some germ-ridden hospital hooked up to machines probably with the same nuns hovering over me again."

She slowly relaxed. She put her feet back on the foot rests.

"It was a protracted battle," she said.

"What was?"

"Giving birth to you. One of the greatest pleasures. It hurt like being crushed and burned but it's not a contradiction. Every cell in my body galvanized together in the cause against you. When you finally came out I closed my eyes so as not to see."

"I'm starting to think Gunnar was right," I said.

"Gunnar knows me as well as anyone. He did."

"He warned me that you were bitter."

"He said that?"

"A bitter old bitch."

"I don't think I am bitter. I am dying."

"Yeah, well you got a strange old heart," I said. "I think I'll just let you get on with your plans."

"Thank you for the courtesy. You derailed my life once. I ask you kindly not to do the same at death."

Eleanor wheeled her chair to the wrought-iron railing at the edge of her stone terrace and placed her hands on it like she was going to try to stand again. Like another wave of the bone-pain was washing through her. A long time went by. I honestly thought to just push her over the wall. I think only her pathetic state stopped me. How had I been so stupid as to come in? She was even worse in real life than the woman I'd imagined. I really was cursed. Sixto had told Hipólito that my problems began before I was born. Well, Eleanor's womb certainly qualified as problematic, from what she was telling me. I remained seated on the cold ground, looked at her back and the shadow of her back spilling on the stones. I could have pushed her. Ending her to end the curse. Yes, that might work. I was so tired I didn't notice my head beginning to nod.

"Milano. Milano."

I snapped awake. Eleanor was right in front of me now, parked in her chair. I got to my feet quickly, wiped some saliva from the corner of my mouth. The outside of my Peacoat was damp with dew. I was freezing.

"What time is it?"

"Late. You can't stay here. That was the deal."

I stood and bent one leg, then the other. Like a sprinter preparing to dash. I couldn't wait to go.

"You understand you'd be ruining my ending," she said.

"I got that. I'm leaving. Where are my friends?"

"Remember my desire for solitude," she insisted. "One day, when your time comes, you might feel just as protective of your own." She smiled ever so slightly, and turned, and rolled herself through the open kitchen doors. It was a smile that said *sayonara*. You were but a brief interruption once, and now again.

I stumbled inside and found the upstairs room where Three Bags and my friends were sleeping. I was going to wake them to leave, but I lay down on a single bed and pulled a quilt over me. I needed just a moment. In the morning Maribel woke us up with coffee and *pan con tomate*. She carried it into our room without knocking, without looking at us, and walked straight out the doors onto the small upper terrace. She set her tray on the table there and came back through. "*Desayuno*," she said.

I sat up, horrified. "Dudes, we gotta roll," I said, rubbing my eyes. I was still dressed, with my shoes on. I went out on the terrace. Massachusetts followed behind. Julien was there, already drinking coffee.

"You ready Julien?"

"What was she saying? About jumping off cliffs?"

"You heard that?"

"I couldn't sleep. I was out on the terrace trying to write a song."

"Yeah, well, if you were listening then you heard."

"Tell, tell," Massachusetts said.

"Guys," I said, holding up my hand. "We need to leave." Three Bags came on to the terrace. He was dressed and red in the face, like he'd been out walking in the woods.

"We leave after breakfast," he said.

"To where?" I said.

"Back to Germany. To your homes."

I glanced over the edge of the wall to the lower terrace, but it was empty. I leaned over further and could see the drapes drawn in front of the kitchen doors and the French doors leading to the living room. I imagined Eleanor still asleep in her darkened room. Or awake, smug with the surety that death would delay its arrival long enough to see us off. I wondered how high it was from this terrace to the one below. For jumping head-first purposes.

"You talk to her this morning?" I said.

"Yes."

"What'd she say?"

"That we can't stay."

"That woman's cold as snow," Massachusetts said.

"Maybe it was a mistake to come here," Three Bags said.

"Mistake?" I said. "Come on! It's been a laugh. Besides, I'm sure you'd considered that possibility beforehand."

"I didn't expect her to be so - so reluctant."

"The sooner we get the fuck out of this witch's lair the better," I said.

On the far side of the sierra you could see clusters of little white houses reflecting the morning sunlight, high up on the green mountainsides. On our way out, we passed right by Eleanor's bedroom door. I hesitated a moment, listening. Was the door as thin as Sixto's? Was she in there calling on her own ghosts for counsel? Or just hiding under her covers? I couldn't hear anything. Part of me wanted to barge in and ruin her ending good. Selfish old hag. Haunting my ass for years. But I didn't really want to go in. I was more scared that the door might suddenly fly open. I was scared of her grindstone soul. Outside Antonio honked. Like we had some schedule to keep. I went after the others, relieved the second I was outside. Eleanor could have her sad victory. My goal was to put as much distance between me and her and her lonely dog's death as I could.

We rode north, the four of us, without talking much. In Paris we didn't even leave the Gare du Nord to walk around. A day later we hit Antwerp. It was getting colder and colder, but I still didn't feel far enough away from her. Three Bags tried to cheer me up by spoiling us with a night in a pension. I washed for twenty minutes in hot water, scrubbing from ears to toes, scrubbing the grime from the puckers of my scar. That night we ate at McDonalds until we were nearly sick, then slept in beds that were not at all damp or lumpy. I dreamed of nothing, as far as I know, but woke up tired still.

We chugged across the German border then on through Essen, Bremen, Hamburg and finally, to Lübeck. We walked out of the station into the dull day. Dark brick and snow.

"Gents," I said. "Say hi to your weirdo families for me."

"Hey," Massachusetts said. "Fuck her. At least you know now."

Three Bags rode the bus with me all the way to Hallersdorf. He was going to catch a ferry there, direct to Oslo, later that night. We walked along the boardwalk, me holding to his arm. I wasn't mad at him. I knew he'd tried his best. I also knew, deep in my heart, that even he couldn't help me. Nobody could. I'd been cursed in utero and had spent my life confirming over and over this thing I felt deep inside even if I'd had no memory of it.

The ice, I was surprised to see, had crept out even further over the sea. There were people way out there on it, waddling like distant penguins. It was as if Spring were still months away.

We went into that bar that served beer and half-chickens and sat down.

"Let me ask you a question," I said.

"Of course."

"Are you going to disappear now?"

"I won't. Except for the big disappearing, when my time comes. I will stay in touch like I always wanted. No one can say no. You are eighteen. That is, if you want."

"I. Yeah, I'd like to. Like you say, until the 'big disappearing.'"

"At least now you know the whole story," he said leaning back. "And from the horse's mouth. Oh!" he said. "I nearly forgot." He loosened the tie on the prayer satchel around his neck, fished around inside with his long fingers. "This year's installment." He set the lugnut on the table, pushed it towards me like a man placing a bet. It was 3/8th inch, just like the others. Going all the way back to Christmas, 1973.

"You?" I said. He nodded. "Why?"

"They're yours."

"I don't get it."

"When you threw your bongos out the window did you mean for them to end up in the trash?"

"I didn't mean to break the window. I only wanted to get your attention."

"It worked. These are the tuning lugs. When I found out you were in jail I didn't mail this year's. I still have one lugnut and two washers to go. The drums I am afaid were destroyed."

"When I was really little, I thought they were from Miriam - never mind."

He shook his head. "From the man who loved her."

And then he was loping back down the boardwalk, toward the terminals, his grey hair bouncing off his backpack, his trombone case dangling from his left hand. He turned once and waved. I took a breath and headed for Chewy's apartment. I figured he'd found out a while ago now that I was officially homeless. He'd have to take me in. For what little time I had left.

Chewy had indeed found out. So had Vietz. Hell, everyone knew. And they knew a lot more than just about my personal troubles at the Wartemann house. In other news, the talk of the town was that Michael Baumann was in jail. The police had found evidence – they wouldn't say what – that linked that shithead to the dead guy on the beach. And as said dead guy had yet to be identified, no one knew what Baumann's motive or role in the man's death might have been. Until they did he'd be sitting tight in the clink. My hail mary pen-drop had netted a fink.

But Michael's seizure didn't have me feeling as good as I'd thought. The reason: It didn't fix anything. And if Halsey knew what I'd done she'd just hate me more. Plus, apparently it had made townsfolk all the more paranoid.

While we'd been away Vietz had hung up a special drop-box, a red metal mailbox, outside the cafeteria into which you could slip notes about suspicious activities of classmates. Hallersdorf's mayor had added an afternoon beach patrol on Wednesdays, which was now obligatory for all *Käsebunker* students, no matter where they lived.

I was now living with Chewy himself in his one-bedroom apartment by the beach. There wasn't time to find me a new host family to cover the last month. And who would have taken me? Thankfully, he asked me very little about what had happened with Jan. I gave him the short version – a misunderstanding – and he sighed nervously, then said "I'll get some sheets for the couch." In the evenings he didn't talk much. Mostly he sat by the big window looking out east over the sea, sipping tea, listening to classical music. He'd grown as morose and silent as Hipólito.

On the first of the new Wednesday patrols students were bussed in from other villages, arriving in big double-deckers that parked along the beachfront. The only upside to this circus was that Massachusetts and Julien had gotten dragged in too. Not ten minutes after setting out a small red helicopter swooped low over our heads, some three hundred feet off the ground. It surprised the hell out of us. It whirred up the shoreline like some advance gunship, it's tail oscillating slightly in the wind, the red lights on its underbelly flashing. When it reached the mouth of the river it banked hard to the south, following the river itself, respecting, just barely, the international border and the batteries of DDR guns hidden beyond it.

"They're bringin' in the Air Force!" Massachusetts yelled.

"It's the town rescue helicopter," I said.

"What's to rescue?"

"The dumb-ass tourists who wander too far out on the ice."

"You're kidding."

The helicopter swooped past again and this time the students cheered. When we reached the promenade a buzz ran down the line of students, for once not about phantom commies and conspiracies, but about a party. Some of our German classmates were suggesting an American-style beach bash the following weekend. In our honor. On a stretch of beach protected from view by grassy bluffs. They would show us how it was done. Ha ha. What a gift, I thought, looking out over the ice. What a send-off.

Beach Blanket Bingo Night came soon enough. I was waiting for Chewy, who like me was showing surprising enthusiasm for the fiesta. But then for some reason he told me to go on without him. "I'll catch up," he said. "I want to finish grading your essays before the weekend starts."

I walked through a thick fog down to the beach, past the universally understood No Fires sign - a rendering of a fire with a red X over it – until I could make out the vague flickering of flames. It was late already, and the kids from school were drunk and really amped up. Everyone was still talking about the whole Michael Baumann arrest, whether it would stick, how they could or couldn't have seen it coming, whether his father might also be a double-agent. The jury was still out on who the Fliehender had been – a simple escapee or a man with a darker mission. I stepped in to the ring of fire, stomped my feet to warm them. Someone put a beer with a ceramic stopper into my hand. From a tape player set in the sand

came a song by some creepy Austrian pop sensation named Falco.
Some of the Germans were singing along.

Der war ein Punker
und er lebte in der großen Stadt/
Das war in Wien, war Viena,
wo er Alles tat/
Amadeus Amadeus, Amadeus…

So much for the American-style beach party. I was looking
around for Julien and Massachusetts, but the fog was thickening.
Only that big bonfire penetrated it. Which was why there was a sign
against fires. Any ferry captain, running south to Lübeck, could easily
have mistaken our distant blaze for a lighthouse beacon and followed
it to disaster.

I wandered within the ring of warmth, wondering whether I
would have the guts for what I was planning, until I made out
Massachusetts sitting on a log, chatting up a beautiful blonde student
from school. She was strikingly thin. Her eyes as blue as TV light.
She looked somewhere between rapt and bewildered as
Massachusetts rattled on a mile a minute, in English.

I finished my beer, interrupted. "You wanna help me get some
firewood?" I said. He followed me into the fog.

"What's up?"

"I don't know," I said. How could I describe the exact wretched
feeling of every single thing gone wrong? I couldn't, so I just told him
about Michael and the pen. Maybe my confession would get him
sprung after I was gone.

"No shit, dude, that deserves a toast – "

Massachusetts' face suddenly went bright. As in, reflecting a huge
amount of light. It was blinding.

"*Polizei!*" I heard someone scream. "*Polizei!*"

We turned and ran. You could hear sirens, and the quiet rustle of
students zipping past us in the dark. Julien went by, a search light on
his back, his black ponytail switching like a horse's tail as he
hightailed it for the scrub-covered cliffs that gave way to the pastures
and farmland beyond. The fields of corn, the fields of kohl. Ahead of
us the German boys were scattering inland too, herd-like. The
searchlight arced over my head and flicked across the backs of the
fleeing students as they scrambled behind Julien up the hill. Losing
them in the fog, finding them again. Massachusetts ran the other way,

out on to the ice, and I followed in his snowy tracks. We were moving in a straight line away from the shore, farther and farther because out here there was nothing to hide behind except maybe the fog. Less than a mile out to sea an enormous ferry was gliding silently toward the coast, as they did two or three times a week, toward the mouth of the river, a quarter mile to our east, and the passenger piers beyond. At first all I could make out was the glow from the ship's windows. Strings of tiny yellow lights swaying gently like a chandelier over the sea. A German policeman barked over and over into a megaphone that we were all under arrest and that we should consider halting where we were. I looked back over my shoulder. Blue and red lights pulsed through the fog but so far no police had appeared to pursue us.

"Massachusetts!" I yelled. "Slow down dickhead!"

"This way!" he yelled, waving an arm. He was losing me.

But then he stopped abruptly in his tracks, panting. He must have realized that we couldn't run forever across the ice. Any further and we'd reach the outer limits of its stability. But that wasn't it. There was a figure moving, ghost-like, some other guy about a hundred feet farther out on the shelf. Walking slowly away from us. A man in a long winter coat.

"Who the fuck is that?" I whispered, feeling very extremely creeped out. "Maybe it's a cop. Let's get the - "

"It ain't a cop," Massachusetts said. The ferry was passing us now, some 50 yards to our right, gliding silently through the dark channel towards the river's mouth. Like some dead captain's ghost vessel. The lights from its cabin windows lit everything like a movie set. Including the white-haired head of the figure walking out to sea.

"Professor Uwingen!" I yelled. Two quick blasts from the ship's horn tore a hole in the night. The force and surprise of it sat me down backwards. A series of deep metallic thuds followed as the side of the ship's hull made sharp contact with the ice sheet encroaching on the lane. Big, oddly symmetrical chunks of ice broke and rose into the air then fell back, submerging and springing back into the air. Rectangles and rhombuses of a puzzle that would have resealed itself in a single day were it not for the icebreakers.

"Professor!" Massachusetts yelled. We ran after him. Was it my imagination or was the ice creaking under our feet?

"What are you doing?" I said, grabbing Chewy's arm. "You're gonna kill yourself out here!"

"Taking a walk," he said quietly. "Seeing how far I can just walk." He'd found out, for all of us: we were a body's length from the open water now. This was it. The edge. Holy shit. The water was dark and choppy in the wind. The cold violence of it freaked me out entirely. Plan aborted. There was no way I was jumping into that.

"How many policemen did they send anyway?" Chewy said. "And how could they have possibly found out?"

"They must have seen the light from the bonfire," Massachusetts said.

"What are you? - Oh, you mean the party."

"What are *you* talking about?" I said.

"Of the certain fact that they will now think I'm a spy."

"Why?"

"Because why else would I be crossing over?" He slipped off his coat. He was dressed like the Fliehender, in a wetsuit and lathered to the hilt with lard. He bent to untie his boots.

"You're kidding me," I said.

"You spyin' bastard," Massachusetts said. He grabbed the professor by the collar of the suit.

"Don't be a fool," said Chewy. "I was being facetious."

But Massachusetts wouldn't let go.

"What should we do with him?"

"Let him go moron," I said. All I was thinking was, he has the balls to leap. He deserves his shot.

And then he did leap.

"No you don't!" Massachusetts shouted, tightening his grip on the wetsuit. But that just meant he was going with. Chewy was a pretty big guy, and pretty big guys entering water tend to drag along whatever's tethered to them.

"What are you doing?" I yelled. Chewy and Massachusetts hit the water and both gasped. At first Massachusetts was trying to detain our 'spy' but in less than a minute his face was stuck in a toothy grimace and his arms stopped flapping. Chewy, floating, got behind him.

"Milo, don't move! Kneel down! I will guide him to you!"

"And then what am I supposed to do?"

"Pull him up."

"Me and what army?"

"Pull him up!"

When Massachusetts was within reach I grabbed him by the hair. But that threw me off balance and I fell forward on the slab, pushing his head under the water.

"Easy!"

"Sorry!"

Massachusetts bobbed to the surface. His teeth weren't even chattering. I grabbed one of his hands and tried to roll my way backwards. With Chewy pushing we managed to get his shoulders out of the water, then his waist.

"If I – ahhhhh!!!" The ice sheet beneath me cracked. This was unbelievable. I had just become one of those people who ended up in the helicopter rescue basket. Except there would be no helicopter now, at night, in this fog. The water felt like acid gurgling up over my thighs and waist.

"Holy fuck is it cold! Chewy, help me!"

"Who? Keep your head above water!" Chewy yelled. I wanted to get sarcastic but fear, I learned a long time ago, reduces sarcasm to urine. For a brief second I could feel my loins again.

"Now what?!" I yelled. "I can't feel my hand! I can't breathe."

"Do you hear it?" Chewy yelled. "Hang on!"

"No," I said. But then I could. The chopper.

"Assholes," Massachusetts whispered.

"Hey! He's alive! He's alive!" I shouted. Then the light was on us.

"*Stehen bleiben!*" someone yelled over a megaphone. Don't move. That was the easiest command I'd ever followed. Now all you could hear was that huge metallic whoosh, the same sound an ant probably hears when a lawnmower passes over him. The rescue bird was holding its position somewhere above us, buffeting us in its downdraft. What the hell are they doing, I thought, taking pictures? Then very gruff hands had me by the belt and the collar of my shirt.

"Massachusetts!" I yelled. "I'm stuck to Massachusetts. I can't let go!"

The hands let me go, and I saw that rescue cage swing out over my head. One of the red-suited guys leaned over and grabbed Massachusetts near the elbow, got some kind of line around him, then wrenched my hand from his wrist. My fingers wouldn't move.

Then the rescue guys yanked me into their basket too and we were all floating up into the brightness. Like being abducted by aliens.

"Wait!" I hissed to the guy lying on top of me. *"Bitte*. My professor is still out there!"

"There's someone else?!"

"Professor Uwingen! White hair. Wetsuit! You can't miss him."

When the Coast Guard duo had me and Massachusetts safely in the helicopter they went back down with the basket. A guy wearing a helmet threw me a blanket and told me to ride co-pilot. I was shivering so hard I thought my head would bust the safety glass on the door. Back and forth we flew, slowly, the rescue basket skimming just above the surface of the water, with me pointing this way and that and back again along the edge of the shipping lane, growing more desperate by the second. Because in ice water seconds are a luxury you don't have. I shook my throbbing hand for proof. I glanced over my shoulder for more. Massachusetts was laid out on the floor, under blankets too, but not moving. "We can't not find him!" I yelled to the pilot. To no one. To the universe. "We can't not find him!"

And then we did. There below us was Chewy, his head like a snowball in ink, doing the crawl toward the eastern shore and the world he'd fled as a younger man.

The phone rang. I ignored it. It rang again. And again. I was alone in Chewy's apartment.

"*Hallo?*"

"Tobias?"

"Uh, no. I'm a student of his."

"Who is this."

"Milo Prieto."

"This is Horace Powders," the voice said.

"Oh."

"Put Professor Uwingen on please."

"He's still at the hospital."

"What are you doing at his place?"

"It's a long story – "

"What did you fuck-ups do over there that my phone doesn't stop ringing?"

"We fell in the water."

"Well here's what it looks like from where I'm sitting. You threw an illegal party. You ran from the police. You nearly caused a cruise ship to crash. You nearly got two people killed."

"None of that is exactly true."

"Congratulations either way, Prieto. AIM's finished. You're the first in Germany to know."

"Wait."

"And don't feel so special. At Zane they set a dorm on fire."

"So now what? How do I get home?"

"That has stopped being my problem. I'm saying goodbye now."

That evening Chewy came home. It had been two days since our arctic bath. Massachusetts was still under observation in the hospital, for shock and hypothermia. In the meantime, the charges against Michael had been dropped, which was a relief. What had raised investigators' eyebrows was the fingerprint-less pen. Even more so his alibi: he'd been with his dad, the retired intelligence colonel, in a crowded sports bar that night.

As for Chewy, all he'd gotten for his trouble was a milder case of hypothermia. To his credit he'd nearly made it across the gap. But the rescue guys were able to get low enough with that chopper and their spotlights to cut his path off. Just as well. All the commotion we were making caused the DDR shoreline to light up like Coney Island. Sirens were howling and distant men barked orders as jeeps whirred back and forth along the fencelines. By some miracle not a shot was fired out of that other world. But I'm sure Chewy would not have gotten the reception he'd imagined.

I helped him get into his bed then made him tea.

"At least you're not a spy," I said, sitting down.

"How do you know?" he whispered.

"Because you wouldn't be home if you were. You'd be hanging by your feet in some soundproof safehouse."

"Astute observation, Prieto."

"So why? Why'd you do it?"

"Family. That's it. To be with my sister again."

"But -"

"When I lost the last of my family, you could say I lost my footing in the world. After all those years I thought I'd learned to accept it. But coming here, being so close again…"

"But even if you'd made it across you'd never have gotten to see her."

"It's not the point. Who's to say she'd have wanted to see me? The young girl I knew no longer exists. You know, she's spurned my every attempt to contact her. She's old now, like me."

"You wrote?"

"Many times. Despite everything. I will tell you something. She was never dragged away. She jumped with me, but that was only because I bullied her into it. When she landed she just stayed put, sitting there on the ground. It was her way of winning our long-standing argument. '*Komm! Komm!*' I yelled. '*Schnell, Bärbel. Wir haben keine Zeit!*' She wouldn't even look up at me. Mila. My own twin. I leapt over the cinderblocks to safety. Some of her friends were with me. We saw the soldiers rushing toward her, but they weren't pointing their weapons. That's when I knew she'd decided against me. She knew the men who helped her up. And she walked away with them, on her own."

"Why the story then?"

"The shame is in the details. So I changed them. I didn't want trouble in my new life. But anyway, what does it matter now?" he whispered. "Its just politics. I would have liked to tell her so. To be there for her even if somehow, now, I am the enemy. Before we're both gone."

"Is she sick?"

"I don't know. Why? One of these days she's going to die, like the rest of us, and then the chance will be lost. To reconcile, to forgive, or at least to try. Or to choke each other to death," he laughed. "Who knows? At least there'd be closure."

I thought to say that I knew how death could leave you world-less. A ghost in your own home. How it could undercut certain opportunities. But a guy like Chewy, he didn't need to listen to me. I thought to say thanks. He'd just given me an idea. I waited for him to fall asleep then ran to the phone and called Three Bags in Norway.

"Threebs!"

"Hallo Milo!"

"I need your help. I got no money to get outta here. And I gotta get outta here."

"The program is over?"

"I'll tell you all about it another time. First I gotta cancel my return trip to New York and get another one."

"You will come to Norway," he said down the line. I could hear faint voices behind him.

"I do have some places I could go."

"We'll go camping."

"I just-"

"You can take the direct flight from Hamburg."

"Indirect," I said.

The flight was long and bumpy and the bus to the downtown terminal even more so. I boarded another bus rolling north. The driver helped me get my pack up on the luggage rack.

"You are Cuban?" he asked me. "Or from the Canary Islands."

"No," I said. "And no."

I took my seat. It was night but it wasn't cold. At some point we began to climb. In a half-sleep I was aware of stopping briefly at a gas station. When I woke up for real we were still rolling and it was still dark. At first light I unfolded my map.

"Hey," I said, walking to the front of the bus. "Is the next stop mine?"

I got out by a small brick vestibule at a crossroads. Again the driver helped me with my pack. If I'd had any extra money I would have tipped him. The sun was still low as I set out, westward, feeling the need to rush but unable to. How could I? I was walking over real mountains. Every once in a while I glanced over my shoulder. I wondered if I'd ever get there. A small, beat up pick-up stopped.

"Where are you headed?"

"To Barranco de Fondales."

"Climb in, then."

The farmer said his name was Gaito, his family name, and that they'd given up on olives two years back to pursue tourism. His 17th century farmhouse was now a bed and breakfast.

"We're joining Europe," he said. "You'll see how things change. We will use the same currency. The tourists will come like an avalanche."

"Spain is Europe."

"So you don't live here," he laughed.

At the entrance to the village I thanked Mr. Gaito and got my pack out of the back of his truck. Then I wet my face at the fountain in the middle of the small roundabout. I was not thirsty but my mouth was dry. I took a breath, bent my knees. Less than a week earlier, sitting next to Chewy, it had dawned on me so clearly that this was the absolute right thing to do. I was trying to ride that conviction, the way he'd hoped to ride the Baltic currents. But with each step now I could feel my resolve wane. I was starting to be scared. I had to move. There might not be another chance.

When I got there my feet crunched on the gravel. At the door I didn't bother to knock. But Maribel was in my face before I'd taken three steps. Her face was contorted with shock.

"*Qué haces aquí!*" she hissed. She put both her hands on my chest like she could stop me.

"Where is she?"

"It is too late," she whispered. "You've come too late."

"No." I fell to my knees. "No…" I put my face in my hand.

"*Quién es?*" came the voice. It was faint. Coming from the bedroom I'd imagined the morning we'd scrammed from here forever. I stood up.

"You can't go in there, *bastardo!*"

"I prefer Gimp."

Maribel grabbed my backpack and wouldn't let go. "For fifteen years," she said, "I have been paid to do one thing." She was struggling so hard against me that a button on her white blouse popped loose, and her blouse dropped down over one shoulder. "And that is," she huffed, "to protect Doña Eleanor's solitude."

"*Doña* Eleanor," I said, "isn't getting off that easy. *Doña* Eleanor doesn't know what's best for her." But I wasn't sure of that at all. I was going to go in there and I was not sure of any single thing except the fact of going. I tipped Maribel over my leg like we were dancing tango, and I let her come to rest on the stone floor. I looked down at her. "Don't make a scene," I said with more fury in my voice than I felt. "Or I'll break your neck." Then I stepped over her and I did it.

Before the door was fully open, the smell. Something sweet, mixed with ammonia. Not incense and medicine but human smells. I saw her feet. They were elevated, and so grey and swollen that you could barely distinguish between them and her calves. They looked like amputee stumps but for the tiny puffed toes.

I shut the door and pushed the latch across into the doorframe. She turned her head. Her eyes went wide. "You," she whispered.

"Have we met?" I said, steadying myself against a rough-hewn wooden chair that faced her. There was a rattling at the door.

"I warned," she whispered. Her breath heavy, raspy. "Not to ruin...."

"Whoa," I said. "Hang on a second." She was so hard to look at. In just three weeks she'd gone deeply to shit. Her eyes were sunk like you couldn't have pried them out with a spoon. Her lips had receded and no longer fully covered her straight, yellowed teeth. She had one arm outside the bedsheets and it was bent like one of those metal desk lamps with the joint in the middle. I thought I might faint, which would have been a disaster. Outside I heard a car start. There wasn't a second to lose.

"What did you... where is Maribel?"

I dropped my pack and forced my legs forward. Lurched from the chair to the edge of her bed. I sat down on it. It was like she'd shrunk to the size of a large doll, something you might win at a fair and carry home with difficulty. I didn't remember it being quite like this. But I could barely remember at all. Only the guilt of it. I was so young. I pulled back her quilt, expecting to feel some small release of heat, and took her other hand. Her fingers were soft and freezing, like partly thawed sausages. She tried to pull her hand away but couldn't even come close. "Fuck me..." she whispered. "Fuck..." She shifted her weak, watery eyes to mine. Watery eyes trying to produce fire. "If... if it's revenge... you don't even ..." Her voice trailed off. She left her mouth open like she was thirsty, or just too done to close it. She looked scared.

"Revenge?" I said. "Call it atonement."

"I've got nothing to atone …"

"You don't understand. I'm not talking about you."

"Get out...please…"

"You see, I've been here before."

"No…"

"I don't mean here, here." I squeezed her hand a little. My throat felt lined with wool. Could you pass out if you were already sitting down? Could you just sit like that, with this person, this person whose imaginary self had dogged you your entire life, who'd tried so hard to snuff you out in the real world and who still only wished you gone, and take this final step? Could I really follow through? I still didn't know, even as I began to speak. "I mean, by someone else's side. At the end. I can't undo what happened. I wish I could. I wish I could."

"This is my ending…"

"Enough with your ending. This time it ends my way."

"Nooo," she said, her voice breaking . "What are you going - ?"

"What I should have done the first time around, Eleanor."

Her eyes went wide.

"Eleanor..."

I brought her hand to my mouth in a kind of kiss. Held my lips against the cold.

Hipólito shook me awake.

"*Tenemo' que irno'*. Come on."

"Where," I said, squinting.

"To the hospital. *Anda ya!*"

It was the second time in a week that my dad had gotten me up in the middle of the night. The first was because Miriam had been screaming like a little girl in bed. An ambulance had come, and we had followed behind in the car. Being in the Cadillac again like that made me feel like an old predator bearing down on some prey I'd only managed to wound. I'd sat as still as I could in the backseat. In the hospital parking garage I'd refused to get out. Hipólito had to open my door, pull me by the hood of my coat. The zipper dug into my neck the way he tugged me along.

"Miriam Prieto Moralez," he'd said at reception, in the emergency room.

"Is she a patient, sir?"

"She's my wife."

"Did she just come in?"

"Two minutes ago. Where is she?"

"We're not going to know where she is at this moment. It depends on what she was brought in for."

"You can't tell me where she is? What is this?"

"I can't tell you yet, sir."

We sat down on orange plastic chairs. A long time later the nurse nodded to Hipólito. He leapt up. Then he came back and sat down.

"I should have left you at home," he said. He closed his eyes.

"Where is mama?"

"Where she was after the accident," he said. "Back to square one."

I thought he'd meant back in the same bed, but before she could get there she would have to have another operation to stop the bleeding in her liver. Which in the end didn't work. Which was why Hipólito was waking me up now for the second time in a week. This time we went straight to a room he knew. She was alone, except for the nurses with their grave faces.

Hotchkiss had said there was one fruit you couldn't take from the bag. That you only had one liver and it had to get better.

"Where is Hotchkiss?" I said to a nurse.

She knelt down. "Who is that, hon?"

"Quiet," Hipólito said. Miriam was asleep, or unconscious. But I didn't want to stop talking. I'd seen her sick and weak for months now, ever since she'd come home, but this wasn't sickness. When I realized it I wet myself. I kept myself pressed up against the side of her bedrail so no one would notice. I was trapped there, clinging to the metal, on the far side of the bed from Hipólito, just as I'd be on the far side of her grave from him a few days later. I was so close to Miriam herself that I could have taken her hand and kissed it.

"Mama," I cried. "Mama." But as much as I wanted her to wake up, I guess I really didn't want that. Because when she opened her eyes and set them upon me I got so scared I dropped under the bed. I lay there, frozen, as the urine that had puddled on the linoleum floor soaked up the front of my sweatshirt.

"Hipo," I heard her say. "Milo."

"I'm here," Hipólito said. He pulled his chair closer. A nurse came in, said something on the intercom, hurried out.

"I'm here," Hipólito repeated.

"*Y Milano.*"

"He just ran out."

"Bring him."

Hipólito stood and went to the door, opened it a little, but stayed in the room. "I don't know where he went," he said.

"Milano," Miriam whispered. She never called me that. It made me feel even more in trouble. She said it again. But I couldn't move. This was all my doing. Hipólito knew exactly where I was. This was going to be his final betrayal before she was gone in the for-good way. Him betraying me, as I was betraying her. That's how this was shaking out. Each time she called my name – softer now, her voice tremulous, the mattress over my head moving a little - I tried even harder to disappear into the cold floor. I knew the way you do that there wasn't much time, that there was basically no time. In her voice it was like she wanted to tell me something. If I closed my eyes I could picture another me, an imaginary me, crawling out from under the bed and rising up and letting her say it. Another better boy, a braver one, giving her that kiss, just a simple goodbye kiss, the little everything gesture I knew she was holding out for with the desperation you experience just once. I can still picture that possibility. It's remained in my head like a scene cut from a movie. Because I did not move. Inches from her but unable to even speak. The same as when the car rolled. The same as just days later, when I'd fall mute on to her coffin.

This was my conundrum. The mess I'd find myself in later and always – on the streets, in juvi, in Germany, wherever I went. It wasn't just about some terrible thing I'd done as a kid, some action I couldn't erase. The chrome and steel smash-up. The accident was part of it, the seed of so many of my problems maybe, but the curse of my childhood, the burden throughout, the weight I'd carried around ever since had drawn its real strength from what I didn't do. The inaction this never-ending flame in my gut. The kind you couldn't snuff out or explain away even if you'd had someone to explain it to. Because you can't undo what you never did.

I did not come out and face the only woman who'd dived in deep enough to surface again feeling love for me. I'd wanted so badly to say goodbye, as much as she did or more, but I could not give her that basic thing because I was too scared. Bats in your chest scared.

Of being alone, even though that was going to happen anyway. Scared that if justice existed you were now marked for the cull. Scared that her last act might be to unforgive me.

So I stayed there in the piss, staring into the back of my hand, withholding myself, trembling like a dog but otherwise immobile, even as she commanded, then begged, using my full name, until I heard Hipólito gasp and I knew that she must have as well and that it was too late forever.

"Let me go…"

She was saying it over and over. Pushing at my face. Feeble, feverish.

"No," I said. "No."

My lips were still pressed against the boney back of her hand. I was starting to think we might be there for a very long time. I closed my eyes and tried to hold my breath. In the darkness I imagined my phantom arm returned, identical to the other. I see Eleanor sitting up, the color returning to her face. Somewhere in the room Miriam tunes her tres and begins to hum. All three of us in imperfect harmony, none worse off for the others. That is possible. It always has been. I can see it. A trinity held however loosely by blood and circumstance.

But I can't hold my breath forever.

I open my eyes, exhale. Eleanor has been mostly still but now she turns her hand around. Her cold fingers move over my nose, my mouth, my wet cheeks. Rigid as sticks. Is she searching for my eyes to scratch out? I don't know what to make of it but I am not going to budge. No one will scare me away. Not this time. Not even me.

Her breathing hastens. From her throat a sound like she's swallowed bottle caps. "Let me go…" she says again. I almost say no for like the fortieth time, but when her fingers curl slowly around mine and squeeze them that last time, I realize maybe I haven't been getting it.

Let me go.

She moves her head from side to side like she's trying to shake something off. She sighs. Then nothing.

"I'm still here," I say at that precise moment, which has been the whole crazy desperate point in coming back. For what I hope might just be a real second chance. The one that I am never going to find in any school or in lock-up. Forgiving the living so that the dead might do the same for me.

"It's okay," I say. "I'm here. I'm right here." Her grip goes slack, her hand wants to slip to the bed. But I hold it still, to make sure. She seems even smaller now. And for the first time she doesn't look bitter or scared or anything. Her mouth is half open, her eyes wide. Unfocused, without judgement or thought. I wonder if she's still in the room. The way I'd hoped Miriam had lingered with us, at least for a while. I cry for them both, even though it feels peaceful. Like everything is nearly where it should be. Everything close to its proper drawer. Possibly even me.

"Goodbye," I say

I actually say it twice. For the woman I'd refused to go to despite her calling, and to the woman I've barged in on who hasn't had this wish even slightly. And it is actually a sort of letting go. It feels like something you might do in a real family. Trying to set something right, restore the balance however late in the game. I think of Three Bags and everything he'd imagined as he lifted me with my bloodied face from Miriam's grave. That ridiculous, illogical hope in the worst of scenarios. I think, maybe I can pull myself up from this. Step up out of this house and figure something out. Find some place to go that makes sense.

I stand and fold Eleanor's hands on her stomach, then pull the blankets up to her shoulders and turn them down a bit. I smooth the bed out as best I can, feeling her tiny frame pass beneath my hand.

I go to the kitchen and drink some water from a dirty glass she might have used that same day. I wash it in cold water and set it to dry upside down on a towel, then go back to her room and pick up my pack. I look at her again. The shell. She is not in the room, I'm sure of it. Maybe I've had something to do with that. Or maybe I'm just projecting. Trying to be her hero like I'd once been Miriam's. For making us a family again, she'd said.

But I've had enough now of heroes. Of seeking them, or of wanting to be someone else's. I snap the waistband of my pack shut. The weight of it on my back feels good. I can recite the exact number of things in it, and the things themselves, and where they are stored, in exact detail. Among them a folded Peacoat at the bottom of the main compartment, the nearly complete set of lugnuts and washers of a drum long lost and the hope I thought lost with it, and an inscribed sink fixture in an inferior zip-pocket, lower left side, stuffed for protection inside two sweatsocks like the ones I'd mailed to Halsey, but clean. Her beginnings, now irremovable from my own.

I figure I'll keep this last item forever. As something to look through each day, into the darkness inside, without falling into the darkness. As a reminder of how much you can leave behind without dying from the leaving, or, who knows, of what you might even try to get back one day, if you ever get your life right.

I have no idea what pipe gauge they use on Norwegian sinks, but I figure Three Bags can help me rig it into place. That is, if he'll make room for me in a permanent sort of way. Like an uncle might. Which is what he once said he was to me.

THE END

ACKNOWLEDGEMENTS

Thanks to everyone who read and commented on versions of the manuscript going back so far in time they may not even remember it: Nora Haller, Sarah Burnes, Bernadette Pampuch Rivero, Michael Signorelli, Victoria Alonso, Alistair Williamson, Victoria Hutchinson, Armando Guerra, Ibon Cormonera, Kyle Minor, Brendan Kiely, David Klein, Christopher Locke, Julie Underhill, Sloan Harris, Lolo Collins, Dan Sullivan, Dean Schwartz, Lois Guberman, Gunnar Vatvedt and the others I've surely left out by mistake. Thanks Sigur Ros for Untitled 6. Thank you, Khyentse Norbu.

Thanks especially to my partner, Mouche, and our own lab experiments run wild: Lula, Nino and Emile.

Cover Design by Michael Romano

ABOUT THE AUTHOR

Gerry Hadden is a journalist and the author of the critically-acclaimed memoir, Never the Hope Itself: Love and Ghosts in Latin America and Haiti (Harper Perennial, 2011). He was born in New York City and went to Colby College in Maine, where he studied German language and literature. On the eve of a semester overseas an uncle warned him to get the travel bug out of his system early. It didn't work. He went on to become a public radio reporter in Seattle, then covered Mexico, Central America and the Caribbean for National Public Radio. From there he and his partner ended up in Barcelona, where he and they are raising their three kids. For ten years Hadden was the Europe Correspondent for PRI's The World, (WGBH Boston public radio). He now makes documentary films. Everything Turns Invisible is his first novel.

CPSIA information can be obtained
at www.ICGtesting.com
Printed in the USA
LVHW110047120522
718567LV00014B/160